LOOKING FOR LOVE—AMERICAN STYLE

BLISS. She always placed the same ad—*Beautiful blond successful designer, 29, seeks equally successful, sophisticated male, 34–40.* She met many men she desired . . . until she met one she feared.

SELMA. She was an unhappy wife looking for a lover—*Vivacious redhead seeks sensitive, mature counterpart.* But the gorgeous man she found wanted more than stolen nights of pleasure.

PEGGY. She hungered for a man more sensitive than the one she married—*Irish-American Venus (with arms) seeks compassionate, intelligent Adonis.* But could she give herself completely to a loving stranger?

WERE THEY ADVERTISING
FOR LOVE—OR HEARTBREAK?

PERSONALS

Susan Lois

A DELL BOOK

Published by
Dell Publishing Co., Inc.
1 Dag Hammarskjold Plaza
New York, New York 10017

To Charlie and Tim
and to all the other
wonderful men in my life

Dell ® TM 681510, Dell Publishing Co., Inc.

ISBN: 0-440-16945-3

Printed in the United States of America

December 1986

10 9 8 7 6 5 4 3 2 1

WFH

1

Selma

OOH, it was delicious! That's so *good*—keep doing whatever you're doing! Don't stop! *Don't stop* . . .

It stopped. Just as she was on the brink.

Selma opened her eyes. It wasn't Warren Beatty on top of her. With her eyes closed, it was easy to imagine gorgeous Warren, hunk of hunks, putting it to her with practiced ease. Eyes open, she saw it was only Jared Galitz, Esq., her lawfully wedded husband—Hizzoner the Mayor of West Falls, Connecticut.

"Why'd you stop?" she moaned.

"Why do you always blame *me?*" he snapped, hurt. "You think I like when this happens?"

Oh, God, she thought wearily. "Who's blaming?" she asked. "I know you have a lot on your mind."

"Damn right." Appeased, at least for the moment, he moved toward her again.

Selma cringed.

But what about *me?* Selma wondered. She closed her eyes and pretended she was Catherine Deneuve in *Belle de Jour,* on her back in the whorehouse. She moved. Automatically. Like the metronome on Olivia's piano. In three-quarter time. She had become the Johann Strauss of the mattress set.

She peered up at him. Jerry's broad face was shiny with sweat, his eyes aglaze with rapture. She felt a stab of envy. *Honi soit qui mal y pense*, she thought. Whatever that meant. Did Catherine Deneuve do this in the movie? she wondered. She couldn't remember . . .

"Whew-whew-whew," Jerry began to whistle.

A sure sign. Dammit, she thought. He sounded just like a woman in labor. Not that he would know how a woman in labor sounded. He had steadfastly refused to attend Lamaze classes with her when she was pregnant with Olivia. Working day and night, he was too busy back then chasing ambulances. "The law is a jealous mistress." How many times had he said that? And how could she argue? After all, she had snagged herself a real go-getter, someone even her father would admire. And Abe Moscovitz was not one to bestow his admiration on just anyone.

Other women had come to class with their husbands, and there *she* was with her cousin Myrna. Halfway through the course, just as they were getting to the crucial "push-blow" technique, Myrna-the-brilliant-Vassar-"gel" eloped with a goy from

6

Queens, breaking Tante Ida's heart and leaving Selma to time her own contractions. Thirteen years ago, and she remembered the humiliation like it was yesterday.

"NOW!" Jerry yelled, scaring the shit out of her. "*Whew-whew-whew-whew.*" He sounded like a locomotive, a goddamn express train, heading straight for the tunnel.

That's *me,* Selma thought. She waited until the last possible second before switching signals and let him slip from her.

"*Shit,* Selma!" he screamed, red faced. "I *hate* it when you do that! It ruins my whole day!"

God forbid he should worry about *my* day, Selma thought. Frustration lingered between her legs like an ache. His capacity for self-absorption knew no bounds. Her capacity to endure it was dwindling. There had to be a better way, she thought. "I'm sorry, Jerry," she said slyly. "You want to try again?"

He stared at her as though she had lost her mind.

So, she thought. The express train makes only one stop a day. She could remember when the train was a real local, stopping everywhere: on the terrace of her parents' condo in Stamford; on the red leather backseat of her father's Continental; against a tree one hot, dark night outside Gerde's Folk City in the Village. Fourteen years next June.

She had loved him once. She was sure of it. She could have sworn he'd loved her, too. Maybe it was all an illusion.

He was up and off her and rushing to the bathroom for a towel. He flung it at her. "Maybe you

7

should wash those sheets yourself, Sel," he said. "We don't want Princess blabbing all over town."

"Maybe we should just fire Princess," she replied, making a face. After all, Princess was not the most discreet housekeeper in the world. She had come with the house after the former owners, the Prentisses, retired to Barbados. According to Princess, they had begged her to go with them. But Princess, never one to mince words, had declined the invitation. "Shee-it. I ain't goin' back dere 'til Ah'm rich," Princess exclaimed. "Dis heah is de lan' o' golden oppo'tunity!"

Princess was determined to get herself some of that gold, and Selma guessed how she would do it. There were rumors that Princess was gathering enough gossip about West Falls's most respected families to write a sizzling exposé. And Selma had an idea that Princess had already begun it. In fact, more than once Selma had caught her scribbling in a little spiral notebook she carried everywhere with her.

Whatever, the book would make Peyton Place seem like Our Town. The Galitzes would no doubt play a major role. Selma shuddered at the thought.

"No way," Jerry called now.

Of course not, Selma thought. How would it look if Hizzoner the Mayor fired a *shvartzeh?* Jared Galitz, the Liberal, the Champion of the Underdog, the Lover of the Downtrodden! She was married to a man who was gearing himself up to be the first Jewish president of the United States of America.

So firing Princess was out of the question. "It

8

wouldn't do my image any good," Jerry hollered from the bathroom.

Image, shmimage, Selma thought. Wrinkling her nose, she removed the sodden sheet and carried it to the sink.

From the shower, Jerry sang at the top of his lungs: " 'Happy days are here again . . .' "

She glanced at his silhouette through the shower curtain. All those Twinkies were beginning to show. She shook her head. A health and exercise freak with a secret addiction to Twinkies. He played racquetball twice a week, swam laps at the YMCA every night, ate sprouts and bean curd until they were coming out of his ears. *And Twinkies.* Every chance he got. When he thought no one was looking. Twinkie after Twinkie.

She filled the basin, then used the dry end of the sheet to wipe the mist off the mirror before dropping it into the water. Well, you're no prize either, *dollink,* she said to her reflection. Alfredo had been experimenting with her hair color for the past eight months. She was a natural redhead, but her hair had begun to fade to a dismal no-color after Olivia's birth. She had tried every home hair color on the market and spent untold hours and dollars in an attempt to revive the natural tone, and nothing had worked. She had succeeded only in turning her hair to straw. Finally, in desperation, she took the problem to Alfredo, who convinced her that it was possible to undo the damage —but only if she would put herself entirely in his hands. So far, all he'd done was turn her hair color to menstrual red. Yech!

Still peering into the mirror, she pulled the skin

on her temples tight. Maybe her mother was right; forty-one wasn't too early for a little lift. And maybe while they're at it, they could do her nose.

Now Jerry was shouting, " 'Tomorrow, tomorrow, I luv ya, tomorrow . . .' "

She put her hands to her ears. Give me a break, she thought. In the bedroom, she began smoothing the spread, which was now decorated with semen spots. Maybe Marimekko will pick up the design, she snickered. The hell with it, she decided. There was a limit to the preservation of image.

She was jolted as the pounding crescendo of the "1812 Overture" crashed the silence of the room. The stereo alarm! "Damn!" Selma muttered, nearly tripping over Jerry's exerciser in her rush to turn down the volume on the Curtis Mathes. The mass of dials and needles and knobs filled one entire wall of their bedroom. They never failed to intimidate her. Quickly, she reached out and switched a dial. The sexy thumping of the Stones replaced the crashing. "Don't get no, Sat-is-faction! I try—and I try—and I try—"

Tell me about it, she thought. She boogied to the closet and smiled into the full-length mirror, mouthing the words along with Mick. Slowly, she slipped out of her nightie and undulated her hips to the music. Mick, ooh Mick! Lay it on me! Now *there* was a man. She sighed. Where were they, men like Mick? And Kris? A man who could make a woman feel like a woman just by looking into her eyes?

But what would she do if one day she should open her front door and there stood Mick—or Kris

10

or even, for that matter, Stevie Wonder, who could turn her on even without looking at her?

She knew what she would do. She let her hands linger over her hips (still narrow), her abdomen (stretch marks, but who cares?), and into the abundance of her bush. She closed her eyes . . .

Lately, her fantasies had taken her into the arms of other men. So far, it was just fantasy, because even if she could find a man, would she have the courage to follow through? Besides, who was there in town? The only possibilities she could think of were Cisco, the lawn guy, and Max Miller from the town council. At least they were single. But every time she even stood near Cisco, she sneezed. Maybe she was allergic to grass seed? Too bad. Cisco looked just like Philip Michael Thomas, that cute *shvartzeh* from *Miami Vice*. As for Max Miller, he was a lovely man, but he was still grieving for his wife even though she'd been dead for two years. Also, he had a daughter about Olivia's age to whom he devoted all his spare time. Where would a woman fit into a setup like that?

She was bringing herself to the point of no return when the bedroom door swung open.

"Hey, Ma, I thought you didn't have to do that after you were married!"

Selma froze in midmotion. "How many times have I told you to knock, Olivia? How many times?"

"Don't freak out, Ma! Be cool," Olivia answered, walking over to her father's wall unit. "How can you stand the Stones, Ma? They're prehistoric. Let's get something good," she said, switching the dial without hesitation.

11

"Don't touch that, Olivia! You know how your father is about his knobs!"

"What about my knobs?" Jerry asked, striding into the bedroom with a towel around his middle.

A nasal voice was blasting relentlessly.

"Don't you just love Johann Paul Jones!" Olivia gushed.

Jerry made a face and turned the radio off. "Olivia, what are you doing here?" He looked at Selma. "What is she doing here? Why isn't she at ballet?"

Selma reached into the closet for a robe. "She has a nine o'clock appointment at Alfredo's. She's been driving me crazy all week with this audition business. You think it was a smart move, Jerry?"

"You, too? Don't start with me, Selma. I'm not in the mood," Jerry answered with a sigh. The whole town was on his head for bringing this movie project to West Falls. Try to do something for the constituents and do they appreciate it? No way. They crucify you. At the same time, they all want to star in the goddam movie. Go figure! Aloud, he said, "Everyone wants to be discovered. Even my own daughter."

"Daddy, how can you say that? This is my big chance," Olivia said, entrechatting around the exerciser. "Is it really true that Michael Jackson is coming to town?"

"Who?"

"Omigod, I don't *believe* you, Daddy! *Michael Jackson!* Don't you even know who Michael Jackson is?"

For a moment Jared looked blank. Michael Jackson, Mahalia Jackson, Jesse Jackson. How could he

12

keep track of all these Jacksons? "I don't know who's coming, Olivia," he said truthfully. For over a month now, rumors had been flying about who was to be the star of this movie. Those moron producers hadn't even had the courtesy to tell him. He made the deal through his brother-in-law's cousin, Nate Greene, the agent. The guy owed him one for the time he got Nate's klepto wife off with just a reprimand. A personal income of two hundred grand and Mrs. Greene has to steal hankies from Bloomie's? Who could imagine such a thing?

So when Nate got wind of this deal, he immediately called Jerry to sit in on the first East Coast meeting. Those boobs were scouting for a typical suburb and had practically decided on Scarsdale when he single-handedly managed to convince them that Scarsdale was hardly typical. West Falls, on the other hand, *was* typical.

Where the hell was West Falls? they wanted to know. It had taken Jerry a couple of expensive lunches at The Four Seasons and a pair of high-priced hookers to convince them that West Falls did exist and would welcome them with open arms.

They should only know. Just about everyone in West Falls was against the project from the word *go*. They were afraid, that's what. Afraid that their precious little town would "go Hollywood."

"We don' wanna them movie big shots snorting cocaine ana fucking ourra women," was how Carlo Battista, the barber, had put it at one of the numerous town meetings at which the issue was discussed. Good old Carlo, actually coming out with

13

the "F" word in public like that. It had been enough to make Margaret Jensen, that fat blue-haired prude, fall right off her chair.

"Carlo, Carlo," Jerry had placated him—after the paramedics had revived old Margaret. "These people may be movie big shots, but they have *hair*. They'll need haircuts! Think of the business!" That gave him something to think about. *Goyisheh kop!*

But it wasn't just Carlo. The entire clergy was up in arms. The ministers and the priests didn't want cameras rolling on Sunday. The rabbi was against filming past sundown on Friday night and all day Saturday. The police were afraid of riots. The librarians were afraid of the noise. Practically everyone was afraid of Communist infiltration. Even Sven Jorgensen, the high school janitor, threatened to quit if one inch of the gym floor was scratched.

Jerry's head was spinning. If it wasn't for Max Miller, he'd lose his mind for sure. Good old Max, the Henry Kissinger of the town council, had persuaded them all to see the light. It would be *good* for the town to have a movie made here, Max had said in his authoritative, diplomatic way. Not just good for business but good for their souls and their psyches. "It's the perfect way to bring people together, to meet each other on neutral ground for a change," Max told them. "In unity there is strength," he said. The townsfolk liked the sound of that—whatever it meant.

For a research scientist without a pot to piss in, Jerry thought, Max Miller sure had a lot of *sachel*.

But not even Max could have foreseen what was going to happen. When the audition notice appeared in *The Marketplace,* the local weekly, the siege began in earnest.

Siege? That was too mild. A regular Armageddon.

The ad had been specific about casting. The producers wanted four teenage girls, period. But either the townspeople couldn't read (and Jerry wouldn't doubt it), or they thought that he, Mayor Jared Galitz, Esq., could work miracles. Mothers came running into his office with pictures of their daughters, some even with pictures of themselves! One or two had even hiked their skirts up past their *pupiks* and showed their legs—and more. It was craziness!

Neighbors rang the bell at all hours. Even Carlo Battista showed up with his grandson, only five years old and a miniature Lou Costello if ever there was one.

"Carlo," Jerry tried to explain tactfully, "they're looking for *girls.*" It was like talking to a wall.

"Just look at those lashes," Carlo cajoled. "We'll put a dress on him, and they'll never know."

Oy. What had he gotten himself into? Now it was Saturday and the audition was scheduled for noon in the high school gym.

And he had to be there.

Olivia was still nudging him. "C'mon, Daddy, you can tell me. It's Michael Jackson, right? Right?"

Jerry shot Selma a pleading look. Turning to his daughter, he said, "Enough! Get dressed and let your mother take you to the beauty shop. You'll get a nice hairdo for the audition. A permanent."

15

"A permanent? Give me a break, Dad!" Olivia screamed, looking at her mother. "Who does he think I am? Shirley Temple?"

"We should be so lucky," Jerry said.

"What does he mean, Ma?" Olivia looked at Selma in puzzlement.

"Go," Selma said, pointing to the door.

"I'm going. I'm *going!* But remember, nine o'clock on the dot! Alfredo will cream if I'm late."

When Olivia had gone, Jerry said, "Cream? She knows from cream?"

Selma rolled her eyes at the ceiling. "Knowing doesn't mean doing, Jerry. They all talk that way." She lowered her voice. "So who's it going to be, Jerry?"

"You, too? What is this?"

"Redford?"

"Selma, please."

"Nicholson?"

It was a nightmare. If he weren't up for reelection in another year, Jerry would drop this project like a hot potato. He'd look for another house in another town. Maybe even in another country.

But he couldn't quit now. What was *that* saying? When the going gets tough, the tough get going?

"Barron Heatter?" Selma asked.

2

Peggy

THE phone rang six times before Peggy Corcoran picked it up. She'd turned off the alarm an hour ago when Morgan left the house for her Saturday morning ballet class.

Her head was pounding and the ringing of the telephone was no help. She glanced across the empty bed. Ten o'clock. Damn! She hadn't meant to sleep this late. But then, she wasn't used to gulping down two double scotches to help her get to sleep.

Could this be how alcoholism begins? Two double scotches before bed?

She reached for the phone and knew, even before answering, that it was Duke. He had called every morning since she'd locked him out of the house two weeks ago. His persistence was beginning to wear her down.

"What do you mean you can't keep the appointment with Dr. Schindler?" he bellowed as soon as she answered. Not even "Hello." She could picture him standing at the pay phone in his service station, shifting from one foot to the other and biting his nails. It was the stance he always took when things weren't going his way. His tone was one he used with customers who were reluctant to take his advice about a new carburetor or a transmission. He had alienated more people with that tone—but did he care? If he thought he was right, he was right. Never budge an inch. That was his motto—and that was why they were still struggling to make ends meet.

Some women minded having to work, but not her. She was lucky. She loved her job as secretary to the Registrar at the community college. Although, to be honest, she liked being able to take free courses even more. Marrying so young, she had missed out on an education. When other girls were cramming for exams and dating fraternity boys, she was changing diapers and waxing floors. Now that Morgie and Wayne, Jr., were almost grown, though, a whole new life was opening up for her, and she was glad she had the job. It kept her mind off the reality of her shattered marriage.

At least I don't have to be a waitress like poor Phyllis DeCaprio, Peggy thought. After Tony left her, Phyl was as helpless as a babe, not knowing which way to turn. So she grabbed the first job that came her way. A waitress in the Agora Diner downtown. But their situations were different. Duke hadn't left Peggy. She'd been the one to lock

18

him out. It was an important difference. And one, she suspected, that was sticking in his craw.

"The appointment can wait," Peggy said, struggling to keep her mind on what Duke was saying. The room was reeling. She put her hand to the back of her head in a futile gesture to stop it.

She had gone along and made the appointment with Dr. Otto Schindler, West Falls's most respected marriage counselor—correction, West Falls's *only* marriage counselor—out of a sense of obligation. But then, just yesterday, she had changed the appointment to next week because of the audition. It was a wonderful opportunity for Morgie, a chance in a million. Why couldn't Duke understand? Maybe it was her fault. She should have *told* him about it instead of just slipping a note under the garage door as she'd done last night. But she'd only just noticed the ad in *The Marketplace* yesterday. And she couldn't bring herself to call him at *that woman*'s house. Just thinking about Barbara Johnson turned her stomach. The bitch had everything. Why did she need Duke, too? But, of course, Peggy knew the answer to that question.

"Duke, can't you see that this audition is important to Morgie?" She sat up and swung her long legs off the bed. The change in position only amplified the cacophony in her head.

"I'm important, too, dammit!" Duke insisted.

"We can start with Schindler next week," Peggy said.

"I knew this would happen!" Duke fumed. "Pie-in-the-sky auditions! I don't want you filling my daughter's head with shit like auditions! It's enough you spend my money on those snooty ballet lessons."

"*Whose* money?" Peggy countered.

"Don't start," Duke snapped.

She wasn't about to. She knew any argument would be futile. But Morgan had real talent, and Peggy was determined to let that talent bloom and flourish even if it meant sacrificing other things to do it.

She had lost track of what Duke was saying. He was off on another tack. He was sweet-talking her now. "Look, Peg, I'm sorry I got angry. But when I saw your note under the door like that . . ." He let the sentence trail. "Okay, okay, it's fine with me if you don't want to start until next week." He paused. "Oh, baby, anything you want." His voice was a husky whisper. "I'll do anything to get you back."

Yes, back in bed, Peggy thought wryly. But in spite of herself, she felt her resolve weakening.

"Peggy, I love you. Let me come over and show you how much," he pleaded.

"Why? Isn't that bitch giving you enough?"

"C'mon, Peg, that's over! I told you, that's over!"

Could she believe him? She ran her fingers through her long black hair and stole a glance in the mirror at the side of the bed. The reflection affirmed what she already knew. She was still pretty—but evidently not pretty enough. She didn't have the kind of seductive sexiness of a Barbara Johnson. Scrimping and struggling had left their mark. Still, her skin was good, and although she was thirty-two years old, she didn't look it. Last

20

week in school, someone had even mistaken her for a coed.

She stood up, the receiver pressed to her ear. Duke's voice had become a hypnotic hum. She studied herself in the mirror. After sixteen years of marriage, her breasts were still firm. Rolls Royce tits, Duke called them. She smiled wistfully. Goddam him. He was the sexiest man she had ever known. She had always suspected about the other women. Some men gambled. Some drank. Her own father had been a drunkard. Some men beat their wives. Duke had never laid a hand on her except in love. She never doubted that he loved her. Until Barbara Johnson. One day Barbara Johnson had driven her shiny new Mercedes into Duke's service station and changed Peggy's life for good. Why was Barbara more of a threat than the others? Because she had money, and money is power. What man could resist that?

And now Duke was begging to be let back in as though nothing had happened. She remembered their first lovemaking in the backseat of his old souped-up Chevy, their young bodies clinging, moving together to Chuck Berry's "Maybellene," Duke's favorite song. And her surprise after, realizing she had actually "done it." But it seemed so right. Duke had whispered how much he loved her, over and over through his kisses . . .

Stop it, Peg! she told herself. Think of Barbara Johnson. And God only knows how many other women, whose names she didn't know. Her eyes filled with tears.

"Peggy, baby, you still there?"

She said nothing.

"Peggy, don't do this to us," he pleaded. "I want you."

Well, she wanted him, too. Dammit, she was wet just from talking to him on the telephone, but then she was always a pushover for Wayne Robert "Duke" Corcoran. She was his, right from the start, loving him even before he knew she existed. He seemed bigger than life, back then, striding around the high school corridors surrounded by girls.

Then, one day in the cafeteria, he plunked himself down beside her and told her he'd be waiting for her after school. There was never a question about her being there.

Peggy's mother had hated him from the start. "He's a hood," she warned. "He'll give you nothing but grief! I didn't move us to West Falls for you to wind up with a lowlife like your father!" Furious, Peggy had shouted back, "You have no right to judge him just because you made a mistake with my father! Duke's decent and hardworking and I love him!" Her mother had snickered, "Love! You'll see how fast love goes when you can't pay the rent!"

When she became pregnant in her senior year, her mother's view softened. "Maybe I was wrong about him," she said. "You're lucky he's marrying you. I hope you have a better life than I did."

Peggy winced, thinking how the tables had turned. Now her mother was the one who had the luck. When Peggy and Duke had been married less than a year, her mother decided to take a real estate course. She got a job with Galitz & Henry, selling houses for the town's largest realtor. Soon after that, she opened her own office. In time she became so successful that she opened branches in Westchester and Long Island. She was remarried now, to George Hanley, a wealthy developer who was ten years her junior. They had often invited Peggy and the children to visit them in Pound Ridge, but they never invited Duke. Of course, Peggy had never accepted.

"Are the kids home?" Duke asked.

He never remembered that on Saturday mornings Morgie had her dance class. "Morgie's at ballet," she told him. "Wayne's still sleeping." Peggy hadn't even heard her son come in the night before. "Duke, you're going to have to do something with him . . ."

"First, I want to do something with *you,*" Duke said softly. And when Peggy didn't protest, he added, "I'll be right over."

She stood with the receiver in her hand for a moment, then placed it carefully on the pedestal and walked into the bathroom. As the hot shower pulsated over her body, she realized she was shaking with excitement. *You are an idiot!* she told herself. Nevertheless, she ran to the front door and unlocked it so the bell wouldn't wake Wayne, Jr.

And then he was there. Striding toward her. Unfastening his belt as he approached the bed. The bulge in his trousers mirrored her own excitement.

"Peggy, baby," he moaned, taking her into his arms. His lips were like fire.

Expertly, without speaking, she reached for his fly and unzipped it. "I've missed you, Duke," she said, taking him into her mouth and sucking him hungrily. Her hands caressed the length of his torso.

He gently disengaged her mouth, and now she was under him and he was stroking her body with extreme tenderness. "I love you, Peggy," he whispered, planting kisses on her breasts, her belly, her thighs. His tongue explored her hungrily, knowing when to probe, when to pause, making her body respond in the way that only he could.

She loved him. She loved him and she would forgive him anything. Dukie, her Dukie . . . her sweet, sweet Dukie . . . And suddenly he was over her and in her, their bodies moving as one, transporting her as far as she had ever been. They came together and she screamed, not wanting it to be over. She was surprised to find tears on her cheeks.

He sighed and kissed her. "Rolls Royce tits," he said, his hands lingering over her breasts. "You're still the best, babe," he said.

It took a moment for the words to register.

"Better than all of them put together."

Her hand, which had been softly caressing his flaccid penis, grabbed it now in a viselike grip.

Howling in pain, he shrieked, "Cunt! What did you do that for?"

"You still don't know, do you?" she sobbed.

"Tell me!" he yelled. "You crazy bitch! What did I do wrong this time?"

"Oh, God, how could I have been so stupid?" she cried. "I don't want to be the best!" she said through her tears. "I want to be the *only! Only! Only!*"

She picked up the telephone and threw it at him.

After he left, she was still shaking. Any minute now, Morgie would come through the door and she would have to hurry. One look and Morgie would know something was wrong. She'd ask if they were still going to the audition.

Of course they were going. Of course. Peggy glanced at the ad in *The Marketplace,* which was open on her dresser—". . . TWELVE O'CLOCK IN THE HIGH SCHOOL AUDITORIUM." She had circled it in red. There would be just enough time to dress. Makeup would hide her swollen eyes.

She glanced down and noticed, for the first time, the personals ads on the adjacent page. Funny, she hadn't seen them before.

Almost as an afterthought, she tore out the page and stuffed it into her purse.

3

Bliss

"DON'T! Oh, Daddy, please . . . please don't!"
But he kept coming at her, his hand raised high,
his face contorted with rage. *Hide! Hide!* But there
was no safe place. She tried to run, but her legs
refused to move. "Daddy, I'll be good. *Please—*"
The hand came smashing down, and Bliss Billington awoke with a start. The pain in her left breast
moved across her chest like a flame. "Oh, God
. . ." she said shakily. Trembling, it took her several seconds to realize she'd been dreaming again.
This was not the pink and white organdy bedroom
in Lake Forest. This was not her father's house.
This was West Falls—*her* bedroom, *her* house, *her*
haven. She looked around as if to verify that it was
so. The pale mauve silk moiré canopy above her.
The soft walls of gray on gray silk–patterned roses.
The tasteful arrangement of anemone and baby's

breath in the graceful swan vase. A calm oasis she had fashioned for herself and for Sunny . . . SUNNY!

She sat up abruptly and glanced at the gold and white filigree clock on the bedside table. Eleven! How could she have overslept? She had set the alarm . . . Or had she? The memories of last night began to close in on her, but she forced them away. Today was Sunny's big day, and nothing—*nothing*—was going to spoil it.

She pushed the call button on the panel beside her bed. It buzzed once and Gladys's familiar brogue came through instantly. "Good morning, Ms. Billington."

Bliss smiled. It had taken months to train Gladys to say *Ms.* instead of *Missus.* "Is Sunny ready? We have to be at the high school by noon . . ."

"Oh, Ms. Billington, I'm sorry, but—uh—"

Bliss shifted impatiently. There was a servile quality in Gladys's voice that never failed to irritate her.

"I believe Sunny said she would be at the library if you wanted her . . ."

Oh, no. "What time did she leave the house?" Bliss's voice was tight with controlled fury. She had promised Sunny she could skip ballet this morning. In return, Sunny had agreed to try out for the movie. The fact that a movie was being made in West Falls was incredible. "Think of it, Sunny!" she had encouraged. "This is your chance!"

She would never forget Sunny's mournful reply. "My chance for what?"

"Oh, come on, honey," Bliss said. In the face of

Sunny's dogged lack of self-esteem, it was not always easy to remain optimistic. "You know you're talented."

It was true. Sunny had a beautiful voice. Her voice coach did not give out compliments freely, but she admitted that Sunny had a pure, natural soprano that was rare in someone her age. "But talent alone is not enough," the teacher added. "There must also be the willingness to perform."

But how could there be willingness without confidence? Confidence was something Sunny had precious little of. Not without reason, Bliss conceded. Even though the last operation had left only a small scar on Sunny's lip.

"Never mind, Gladys," Bliss said into the intercom. "I'll stop by the library on my way to the high school."

There was hardly time, but Bliss felt compelled to shower. She could still feel last night's sex clinging to her like a grimy film. Last night—early morning, to be precise—she had soaked in a steaming tub for what seemed like hours. It hadn't been enough. The creep had gotten into her pores . . .

Well, that was *it!* No more ads, no more taking chances. Come to think of it, it was a miracle that nothing like last night had happened before. She'd lost count of how many men she'd met through the personals. She always placed the same ad:

Slender, sophisticated successful designer, 29, seeks equally successful, sophisticated male, 34–40. Urbane, witty, appreciative of the finer things in life. Photo a must; ditto short bio. Reply **Box 2122.**

It never failed to bring more replies than she could ever respond to, no matter where the ad was placed. She had her own system for weeding out the ineligibles. The ones without photos. The ones written in crayon. The admittedly married, and the ones who merely implied that they were. The ones she knew instinctively were weirdos.

Steve's photo and bio had seemed normal. Actually, better than normal. His letter was intelligently written, and he was gorgeous. When she phoned him, he sounded pleasantly surprised, but not overwhelmed. He was a stockbroker, thirty-seven, in the process of getting a divorce, he said. He had no children, but he did have two tickets for Forest Hills in June. Did she like tennis? Would she care to meet him for a drink at The Pierre? Just to get to know each other.

"No," she said, "there's a great place around here." She liked to meet them on home ground, first time out. It gave her the necessary feeling of control.

The Royal Palm, across from the mall, was the place she usually chose. It was large but intimate, and it had the proper ambience of anonymity.

Steve had not been a disappointment. In fact, at first he seemed too good to be true. No photograph could have captured his slow, languorous smile. There was nothing blatant or strident about him. He was confident and assured as he took her elbow and guided her to their booth.

Earlier, she had approached him at the bar. She recognized him immediately from his photograph. "Steve?"

His expression mirrored frank delight. "Bliss? Why—you're beautiful!"

Men had been telling her this all her life. Still, the way Steve said it made her blush. She was turned on by strong, masterful men, men who knew what they were doing. Steve was no exception. There was none of the usual awkwardness between them. When the waiter brought their drinks, they toasted each other in mutual appreciation.

"To unexpected delights," Steve said.

"And mysteries to unfold," she added.

They looked into each other's eyes and smiled.

He was impeccably dressed in a blue wool blazer with silver monogrammed buttons. A red silk tie that could only have been Countess Mara. Shiny dark hair and a tanned complexion. She couldn't keep her eyes off him.

"It's funny. Your call came just as I walked in the door," he said. "You wouldn't think a week in Cannes could be boring, but when you're talking tax shelters with fat old men, even the Riviera begins to pall."

"I wish someone would bore *me* like that," she replied. "Poor Stevie."

Suddenly the smile was gone. "Don't call me Stevie!" he said sharply. "My name is Steve."

Then the moment passed and he was charming again. A faint warning signaled in her brain, but she ignored it. That would prove to be one of the biggest mistakes of her life.

After dinner, he took her hand. They stood for a moment in the moonlight. All around them, West Falls was putting itself to sleep. Almost shyly, he asked, "What now? I'm not very experienced at this. Where do we go from here?"

Bliss, baby, she thought, you've hit the jackpot. She squeezed his hand. "I know a place where noboby will bother us."

He smiled. "Good. I hate to be bothered."

Their footsteps echoed hollowly in the empty shopping mall. Somebody else might have found it eerie, being alone in such a vast emptiness, but Bliss found the absence of crowds a comforting change. Fishing her key from her purse, she unlocked the rear entrance to her shop.

"A knitting store?" Steve asked in surprise. "You don't plan to knit me a sweater, do you?"

Maybe someday but not tonight, she thought. "This is my shop," she explained. "I have a hotplate in back. I'll make us some tea."

The glow of the window lights at the front of the store was enough to show the way around the curtained alcove that was her office. On the floor, she'd strewn overstuffed pillows. The smell of incense hung sweetly in the air.

"Umm," Steve sniffed. "Pot?"

"Incense," she replied, laughing.

"So I made a mistake! So?" There it was again, that strange intensity. All this time he had not let go of her hand, and now suddenly he pulled her roughly to him. "You weren't laughing at me, were you?"

"Of course not. Hey, what is this?" she asked. He

31

was breathing heavily, and she could feel his hardness against her. For a fleeting moment, she was flattered that he needed her so immediately, but there was something wrong. He was going too fast. He slipped his hands under her sweater and was deftly unhooking her bra. Her breasts swung free.

"Nice," he breathed.

All right, Bliss, go with it. Skip the amenities. She was as attracted to him as he to her.

His tongue parted her lips and insinuated itself too quickly into her mouth. There was something unsavory about the way he was coming on. She tried to respond as best she could, but she couldn't keep up with him. He began to rip at the delicate pearl buttons of her sweater.

"Wait! Let me do it," she said.

"Hurry up!" He flung his blazer on the floor and started to remove his tie.

She felt a stab of disappointment when he removed his shirt. She always preferred men with hairy chests. "Why are you in such a hurry, all of a sudden?" she asked.

He turned to her with a sneer. "Don't tell me you want to make small talk, a cunt like you who has to advertise for sex?"

"Now wait a minute—" she started to say, but he was forcing her down to the floor.

"I don't like waiting, baby." In a moment, he had pushed up her skirt and had ripped off her panties.

Oh, God . . . Oh, God, oh, God, don't let him hurt me! He was moving on top of her, rhythmically, and then suddenly, she noticed. His pants were still on. Maybe she could stall for time . . .

"Aren't you going to take off your pants?" she asked. When he did, maybe she would have an opportunity to escape.

Instead, he remained rigid on top of her. After a moment, in a voice she hardly recognized, he said, "You'll laugh."

"No, I won't," she hurried to assure him. Her heart was beating frantically.

"Yes, you will," he insisted. "If I take off my pants, you'll laugh."

It was a *child's* voice! She had a full-bloomed psycho on her hands.

"If you laugh, I'll kill you," he said.

"I won't laugh—I promise." Her skin was clammy with fear.

Slowly, very slowly, he began to pull his trousers off.

"There," she said, stalling for time, "isn't that better?" Instinctively, she caressed his torso. She felt a shudder run through him. Her hands slid down to his buttocks and touched . . . ruffles. *Ruffles?* And lace. *Bikinis!* As delicate as the ones she usually wore. In spite of herself, a giggle escaped her. "I'm sorry," she said immediately. "Really, I didn't mean—"

"WHORE!" His scream was as sudden as the fist that slammed across her face, bringing tears to her eyes.

She opened her mouth, but no sound came out. "Please," she said finally, her voice only a bare whisper. She tried to sit up, but he pushed her down again and she was trapped beneath him, helpless as prey.

"I'll teach you to laugh, bitch!"

She started to cry.

"Shut up, shut up, shut up!" he screamed.

He forced her legs apart with his knee. His fingers jammed into her without warning. The pain was worse than anything she had ever known. She gasped reflexively, but before she could scream, his free hand clamped down over her mouth.

She struggled in vain beneath him.

"Whining bitch," he hissed as his fist plunged into the creamy softness of her breast. He did it again. And again.

She was going to die. She would never see Sunny again. Her sweet Sunbeam, the only good thing that had come out of her miserable life. Sunny. Sweet Sunbeam, oh, my baby. I'm so sorry, so sorry . . .

She lapsed into unconsciousness and didn't know when the beating had stopped. She could hear him breathing, though, in the dark. His breath was noisy, spasmodic, as though he had been crying. How long had she been lying here? She was a mass of pain, everywhere.

"That was good, baby," she heard him say. She lay unmoving on the floor and heard the sharp zip of his fly. His smell was everywhere. It had permeated her skin. Her hair. She could taste it.

"I'll let myself out, pretty one," he said. "See you around."

Oh, God, she prayed, *please* let him go.

It wasn't until she heard the door slam that she permitted herself to cry out loud.

"Daddy," she sobbed, "I'll be good."

* * *

The April sunlight was too bright, and she
reached into her purse for her sunglasses. Sliding
onto the soft leather seat of her silver Porsche, she
glanced into the rearview mirror. "That *bastard,*"
she muttered. At least the makeup hid the bruise
on her cheek.

Don't think about it, Bliss, she told herself. Concentrate on the present. The cherry blossoms
were shedding on her front lawn. She mustn't forget to ask Gladys to call Cisco, the gardener. Now,
there's a creep, she thought. Always giving her the
eye, scrutinizing her. She sensed something dis-
turbingly primitive about him. But he was probably no different from any of the others. She had yet
to meet a man who was truly gentle or kind. Or
sane, for that matter. Sojourn had come close,
though, but even he had used her.

The car purred smoothly along the wide, quiet
streets of West Falls. The serenity of the town was
what had drawn her here—and kept her here—
although she had yet to make a single friend. But
then, she'd never had many friends. She had found
out early that women felt uneasy in the company
of a beautiful woman. But that was beside the
point. She would stay in West Falls because it was
the perfect place to raise her daughter. It had
none of the phoniness of Lake Forest, none of the
snobbery. How she'd hated Lake Forest, hated it
enough to run away from her father's elegant lake-
front mansion at age sixteen. She ran as far as she
could, right into the rough backwoods of Tennes-
see, where she found temporary solace in The Settlement. It was another life. A life without ameni-

ties, a life where Truth and Beauty mattered more than money.

She had begun her tenure there working the fields from dawn to dusk, slowly making her way into the closed circle of the communal family. After her duty in the fields was over, they rotated her to the kitchen. And then, finally, one night when Sojourn had come in for a midnight snack, he'd discovered her special talent.

Afterward, lying on his pallet, she had fingered the rough muslin of his shirt. "Doesn't this chafe your skin?" she asked. "I could weave something softer for you. I'm very good with my hands."

A grin had lighted Sojourn's long, bony face. "No kidding?"

"Seriously. I can knit and I can sew. I've won prizes for my weaving . . ."

"I don't doubt it for a minute, baby. If you knit the way you fuck, you can knit for the whole community." Sojourn had said it in jest, but it wasn't long before they had appointed her Mistress of the Cloth.

By the time Eric drifted into their midst and was told to report to her for a fitting, Bliss could tell at a glance what size shirt he would need.

Eric. Lanky and easygoing, he reminded her of Sojourn, with whom she was hopelessly in love. Eric, however, was available, whereas Sojourn was communal property. Eric was also hot-tempered and moody. One day kind and gentle, the next brutal and insensitive. When Bliss told him she was going to have his baby, he wept with joy and told her he would love the both of them forever. But

36

the next morning, he was gone without a trace. No note. Not a word to anyone. Just gone.

She had mourned for months, until Sunbeam was born, and for the first time, she knew what happiness was.

Through the years, she had often wondered what had become of Eric. The years had altered her perception of him, and she was able to think of him with fondness. When Sunny was small and asking where her father was, she had been tempted to try and track him down. By that time, though, she was living with Joan Hobbs on St. Mark's Place, knitting day and night, trying to place her sweaters at Bendel's and Bergdorf's.

"Don't look for that bastard," Joan had told her. "He was bad for you then, he'll be bad for you now." She smiled wistfully. "Besides, *I'm* a better father than Eric could ever be. Right?"

Bliss smiled. Good old Joan, always so practical. She hoped that Joan was happy with her new lover in California.

She stopped for a light at Elmwood Terrace just as Mayor Galitz was leaving his house. He waved and flashed his politician's smile. Bliss smiled back and shifted gears. The light was changing. She still couldn't believe it. West Falls with a Jewish liberal mayor. She had voted for Jared Galitz—even worked a telephone campaign with some of the other women in town.

Bliss turned a corner and drove into the library parking lot.

Sunny had *better* be there, she thought.

4

The Audition

SUNNY had never seen anything like it in her whole life. The auditorium of West Falls High had about a thousand seats. It was nothing like the dinky auditorium at Miramar-Bromley, with its old-fashioned stained-glass windows and hard wooden pews like a church. Everyone thought those windows were so beautiful, but Sunny couldn't stand looking at them. There were scenes of Crusaders plunging javelins into heathens. Blood all over. *Ugh.* And all the kids so snobby with their Gucci loafers and their chauffeur-driven limos. Maybe she could convince her mother to let her transfer to West Falls High next year. *Maybe.*

"Sunny, please, your hand."

Immediately, Sunny took her hand from her face. She hardly knew she did that anymore, but she could always count on her mother to remind her. *Sunny, your hand.* Maybe she would have a T-shirt made up with that slogan on it: SUNNY, YOUR HAND. And under it a picture of a girl with a twisted mouth . . .

She looked at her mother. Perfect, as usual. Every hair in place, the subtle, expensive perfume somehow just right to complement the exquisite knit jacket her mother had made in less than a week. She's incredible, Sunny thought. Nevertheless, she had a feeling that something was troubling her mother today.

Of course, if something were wrong, Sunny would be the last to know. Her mother never confided in her. Never.

Bliss was frowning now, surveying the crowded room. Maybe she had a headache, or maybe her period. Sensing the possibility of advantage, Sunny said, "Mother, please, let's go! This place is a zoo."

Privately, Bliss agreed. This was not what she had expected. This was pure pandemonium. But she said, "Wait. Let's give it another five minutes."

The auditorium was packed. People were crowded against the walls, in the aisles, blocking doorways. If a fire broke out, they'd all perish. She turned, and across the room she thought she saw a familiar face. Peggy Corcoran. And wasn't that Morgie, her daughter, with her?

"Sunny, isn't that the girl from your ballet class?"

Sunny followed her mother's gaze. It was Morgie Corcoran. Today her long dark hair was pulled back in a ponytail, which made her look prettier than ever. At that moment Morgan turned and smiled at her. The girls waved at each

39

other. Sunny felt a rush of relief. If Morgan was here, she thought, maybe she'd stay. She didn't know many girls in town, but she had met Morgan at Miss Priscilla's École de Ballet. Once, when the elastic on Sunny's ballet slipper had come loose, Morgie had lent her some thread. When Morgie had asked about her mouth (as they all did), Sunny had sensed true sympathy, and not just curiosity. So she didn't mind telling her: "It happened when I was a baby. It was an accident. I crawled up to a socket and I guess it must have looked good enough to eat . . ." Tears had come to Morgie's eyes. "It must have hurt terribly," she said.

Sunny shrugged. "I was just a real little kid. I don't remember." And that had been the end of it.

Bliss looked at her Baume & Mercier watch. A surprise Christmas gift from a man she'd gone out with only twice. He'd seen her ad in *Gothamite* Magazine and had fallen instantly in love with her. He was charming, a wealthy furrier in his early sixties, but he had a wife. He couldn't understand Bliss's reluctance to see him again because of that.

"My dear, in this day and age, surely you're sophisticated enough not to hold that against me." He had presented her with the watch. "Perhaps this will help change your mind."

She had smiled, kissed him tenderly on the cheek, and told him, "Whatever I am, I'm not a home wrecker."

She had tried to give him back the watch, but he had refused to take it. "I admire a woman with principle, Bliss," he said.

40

They had been here almost forty-five minutes, and the heat and the noise were finally getting to her. Maybe it was a mistake to come, after all. Onstage, an aging fag in a white turtleneck sweater was trying to get things started. Evidently there was something wrong with the microphone. The room filled with a series of ear-splitting hums and buzzes.

The man began to gesture wildly. Bliss stared in fascination. It was like watching a silent movie at double speed.

BZZZZHUMMMMGLLLAAAAAAHH-HHHH . . .

The noise crescendoed in a vibrating wail.

"PHYLLIS, FOR GOD'S SAKE, PULL THE FUCKING PLUG!"

Andy ffrench froze as his words suddenly bellowed loud and clear. A sea of stunned faces glared at him.

"Ha, ha," he began, laughing weakly. "Well, thank goodness we finally got it to work." The rubes didn't crack a smile. His hand went reflexively to his head. The old wigeroo was still in place. For fifteen hundred dollars it had better be! Mr. Rudolph, Perukier to the Stars, had assured him it was better even than the one he made for Sinatra.

They were still staring at him. The bumpkins reminded him of a lynch mob. "Bear with us, folks. We'll get the road on the show in another minute." They started talking to each other again, and he could breathe. He still couldn't believe the size of the turnout. Not only teenage girls, as he'd specified, but toddlers, babies, boys, mothers, grandfathers, the whole fucking town.

He was beginning to have doubts about this project, but did he have a choice? Nate Greene had assured him this was going to be a top-drawer production, the big time at last. But Andy wondered. He still couldn't believe it. Barron Heatter, the biggest box-office draw in America, directing a rock remake of *Little Women!* He shook his head. Maybe they knew something he didn't. He'd been in the business twenty-five years and thought he'd heard everything. Evidently, there were still some surprises left. Well, the old adage was true: There's no business like show business!

He glanced at the clock on the wall. Nearly one o'clock. Where the hell was that frigging mayor, the guy with the curls like Gorgeous George? Glitz, or whatever his name was. The natives were getting restless.

"Mothers, children, everyone—please control yourselves," Andy begged. The brats were running up and down the aisles. A couple of them had even climbed up onto the stage and were making faces at him. If they tripped on the wires, who would they blame? Andrew ffrench! This was much worse than the audition in Burbank, when they were casting for *Annie* with the Sunrise Rep. There, at least, the mothers had known enough to wait in the car.

But this place was something else. West Farts, Connecticut. Hey, he thought, that's a good one. He laughed. He'd have to tell that one to Barron. He could only hope Barron knew what he was doing. In addition to directing the picture, Barron was also producing it. He was also writing it. And it was Barron's idea to use unknowns. Already, unbeknownst to the general public, a huge media blitz was being planned around the four kids, whomsoever they might be. It was up to him, Andy ffrench, to find them.

No big thing. All he had to do was discover four adolescent girls who could sing and dance and act like June Allyson and Elizabeth Taylor and Margaret O'Brien and Jeanne Crain. Except they couldn't be professionals because they had to be unknowns. They also had to be beautiful and poised, and the camera had to love them. He was expected to accomplish this miracle in the space of a single afternoon.

If he failed to deliver, he could kiss his career good-bye. Not to mention his ass.

His ass had gotten him into this predicament in the first place. Ever since that fiasco in San Diego two years ago, he hadn't worked diddly shit.

Once they found out about San Diego, it was good-bye, Andy. Did they care that he was innocent? No way. All they cared about was that he had a record. Big deal. He had spent three months in the local brig fending off every King Kong clone in the county. So what? He'd been framed, pure and simple. How was he to know that sweet-faced little sailor was a hustler? He came on so innocent, but then, he did suck cock like a real pro. Still, Andy had been surprised when the guy demanded "five hundred dollars, cash money—no check!" And Andy had said, "No way, José." The guy, all four feet seven of him, opened the hotel window and, at the top of his lungs, began screaming "RAPE!"

Wouldn't ya know, the judge believed the little punk. One lousy weekend of less-than-glorious sex had been Andy's ruination.

Nate Greene had been his salvation.

After months of pounding on closed doors all over Hollywood, Andy had fled East. There was always off-Broadway, and even off-off-Broadway. He'd sublet a roach-infested studio on Leroy Street and taken a part-time job as a waiter in Felicia's Trattoria on Mulberry Street. The pay was zilch, but at least he was entitled to free lunch.

One afternoon, Nate had come in, looked up from his Fettuccine Felicia, and recognized him. Nate blinked. "You," he said, pointing with his fork. "I know you. You're the one who coproduced *Annie* with the Sunrise Rep, ain't ya?"

ffrench tried to smile. Who *was* this guy? "How absolutely marvelous of you to remember," he said. Christ. He *did* look familiar. Was he a director? A producer? A vice cop?

"Remember? How could I forget? You were the genius who cast my client, Rosa McKern, in the lead. May she rot on the spot wherever she is."

ffrench stared openmouthed. "Rosa was *your* client?" A touch of respect came into his voice. Rosa McKern was the most talented midget he'd ever met, although nobody suspected she was nearly forty. She didn't have one of those high-pitched midget voices that turned everyone off; Rosa sounded just like a normal child. And she looked like one, too.

"I hear she's playing Stallone's granddaughter in *Rocky VIII,*" ffrench said. "She's going to be a big star!"

44

"Star, my ass. The ungrateful bitch left me for Sue Mengers. Another beauty." Greene made a noise like a wounded mountain lion. For a moment the two men commiserated in silence. Whoever said show business was glamorous?

Greene squinted at ffrench as if struggling to remember something. "Dincha once have some union trouble in San Diego? Somethin' like dat?" he asked.

ffrench sank slowly into the chair beside Greene. So. His reputation had followed him all the way to the Apple. He was doomed. "Union trouble, right," he replied, sighing.

His heart was pounding so violently that he almost didn't hear Greene ask, "Hey, you wouldn't by any chance be lookin' for work?"

Andy was not a religious man. In fact, the last time he prayed in earnest was back in sixth grade when a bunch of mean girls cornered him in the schoolyard and tried to pull his pants down to see if he had one.

But he prayed now. With his fingers crossed behind him, he prayed. "Well, I'm always open to new opportunities," he said.

"Yeah?" Greene said. He seemed to be pondering whether or not to disclose some information. He lighted a long cigar, drew on it, took it from his mouth, and waved it in front of Andy. "Well, ya gotta promise to keep this on the QT. Nothing is set yet, but there's a big project in the works. If it gets off the ground, I'm in for a percentage and credit as line producer. I hear you're good with little people."

Oh, shit. The creep was putting him on. All

45

right, he'd play along. "Little people?" he asked, trying to look nonchalant.

Nate stared at him. "Yeah, *kids*. I once heard someone say you liked kids." He tapped a pudgy finger to his head. "Old Nate Greene never forgets what people tell him. It's all up here."

Andy had lost so much already that there was nothing left to lose. He nodded. "It's true. I do love kids," he admitted. *"A lot.* I've always regretted never having any of my own."

Nate seemed satisfied. "Good," he said. "Because not everyone is willing to work with kids, and this thing is *big*, my boy."

Any minute now, the punch line would come. "How big?" he asked.

Greene leaned forward conspiratorially, although they were the only ones in the restaurant at this hour, not counting Felicia, who was glowering at them from the kitchen. "We're talking Academy Awards, pal."

Sure, Andy thought. *Sure.*

But Nate Greene wasn't kidding. Good grief, the guy was serious. Swallowing hard, Andy said, "Wow, that's pretty big, Nate." From the corner of his eye, he could see Felicia waving a dish towel at him, her signal for him to get his ass moving. Reluctantly, Andy stood up. Tearing off a corner of the grease-spattered placemat, he scribbled his phone number. "Call me," he said. "We'll take a meeting."

Greene nodded. "It may not happen overnight," he cautioned him.

Andy could wait. He had been waiting his whole

life for something like this, and he could wait a little longer.

As it turned out, it was six weeks before Greene called. Andy had almost forgotten about it. "We got the green light," Nate had said. "Be at The Plaza for breakfast on Monday, eight sharp."

So there he sat at the same table with Greene; Spyros Andropolis, the cinematographer; Phyllis Sawyer, who would be Andy's assistant; a couple of script people; and Barron Heatter himself. It had made his head spin, being with doers for a change instead of do-nothings.

Everything was all set—everything, that is, except the casting of the main roles. The four unknowns.

God help him.

The polite applause of the crowd brought him back to the present. Almost reflexively, ffrench started to take a bow when, from the corner of his eye, he caught a glimpse of plaid pants. Plaid pants and a forest-green blazer. Unbelievable.

"Ladies and gentlemen, let me introduce you now to someone you already know and love—your very own mayor, Hizzoner the Mayor Glitz."

"That's *Ga*-litz," Jerry whispered into Andy's ear. "*G-a-l-i-t-z.*"

For a second, Andy felt a dangerous stirring within himself. Whispering in his ear always turned him on. He stepped back. He couldn't afford another San Diego. But, he had to admit, the man's curls were a wonder to behold. What a tragedy the guy was straight. Only straight men would be foolish enough to appear in public in a getup like that. Life was so unfair.

The mayor took over the mike. "My gracious constituents," he began, "I can't tell you how gratifying it is to see so many of you here today, all bright-eyed and bushy-tailed . . ."

ffrench forced a grin. "Uh, we're running late, Mayor, so if you could just speed it up a bit . . ."

Jared nodded. "Of course, of course, this won't take but a minute. I just want to make sure all these good people know how fortunate we are to have been chosen as the location for a film that will surely go down in cinematic history."

Suddenly someone in the back yelled out, "Hey . . . What's it about?"

"Yeah, tell us. Where's Michael Jackson?"

A great roar swelled from the audience. Jared looked at ffrench for help.

"Uh-uh-uh," ffrench began in a singsong voice. "That's a no-no! We'll all find out soon enough!"

A wail of disappointment replaced the roar.

Jared made a placating gesture. "Now, now. Let's show Mr. ffrench how well behaved we can be. I'm sure you all know Mr. Andrew ffrench, who has come to us directly from Hollywood, where he was casting director on such never-to-be-forgotten films as—" Jared fumbled through his pockets for the list. Greene had given him a list of ffrench's credentials, but where the hell was it? "Uh—some very famous motion pictures too numerous to mention. I hope you will give him your full cooperation and make us all proud of our wonderful town, West Falls. Let's hear it for Mr. Andrew ffrench . . ."

One or two people in the crowd applauded, and Andy stepped forward eagerly. Evidently, though, the mayor was not quite finished. "But before I leave you today, I would like to take this opportunity to have my family extend their own special welcome to you, Mr. ffrench, and to your entire company." The mayor pointed to the front row. "Selma, dear . . . Olivia, darling . . . come on up and welcome Mr. ffrench."

Andy ffrench looked to the wings where Phyllis Sawyer stood hugging her clipboard. She seemed to be enjoying his suffering. He'd seen ugly women in his time, but Phyllis was bowwow city. The minute he laid eyes on her, he knew she'd be a royal pain. But Nate Greene had insisted she was *also* great with kids. Naturally, two people who were great with kids would make a wonderful team. And Phyllis had credentials. Big deal. So she once worked for Soupy Sales and, before that, Pinky Lee. ffrench wasn't born yesterday. He knew Greene was *shtupping* her. How even a low-life agent could dip his wick into that pot of glue was beyond comprehension. She was a bleach blond with a face full of warts and the longest earlobes he'd ever seen. They hung down practically to her titties. Phyllis Sawyer made Phyllis Diller look like Phyllis George.

But wait. What was *this* coming onstage? He couldn't believe it. Good Lord, it was a younger version of Phyllis Sawyer minus the warts and the earlobes!

Olivia Galitz, centerstage, grabbed the microphone from her father. "So glad to meet you, Mr. ffrench," she said in a gravelly voice that gave him gooseflesh. Her pudgy hand was extended. "On behalf of my mother and myself, I just wanna say how absolutely euphoric we are to have you here in West Falls."

More scattered applause.

ffrench couldn't take another minute of it. He seriously wondered if he could last out the day. Maybe he had died and this was hell. Maybe he was in the Twilight Zone. All he knew was, the sooner it was over, the better. He gave Olivia's hand a limp shake. "We really must get started, folks," he said. "Time is money in this business."

When at last he was alone again on the stage, he plunged right in. The first thing he had to do was thin the ranks.

"Will the following people please excuse themselves: all boys, please leave."

There was a rising murmur that he knew would keep rising as he continued.

"All girls younger than twelve and older than fifteen, please leave."

The murmur became louder.

Now he was getting to the nitty-gritty. Fools rush in where angels fear to tread, he thought, but sometimes you have to be a fool. "All girls who wear larger than a size thirty-four bee bra, out." Galitz's kid glared at him from the first row. He cleared his throat. "Uh . . . make that larger than a thirty-six cee."

Now he began to hear shouts of "unfair" and "discrimination!"

He turned a deaf ear. "Girls with braces, girls with glasses, girls with hearing aids, girls who limp, go!"

50

The hostility was tangible now. It was a monster waiting to pounce on him. He could feel the sweat dripping from his scalp, and he prayed that Mr. Rudolph wasn't shitting him about the waterproof glue. He waited while the rejects filed out of the auditorium and some measure of order descended once again.

He glanced at Phyllis Sawyer. She gave him the nod. He took a deep breath. Here comes the big one, he thought. "Okay, all you beautiful moms, out. OUT! See you back here at four thirty."

There were shrieks. There were howls. Andy ffrench, the professional, rendered himself impervious to the cries of the masses.

"O-kay," he said. "Everybody else—let's move to the gym."

Sunny Billington couldn't believe it. There were only a handful of girls left, and she was one of them. She didn't wear braces or glasses or a hearing aid, and she was still wearing a training bra. She didn't limp. But what about her mouth? Would the scar count? The man hadn't said anything about a deformed mouth.

She stood uncertainly, wondering what to do, when a voice said, "Hey, Sunny, isn't this great? We're really going to get a chance to audition!"

Morgan Corcoran smiled and took her hand. Together they walked into the gym.

5

The Royal Palm

PEGGY stood squinting in the bright sunlight. The steps of the high school were crowded with mothers who suddenly had no place to go. She looked at her watch. Almost one thirty. Maybe she should have kept the appointment with Dr. Schindler after all. Well, the *hell* with that, she decided. She'd wanted to kill Duke this morning. He would never change. But she had. After sixteen years, she had finally reached the end of her patience. What Duke thought was love was nothing more than animal passion. And it wasn't enough. If she let him back into her life, he would go on with his infidelities, and she would go on feeling used. And maybe one day, she really *would* lose control and then it would be too late for both of them.

Absorbed in her thoughts, she jumped as she felt a hand on her shoulder.

"Peggy?"

The woman seemed vaguely familiar. Where had she met her? She was obviously wealthy. That knit jacket sure didn't come from K-Mart.

"I'm Bliss Billington," the woman said, offering her hand. "Our daughters are in the same ballet class."

A smile of recognition crossed Peggy's face. "You're Sunny's mother."

"Please call me Bliss," the woman said. She gestured to the crowd. "Isn't this something?"

Women were still pushing their way out of the building. Some had gathered in tight little groups on the steps. They looked confused and angry. Children were crying. It was a bad scene.

"I don't think this thing was handled properly," Peggy said.

Bliss shrugged. "That's an understatement, to say the least."

Peggy smiled. "Is this what they mean by 'show biz'?"

Bliss laughed lightly. "So," she said, "what are we going to do with all this extra time?"

Peggy hesitated. She could think of several things. That paper on Sylvia Plath, for one. It was due on Monday. God, talk about depressing. "Maybe we should get drunk."

Bliss chuckled. "Not a bad idea."

There was a sudden loud roar at the far end of the parking lot. Jared Galitz's white BMW sped into the flow of oncoming traffic.

"There he goes," Peggy said. "Our illustrious mayor, about to cause a major collision. Do you think he knows what he's doing?" she asked.

"When he made Hoover Parkway one-way, all those stores went out . . ."

"I think he knows what's good for the town," Bliss replied.

"I'm glad you think he's good for something," said a voice behind them. Startled, they turned to see who'd said it.

Uh, oh. When will I learn to keep my mouth shut? Selma felt her cheeks reddening. But I'm so *pissed* at him I could scream.

The women were still staring at her.

"Mrs. Galitz?" the one in the knit jacket asked.

"Don't mind me," Selma stammered. "I'm always putting my foot in my mouth." Among *other* things. "It's just that I had a very rough morning."

"You've had a rough morning?" the other two said in unison. The three of them laughed.

"Shirley, isn't it?" Bliss asked, reaching out to shake Selma's hand.

Selma made a face. "Close enough, but it's Selma, as in Alabama." How she hated the name. She'd given her own daughter a lovely, mellifluous name. *Olivia* reminded her of apple blossoms and starry nights and romance. Was it her fault the girl was a carbon copy of her father?

Where did she know these women from? The town council? The League of Women Voters? The temple? These days you couldn't tell who was and who wasn't. She shaded her eyes for a better look.

"I'm Bliss Billington and this is Peggy Corcoran. I think our daughters are in the same dance class. And I worked for your husband's election during the campaign."

"So did I," Peggy chimed in, looking at Bliss.

54

Well, hotsy-totsy for you, Selma thought. But she smiled. "Oh, yes," she said. "Now I remember." Hundreds of women in town had worked on Jerry's campaign. Was she supposed to remember every one of them?

"I'm Morgan's mother," Peggy said.

"Oh, *Morgan,*" Selma gushed. She knew from Morgan. Olivia couldn't stop saying how much she hated Morgan because she sucked up to Ms. Priscilla, and so Ms. Priscilla let her have all the solos. "My Olivia has told me that Morgan dances so beautifully. Like a swan."

Peggy was warmed by the unexpected compliment. The mother seemed to be cut of a different cloth than the daughter. Morgie had told her what a show-off Olivia was, always racing for the best place at the barre, never heeding Ms. Priscilla's instructions.

For a moment the three women stood in awkward silence. "We were just talking about going for a drink," Bliss began. "Would you like to join us?"

Peggy looked sharply at Bliss. *Us?* Had she agreed to a drink? Oh, why not? Sylvia Plath could wait.

There was something deliciously *verboten* about sitting in a bar in the middle of the afternoon. Selma loved it. Her arms were covered with goose bumps, partly because there was so much excitement and partly because she had just finished her third whiskey sour. In her whole life, she'd never had more than two drinks at one time. Even at Olivia's Bas Mitzvah, she had limited herself to a cup of wine at the kiddush. Always so afraid of losing control. Well, Selma, it's time to grow up.

There was a pleasant buzzing in her ears, like the hypnotic drone of insects on a warm summer's day. Next to her sat her good friend Bliss, a woman she hadn't even known two hours ago. What a gorgeous woman, that Bliss. And look at that jacket around her shoulders! "That's the most beautiful jacket I've ever seen," she said, fingering the soft wool. "Beautiful, beautiful."

Bliss smiled. "Thank you. I made it. If you like, I'll make you one, too."

Peggy leaned forward with interest. "You *made* that? Oh, my God, don't tell me—you're Bliss Knits!" How many times had she passed by that shop, right across the street in the West Falls Mall, and wished that she could afford to buy something there?

Bliss Nitts? Selma wondered. What kind of a name was *Nitts?* She could have sworn her name was Killington, Millington, something like that. Who cared? These were her friends. They were one for all and all for one. The Three Musketresses. Selma dissolved in a burst of laughter.

The women turned to her. "What?" Peggy asked. It was funny to see the mayor's wife so totally smashed after only three drinks. But she liked her. "Let us in on the joke."

"I bet your name is really Nitskovsky. Right? And you shortened it to Nitts so nobody would know." Selma leaned forward with a finger to her lips. "You don't have to worry," she whispered. "I won't tell anybody. Scout's honor!"

Bliss laughed heartily. It was the first good laugh

she'd had all day. After last night, she hadn't ever wanted to see The Royal Palm again. When Peggy had suggested they come here, she couldn't think of a way out. After a couple of drinks, however, the place seemed harmless enough. An ordinary bar. Nothing sinister about it.

Fred the bartender appeared at their table with a fresh round of drinks. "Compliments of the gentleman at the bar," he explained.

The three women simultaneously looked toward the bar. There was one man, an unkempt-looking fellow in a tweed jacket that was worn through at both elbows. He raised his glass to acknowledge them.

"Creep," Peggy said. "He sees three women alone, and right away he figures we're on the make."

Selma squinted through a golden haze. Everything seemed blurred and pleasantly soft. "Wait," she said. "I think I know him." She couldn't be sure, but wasn't that Max Miller?

"Who is he?" Bliss asked. She thought she'd seen him around town. He looked harmless enough, but of course since last night, she knew that looks were no criterion for judging sanity.

Selma took a sip of her fourth whiskey sour and grinned. She couldn't feel her tongue. You're *shikker,* my love, she giggled to herself. "That's Mill Maxler . . . Oooops," she whooped. "I mean Max Miller. A real *Mensch.* Capital *M.*"

Peggy looked at her quizzically. "What's a 'mensch'?"

"Oh, my dear, that's a question even Hillel had trouble answering," Selma replied somberly. "A mensch? A mensch is a man who doesn't care about his image." There were tears in Selma's eyes. She had hit it right on the head. She was forty-one years old, and she was married to someone who didn't know the meaning of the word *mensch.* She was stuck. Stuck with a schmuck. Stuck with a schmuck who made her suck. She laughed. She was crying and laughing at the same time and hoping that this wonderful afternoon would never end.

She must have dozed off. The buzzing in her ears had disappeared, and Peggy's voice was saying, " 'Married female, white, 41, desires a little "afternoon delight." Discretion a must! Sincere, sensitive, sexy. Please send photo, short bio to Box 4012.' "

Selma shook her head. "What *is* that?" She squinted at the newspaper Peggy had spread out on the table. "How long have I been asleep?"

Peggy smiled at her. "Not long. Look at this. Right here in *The Marketplace.* Personals ads! Can you believe it?"

Selma blinked. She always looked at the back pages of *The Marketplace.* There were always wonderful-sounding ads for garage sales, domestics, antiques. So how come she never noticed "afternoon delight"? "Does that mean what I think it does?" she gasped.

"Not always," Bliss replied, an edge of bitterness to her voice. *Never again,* she promised herself once more. Her tit was killing her. If it didn't stop hurting, she'd have to go to the doctor . . .

Peggy watched her with interest. "Have you ever done this? Answered an ad, I mean?"

Bliss stirred the ice in her vodka collins. "Let's drop it, okay?"

"Oh, come on, they sound harmless enough," Peggy said. "Listen to this one: 'Quiet, refined, middle-aged stockbroker seeks soul mate. Warmth and understanding more important than looks. Mutual interests a must. Prokofiev, Pirandello, Picasso . . .'"

Bliss shrugged. "Don't believe everything you read."

Peggy glanced at Bliss's ringless finger. "When did you get your divorce?" Peggy asked. Perhaps she shouldn't have asked. After all, they hardly knew each other. Still, she felt a curious bond with these women that was only partly attributable to the drinks and to the fact that their daughters were members of Miss Priscilla's École de Ballet.

"A lifetime ago," Bliss replied. "You can learn a lot in a lifetime."

They lapsed into a ruminative silence that was broken when Selma said sadly, "They didn't have ads like that when I was single."

Well, they do now, Peggy thought. "It's easier to be single today," she said. After a pause, she confessed, "My husband and I are separating."

"Oh, I'm so sorry," Selma offered earnestly. She began to cry.

Tears filled Peggy's eyes. "Don't," she said, taking Selma's hand. "Don't you dare cry or I will, too."

Only by concentrating on the pain in her chest did Bliss manage to keep from breaking down. "It's all these drinks. They're doing it to us . . ."

"Excuse me," said a deep voice. "Is everything all right here?"

The three women looked up into Max Miller's concerned face.

"Max!" Selma exclaimed. "It *is* you! Girls! It *is* him!"

Somehow Bliss found her voice. She held out her hand. "Thank you for the drinks, Mr. Miller. This is Peggy Corcoran . . ."

Peggy nodded hello. "It was kind of you, but I'm afraid it was one more than we could handle."

"Speak for yourself," Selma slurred, grinning. She stood up and fell against the table. She sank back into her seat with a groan.

"I don't think she should drive," Max said. He had not let go of Bliss's hand. "Maybe I should drive her back to the high school."

Bliss stared at him. "How did you know we're going back to the high school?"

Max, reddening, admitted, "I'm afraid I didn't get your name, but I couldn't help noticing you at the audition."

She couldn't help but smile. He was so ingenuous, so caring . . . *Oh, no!* She refused to be taken in again. The smile froze on her face. "Bliss Billington," she said coolly, and took her hand from his.

Max was devastated. Obviously, he had offended her in some way. It had been so long since he'd even seen a woman he'd like to know better, and now, somehow, he'd spoiled it. She was the most beautiful woman he'd ever seen—more beautiful, even, than Audrey. God forgive him.

"Ruthie is at the audition?" Selma asked disbelievingly.

Max had to smile. "What can I tell you, Selma? It was like pulling teeth. She wanted to go to the softball game." He turned to Bliss. "My daughter, Ruthie, is catcher for the Bluebirds. She says softball is her life. Do you have that problem with your daughter?"

Bliss laughed. "Not quite. But I have other problems."

"Well," Max said softly, "maybe we can discuss our daughters' problems over dinner someday." He looked at his watch. "Hadn't we better get back? It's past four thirty . . ."

Bliss and Peggy got to their feet in a hurry.

"I don't believe it," said Peggy.

"Believe what?" asked Selma, leaning against the table for support.

Bliss and Peggy exchanged glances. "It's time for us to leave now, Selma. Do you think you can make it to the car?"

Selma nodded wordlessly. Her head was beginning to feel very heavy.

Bliss remembered they hadn't paid for their drinks yet. "What about our bill?"

"I took care of it," Max replied quickly.

"You shouldn't have done that," she said. "Really, you shouldn't have."

He took her hand. This time she did not resist. "Maybe I shouldn't have," he conceded, "but I wanted to. Please don't be angry."

She wasn't angry. She didn't know what she was.

61

6

Selma

Vital, vivacious redhead seeks sensitive, mature counterpart capable of appreciating the better things in life: love, friendship, kindness. No raving beauty but personality plus. Good cook, good listener, good-hearted. No photo necessary. **Box 7321.**

"YOU'RE the most beautiful woman I've ever seen." He kissed her eyelids. The tip of her nose. Her cheeks. Her chin. His lips brushed hers.

"Ooh . . ."

His sensitive fingers caressed her nipples. "Beautiful, beautiful," he murmured.

"You like them?"

"What's not to like?" His teeth flashed. Perfect. No gaps. He moved on top of her, light as a feather. "Look at me," he demanded.

She looked. "I love you," she said. "I've always loved you, especially in *Belgian Affair.*"

"You're magnificent," he told her. "You were made for love."

"And to think I almost lost you," they said together.

The music crescendoed and Selma woke up.

"Shit!" she said. Every night this week, she'd dreamed about him. Barron Heatter. Hunk of hunks. The Gorgeous Goy. In town for a whole week, and she still hadn't met him. So near and yet so far.

The moistness between her legs was real enough, though. With her eyes still closed, she let her fingers slip between her thighs. "Oh, Barron . . ." she crooned, undulating to her own private rhythm.

The door burst open. "Miz G'litz, ain'tchu up *yet?*"

Selma blanched. When would Princess ever learn to knock? She was as bad as Olivia! "What is it, Princess?" Selma asked.

"Ah needs money! Hizzoner fo'got agin, and widout money, how's I s'poze to buy food?" Princess, one hand on her hip, the other extended under Selma's chin, cracked her gum loudly.

Selma pushed Princess's hand aside and reluctantly stumbled out of bed. Her head was spinning. What was the matter with Jerry anyway? Today was Monday. Monday was the day Princess got the food money for the week. Why couldn't he remember a simple thing like that?

Princess tapped her foot impatiently. "Ya wanna

step on it, Miz Gee? Ah has to be back at eleven for *The Price Is Right!*"

Selma fished in her purse and thrust some bills into Princess's hand. "What time is it?" Selma asked, yawning.

Princess sighed. She looked at the slim gold watch she always wore. A damn good copy of a Piaget, Selma thought. If she didn't know better, she'd take it for the real thing. "Ten aftuh ten, Miz Gee," Princess informed her, eyeing her closely.

When she looked at her that way, Selma always felt vaguely uncomfortable. She forced herself to return the stare. For a brief moment, Selma wondered what Princess was planning to write about her in that exposé. She shook her head. Maybe the exposé was only a rumor. Just look at that stupid expression. Look at that dumb red Afro. Selma shrugged. Without the red hair, without the vacuous look, Princess would be a real beauty. She had a good figure. If only she didn't insist on wearing those *shmattes* that looked as though they had come from some thrift shop. Which they probably had. Selma had offered Princess some of her own clothes, but unlike other *shvartzehs* she had known, Princess had steadfastly refused them.

"Me? Ah don' wear honkie clothes!"

So Selma had stopped offering.

Princess shoved the bills into the pocket of her Army surplus shirt and sashayed out of the bedroom.

Again Selma wished they could get rid of her, but of course, Jerry wouldn't hear of it. These days, Jerry wasn't hearing much of anything. He wasn't hearing; he wasn't talking; he wasn't *doing*. He

64

hadn't touched her in more than a week. He was still furious.

Sighing, Selma crawled back into bed and closed her eyes. The headache was back. Actually, it had never left. A week of pounding, on-again, off-again headaches, ever since that afternoon at The Royal Palm. It must be the longest hangover in recorded history. It was her punishment from God, for going out drinking with shiksas in the afternoon. Would Jerry ever let her forget it?

It was bad enough she'd gotten drunk in public. Bad enough she'd puked all over Bliss Billington's silver Porsche. Bad enough Peggy and Bliss had practically carried her up the high school steps. But when she'd passed out cold in the high school gym and Max Miller had to carry her to his car and drive her home, she'd crossed the line. Jerry's sacrosanct image had been tarnished forever.

"A member of the town council, Selma!" he'd raged. "He had to sling you over his shoulder like a common drunk! My wife! My helpmate! My partner! *Feh!*"

In vain, she had tried to convince him that it wasn't the end of the world, that Max Miller was a real *mensch*, a true gentleman. He would understand.

"What's to understand?" Jerry had screamed. "I can't walk down the street without people giving me looks! My own secretary turns away when she brings me coffee! The whole town knows I have a *shikker* for a wife!"

Selma shook her head. She couldn't believe he was making such a megillah! If being the mayor's wife was like this, she thought, what would it be like to be married to the first Jewish president of the United States? For the first time, she thought she knew what drove Betty Ford into the clinic.

But getting drunk in public was only part of the problem. The audition was another story. It still seemed unreal. One minute she was passed-out drunk, the next minute she woke to find herself the mother of a star.

Her Olivia—among the *chosen!* Olivia had beaten the odds and landed one of the leads—Jo March—in Barron Heatter's *Little Women* epic. And not just Olivia; Sunny Billington, Morgie Corcoran, and most surprising of all, little Ruthie Miller, that scraggly wild child whose hair cried out for a comb. (Not that it was her fault; the poor baby had no mother.) How to explain it? It was *more* than a coincidence—it was a miracle. All their babies plucked like plums for stardom!

She would never forget the sight of Olivia dancing on the kitchen table with all the lamps in the house brought into the kitchen and focused on her as Princess held the telephone aloft. "Listen, Bubbeh, this is how it goes. I memorized the whole thing already: 'Poor little us. No mon-eee, but we've got each otherrrrr! Meg, Jo, Amy, Beth, and Motherrrrr!'" Olivia belted out to her grandmother.

Oy. Such a *geshray!* Her head splitting, Selma put her hands over her ears. "What's going on?" she had asked hoarsely. Her mouth felt as though it were stuffed with cotton.

"I got the part, for your information," Olivia had said coldly. "Or are you too drunk to understand?"

Selma felt as if she'd been slapped. Princess set

66

the phone on the table and put her arms around Selma. "Yo' need yo' rest, Miz Gee," she said, leading Selma back to bed. Behind her, she could hear Olivia bleat into the phone: *"Bubbeh,* I'm glad you and *Zayde* are coming. Mommy has a terrible drinking problem . . ."

That's when the pounding in Selma's head had begun in earnest.

The next day brought nausea, more dizziness, and the doting grandparents—Bea and Abe Moscovitz, the Flanken King himself. They arrived at the door with six dozen long-stemmed American Beauty roses for their American Beauty granddaughter and a copy of "The Twelve Steps" from Alcoholics Anonymous for Selma.

"Get ahold of yourself!" Bea admonished Selma. "After all, now you have your daughter's future to consider! This is not the time to become a *shikker!"*

Was there ever a good time for that? Selma wondered. Well, it *could* be worse. Abe and Bea could be staying with them. At least they had kept the condo in Stamford. Even so, they spent most of their time in West Falls. They had appointed themselves Olivia's official cheering squad. They even brought their own director's chairs—labeled *"Zayde"* and *"Bubbeh"*—to the set each morning. Abe wore sunglasses and a beret. Bea carried a clipboard and a thermos of lemonade with honey for Olivia's throat.

Every morning, at seven o'clock sharp, they arrived to whisk Olivia off to work in the salmon-colored Continental with vanity plate: FLANKEN-1.

FLANKEN-2 and FLANKEN-3 on the Mercedes and the Alfa-Romeo, respectively, were, thank heaven, still in the garage of the Palm Springs house. When Selma was a child, there had been only one FLANKEN—a black-and-white Buick with the four holes. But that was when Crazy Abe's Flanken City was just one kosher butcher shop in the Throg's Neck section of the Bronx. Now, of course, there were hundreds of Flanken Cities all over the country.

The FLANKEN plates didn't embarrass Olivia, but they still bothered Selma. Even after all these years, she still remembered her sweet sixteen party at The Plaza, and how she'd resisted getting into the car to get there.

"You think *FLANKEN*'s bad?" Bea entreated. "Your father wanted *BRUST!* Can you imagine? I had to beg and plead. 'Anything,' I said, 'anything is better than *BRUST! KISHKE,*' I said. 'Abe, make it *DECKEL, HELZEL—BRUST* is not nice!' You know your father—stubborn as a cheap steak under the knife.

"Thank God there was a guy named Goldstein at the Motor Vehicles who said, 'You ain't gonna get avay wid it. Dey don' letcha do dat. *BRUST* is *tits*, plain and simple.' Your father offered him money, but the guy was just as stubborn as he was. So we settled on *FLANKEN*. Thank your lucky stars!"

Selma sighed, remembering. She was grateful for the silence in the house. Everyone was gone, and she liked it this way. Jerry's Curtis Mathes beckoned. Did she dare? Should she? What the hell? He wouldn't know the difference anyway.

He had other things to worry about. First, there was the hubbub about rerouting the traffic from Coolidge Boulevard to Hayes Road, over by the railroad tracks. Carlo Battista was screaming bloody murder. His barbershop happened to be on Coolidge Boulevard. "Itsa da enda my businessa! Jes' lika da shops onda Hoover Parkway!" he had raged. This morning, Selma could hear Carlo's words blasting through the receiver as Jerry stood there, dripping wet from the shower, trying to placate the little man.

"Carlo, Carlo, this is different," Jerry had soothed. "You've been in business thirty years! A few days without traffic isn't going to hurt you! Trust me!"

Yesterday there was a call from Dr. Marcus Silver, the orthodontist, asking what was it with the guy who was discriminating against girls with braces. And then the front doorbell rang and there stood Harvey Glass, O.D., the head of the Fairfield County Optometric Association, waving a petition with nearly a thousand signatures on it. "We're gonna get the Civil Liberties people on you if this situation isn't remedied," Glass had sputtered. "I've never heard of such blatant discriminatory tactics. Who the hell do you think you are?"

Poor Jerry. "I'll see what I can do," he promised.

As if that wasn't enough, Roger Ridgeway, their neighbor from two houses down, was on a rampant antilitter campaign. Nothing new there. Roger had an obsession with neatness. He couldn't stand to see as much as a blade of grass out of place anywhere. Two days ago, still in his bedroom slippers, before the sun was even up, Roger had rung their bell to complain about the litter on the high school grounds.

"All those idiot women with nothing better to do than hang around waiting to see that movie star, What's-his-name! The grounds are littered with their garbage! Styrofoam cups! Cigarette butts . . . *Gross!*"

Jerry had tried to calm him. "Sven will take care of it, Roger. That's what we pay him for!"

Roger wasn't appeased. "Don't mention that Swede's name to me," he said. "He's a walking pigsty!"

Selma almost felt sorry for Jerry. But hadn't he brought this whole thing on himself? Making a movie in West Falls was his idea in the first place.

She reached out and turned on the stereo.

It was Mick, orgasmically demanding that she look at him.

Oh, God, she thought, recalling the dream she'd had of Barron Heatter, telling her to look at *him.* At this very moment Barron was here in West Falls, breathing the same air, hearing the same sirens, washing his hands in the same unfluoridated water. Her own parents were probably looking at him right now, in the high school gym. Olivia was looking at him. *Everyone* was looking at him. Everyone but me, she thought. Well, she'd had her chance that day at the audition, but she blew it. He was there and she was there—in the same room—and she'd been too drunk to know.

Olivia was no help at all. "Stay away from rehearsals, Ma," she'd ordered. "I don't want my

70

friends laughing, waiting for you to pass out again. Once was enough!"

So stay away she did.

When Olivia came home at night, Selma tried in vain to find out about Barron.

"Is he really tall?"

Olivia shrugged.

"Is he as good-looking in person?"

"If you go for *old*, Ma. He must be thirty, at least."

"So what was he wearing today?"

"I didn't notice."

"How could you not notice?"

"Ma! Leave me alone!" Olivia screamed, stomping off to her room.

She couldn't talk to Jerry. After their argument last night, she might never talk to him again.

"How could you *do* this to me," he had raged. "Don't you care about my image?"

She'd had about enough. How long was he going to punish her for what happened with Bliss and Peggy?

Before she could stop herself, she said it. "I'm sick of your image!" It had taken them both by surprise. In fourteen years of marriage, she never thought she'd find the courage.

Once she began, however, she couldn't stop. The words tumbled forth in an avalanche. "All you ever think about is your image! Did Harry Truman bug Bess about *his* image? Did Lincoln yammer at Mary Todd about his? Would Martha take such crap from George?"

Jerry's broad face reddened. His eyes bulged

71

goiterously. He wagged a finger in her face. "Watch it, Sel. You're on thin ice."

"No, Jerry, this time you watch it!" she had screamed. Jabbing a finger into his paunch, she warned, "One more Twinkie and you're going to burst!"

"How dare you!" he yelled, backing away. "I'm not going to listen to any more of this! I don't have to take such talk from my own wife! Bad enough I've got the whole town on my head!"

"*Your* head! *Your* image! *Your* future! *Your* schlong!"

He stared. "What does my *schlong* have to do with anything?"

Had she gone too far? She remembered an article she had read in *Cosmo* about never using the penis as a bargaining tool. But she didn't care. She had come this far, and she wasn't going to stop now.

"You *really* want to know about your *schlong*, Jerry? You put it *where* you want and *when* you want, and never once do you think about what *I* want!"

The blood drained from his face. A vein throbbed dangerously in his forehead. His hands were trembling. Evidently, she had hit a nerve.

"You're supposed to want what *I* want," he had whispered hoarsely. "You're my *wife*, aren't you?"

She groaned. It was useless. They weren't communicating. Maybe it was time she realized that. Maybe she should do something about it.

Meanwhile, things were going from bad to worse. This morning, he'd even closed the door when he went into the bathroom. Last night, he'd undressed in the dark. The way things were going, she might never see hide nor hair of his *schlong* again. Would she miss it? She wondered. What happens to a woman when she has no access to a *schlong*?

She thought of Peggy Corcoran. Had she finally separated from that mechanic husband of hers? And what about Bliss Billington? Did she enjoy the single life?

She thought back to that afternoon at The Royal Palm. How they'd laughed over those ads in *The Marketplace*. How ridiculous they were! "Afternoon delight!" Imagine! She imagined. Hmm. Maybe it wasn't so ridiculous after all . . .

Mickey David's sexy baritone flooded the room. "Take a chance on love," he urged seductively. "It won't hurt you . . . to take a little chance . . ."

Those ads didn't just *appear* in the paper, she thought. They were written by real people. Lonely people. Misunderstood people. People like *me*, Selma realized.

". . . So take a chance, myyyyy baaaaa-by. Take a chance and . . ."

"Why not?" Selma said aloud.

7

Peggy

Irish-American Venus (with arms) seeks compassionate, intelligent Adonis for dialogue and Dionysian pursuits. Sincere, separated student of philosophy needs soul mate. Let's toast the gods together. Send bio to **Box 6810.**

PEGGY shifted in her chair. The session was not going well. In fact, it wasn't going at all. Five minutes had gone by and Duke hadn't said a word. It was his turn, but he was sitting in the chair next to her with his legs splayed out in front of him, biting his nails. It was a gesture she knew well. She resisted the urge to tell him to sit up straight, to grow up.

When they'd come into the office, Dr. Otto Schindler, F.C.A.A.S., P.C., had laid out the ground rules: "First, one of you speaks, then, please, the other." He had pointed a long, bony finger toward Peggy. "And the other must remember, please, never to interrupt." Then he had pointed the same skeletal finger at Duke and said, "Wayne, why don't you tell us what circumstances brought you here today?"

A vein in Duke's temple began to throb. He looked confused.

Dr. Schindler encouraged, "It's perfectly all right, Wayne. You needn't be afraid."

Duke took his fingers out of his mouth. "I ain't afraid!" he insisted belligerently. "And I ain't Wayne! Wayne is my son. I'm Duke."

Peggy watched as Schindler began to scribble madly in the notebook on his desk.

"Yes, I see. Wayne. Duke. Ah, the machismo of the American male," Schindler mused. "You're a fan of his, I take it?"

Duke stole a quick look at Peggy. She shrugged. "A fan of whose?" he asked.

"Why, John Wayne, of course. Wasn't he the Duke?"

"I never thought of that," Duke replied. He reached into his shirt pocket and pulled out a cigarette.

Schindler's bony finger made its appearance again. "Uh, uh, uh," it wagged. He pointed to a framed needlepoint square on the wall: HE (OR SHE) WHO SMOKES IS MASTURBATING IN PUBLIC.

Duke quickly put the cigarette back into his pocket.

Schindler leaned back in his chair. Peggy had

never seen anyone quite like him before. He was tall. Very tall. When he stood, his hairless head nearly grazed the ceiling. He was also reed thin and slightly stoop shouldered. He spoke with an accent—German, probably. He had a penetrating stare that made her feel more than a little uneasy. She could understand why Duke was having such a hard time communicating. She was going to have trouble, too.

The silence in the office was punctuated by the ticking of the clock on Schindler's desk.

Duke cleared his throat nervously.

"Take your time," Schindler said soothingly.

"Well . . ." Duke began at last, "she—"

"Who?" Schindler interjected. "We don't say 'she' here. We use names," he explained, smiling a cool smile.

This was a *big* mistake, Peggy thought. The man was not easy to talk to. She didn't know why Duke had insisted they come. She suspected no amount of counseling would help their marriage. Why couldn't Duke just accept that?

Visibly uncomfortable, Duke tried again. "Well, Peggy, my wife—her, over there—I mean, she— uh—Peggy—she threw me out!"

"Go on," Schindler urged.

"Well, uh, I mean, she found—uh, she, Peggy, she—uh—look, Doc, I'm not good with words, ya know?"

Schindler nodded. "I can see that, Wayne," he said. Frowning, he added, "I must please ask you not to call me 'Doc.' Doc is a bunny, and I am not a bunny."

Peggy and Duke exchanged glances. "Excuse

76

me," Peggy said to Schindler, "I think you have that a little mixed up. The bunny you're thinking of is Bugs. He says *Doc* a lot, but his name is Bugs."

Duke stared at her. Seventy-five bucks an hour, and they were discussing Bugs Bunny? "Wait a minute, can we please get back to the problem?" Duke demanded.

"Now, now, Wayne," Schindler advised cautiously, a professional, knowing tone to his voice, "let's not be hasty. Everything we say in this office has meaning."

Duke wondered what meaning Bugs Bunny could have in his marriage. But this guy was a doctor, and he must know. He inhaled and tried again. "So she—Peggy—threw me out. I mean, one minute we're doing it, and the next minute I'm out on my ass on the sidewalk!"

"Now wait a minute," Peggy interjected. "That's not—"

Schindler smiled benevolently and wagged the bony finger. "Now, now, Mrs. Corcoran, you must wait your turn." Turning to Duke, he said, "Let's backtrack a little. You were doing *what?*" He leaned forward eagerly.

Peggy saw the flush rise from Duke's neck and spread across his face. He didn't know what he was letting himself in for, Peggy thought, feeling sorry for him.

Duke gestured emptily in the air. "*It.* You know. *It!* We were making it, making out—"

"Well, which was it—*it* or *out?*" Schindler pressed.

Lowering his voice almost to a whisper, Duke said, "We were screwing. You know?"

Schindler shook his head. "No. I don't know. Why don't you explain?"

Duke slapped a hand to his forehead. "Doc! You don't know what *screwing* is? And you're a sex doctor?"

"Human sexuality is my field, yes," Schindler replied as he nodded, then began scribbling again. An alarm sounded. He pointed to Peggy. "Your turn," he said.

Duke stood up. "Hey, wait a minute! What is this?" he bellowed. "I'm not through! I'm paying seventy-five bucks an hour and I want my money's worth!"

"This is not a fire sale, Mr. Corcoran," Schindler answered brusquely. "Your 'money's worth' here is not measured in quantity but rather in *quality*. Please be seated."

Duke sat down in a daze. Peggy reached out and touched his arm, but he shrugged her off. "Duke, please," she said, "take it easy."

He turned to her. "Don't tell me what to do! You're always telling me what to do!" He was on his feet again, his hands balled into fists, his eyes blazing. "I'm sick to death of your being such a smarty-pants! Mrs. Big-time College Girl! You take a couple of pissant courses and you think you know it all!" He was screaming now.

Peggy stood and said, "This is ridiculous. I'm leaving." She turned to go.

"Oh, no, you're not! You're not going to pull that one on me!" Duke bellowed, pushing her back into her chair. "If anyone's leaving, it's gonna be me!" He stomped to the door. Then he turned. "And, Doc," he added, "you can take your bill and put it where the sun don't shine!" He slammed the door behind him. Hard.

Peggy burst into tears. "Oh, God!" She began to weep. "Dr. Schindler, I'm sorry you had to see this."

"That's all right," Schindler replied soothingly. "I see this kinda stuff all the time."

It was a lie. He *didn't* see this kind of stuff all the time. A dish like Peggy Corcoran walked into his office maybe once in a lifetime.

Under the desk, his long legs were crossed to sustain a powerful erection. Trying to keep his voice as calm as possible, he asked, "Do you always feel responsible for your spouse's infantile shenanigans?"

She looked up. He handed her a tissue. "Thank you," she said meekly. "I didn't want to come here today. I knew it would end up like this. The whole situation is pitiful."

"Well, I'm glad you came here," Schindler assured her. He stared at her. This Peggy Corcoran was one juicy piece. Usually they were worn-out, washed-out baggage whose husbands deserved a medal for staying with them for even a night. *But this one!* God! Tits that would have Freud salivating all over his beard. Shiny black hair that hung past her shoulders. He wondered what color her pussy hair was. Black, too, he bet. But you could never tell. He had slept with blonds who had black pussy hair and redheads with blond pussy hair and all combinations in between.

He recrossed his legs to heighten what he liked to call the "duality of response": above the desk, cool and analytical; below, a colossal jack-off. He hoped he could keep her in her chair a while longer. Maybe even get her to part her legs a little.

"I'm so ashamed," she said.

"Don't be," he comforted her. "These things happen."

"Not to me, they don't," Peggy insisted. Much to his dismay, she rose and headed toward the door. "I'm sorry we wasted your time, Dr. Schindler."

He stood up. "Wait!" he called desperately. "Please, Mrs. Corcoran—Peggy . . . May I call you Peggy?" he asked as he lunged awkwardly toward her.

"Are you all right?" she asked. "You're limping."

Schindler shook his head. "It fell asleep. My leg. It always falls asleep. Sleepy leg syndrome," he babbled.

Peggy looked at him with interest. "Really? I've never heard of that."

"An occupational hazard," he explained. He was standing very close to her. Maybe *too* close.

Was she imagining it? Or was there an enormous bulge in his trousers? She didn't dare look.

"Perhaps you'd consider coming here on your own?" he asked hopefully.

She didn't answer right away. "I'd have to think about it," she said. She put her hand on the door-knob.

Schindler's hand covered hers. It was a big hand —and very warm. "You may find it of *great* bene-fit," he said, pushing suddenly against her. "I can see how much you've suffered all these years."

What was happening? Was he supposed to come on to her like this? Was it some kind of therapy, or was he merely being nice?

"It's obvious your husband is still functioning on a primitive level. In other words, he's a big baby. I don't see how you've put up with him all these years," Schindler went on dramatically.

Her expression hardened. When she spoke, there was an edge to her voice. "Duke—Wayne—is basically a good person. I loved him very much . . . once."

Schindler cursed his luck. In his desperate ploy to keep her there, he hadn't counted on her loyalty to that ape husband of hers. Not only was she stacked, but she had character, too. His luck. Oh, well, he'd have another turn with her someday.

He didn't know when or how or under what circumstances. But when Otto Schindler made up his mind about a woman, she didn't stand a chance.

8

Bliss

IT was one of those days when nothing seemed to go right. One of the knitters had turned in a batch of sweaters with mismatched seams. She'd been forced to fire the woman, but a replacement would be hard to find. Luckily, it was summer and there was still time to prepare for the winter rush of orders.

What she could use now was a vacation. A change of scene. But Sunny was so busy these days that it was out of the question. Not that she wasn't grateful; the thought of Sunny being so happily involved for once was cause for celebration.

The transformation in her daughter's personality was incredible. In fact, Bliss couldn't remember the last time she saw Sunny put her hand to her mouth to hide the scar. It just didn't happen anymore. Not since that day when she and Selma and Peggy had returned to the high school from The Royal Palm.

Sunny had run up to her, shouting, "You won't believe it, Mother! I have a part in *Little Women!*" Bliss could hardly believe her ears, but Sunny rushed on: "Mother! I get to play Amy! Mr. ffrench said I sing like a nightingale!" Bliss scored one for Mr. ffrench. She knew she had been right to push this. Maybe this was just what Sunny needed to give her confidence.

But there was another side to the coin—negative factors Bliss hadn't counted on. The media, for one. That pushy reporter from *FOLK* Magazine, Myra Schick, kept calling day and night, asking for an interview. *People, Time,* and *Newsweek* had already been to see the four "Little Women" on the set, and the *Time* piece was on the newsstands right now. The phone at home didn't stop ringing. It was scary, so much instant fame.

Now the phone was ringing at the shop as well. Lynda Szyszyc, her assistant, was out to lunch, naturally, and that meant Bliss would have to answer it herself. She hated dealing with customers on the phone. And suppose it wasn't a customer? Suppose it was another nosy reporter—or another fan of Sunny's. Or even Selma Galitz calling *again* to apologize for throwing up all over her Porsche. The poor woman had been so embarrassed. Obviously, she wasn't used to social drinking. Still, there was something immensely likable about Selma—she was so up-front, so totally honest, so different from her husband, the mayor.

Almost absently, Bliss picked up the receiver.

83

She was unprepared for the breathy voice that taunted, "Are you still laughing, Bliss?"

A chill ran through her. "Who is this?" she demanded. But she knew, of course.

"So the slut has a daughter! You didn't mention that when you were making fun of me."

Her heart was beating frantically. "Listen, you," she warned, "I don't think this is a bit funny! What do you want from me?"

He ignored the question. "So there I was, reading my copy of *Time*, and who do I see but the slut! And her daughter! So, Bliss, did you tell them everything? How you advertise for love? How you take men to your shop? How you tease them with your soft white skin . . . your big tits . . . that creamy white ass of yours . . . ?" His breath was coming faster.

The bastard was jerking off, damn him!

She slammed the receiver down as hard as she could. Oh, God, she groaned. For the past couple of weeks, she had almost convinced herself that the episode with Steve Gordon hadn't really happened. But she could no longer deny it. He was real, all right, as real as the knot of pain in her breast.

The phone rang again. She stared at it, willing it to stop. Maybe he would get tired and find someone else to torment.

The ringing stopped at last.

Lynda Szyszyc returned and found Bliss still staring at the phone. "Bliss? Are you all right? Did anything happen?"

Bliss shook her head. "No, nothing happened," she said. "I'm fine."

9

Barron

THEY were here again today. Not even the rain could keep them away—and some of them didn't even have umbrellas! Through the tinted-glass window of the limo, Barron Heatter saw them lined up on both sides of the street in front of the high school. He felt a familiar twinge of panic.

What if the barricades didn't hold? What if Enrico couldn't slip him into the building fast enough and the women got to him and started ripping at his clothes? What if they took down his pants like that time in Brussels when he was making *Belgian Affair?* He broke into a cold sweat just thinking about it. He glanced at Enrico through the partition. The driver seemed his usual, catatonic self, calmly maneuvering the limo up the winding driveway to the entrance of West Falls High

School. Would Enrico know what to do in an emergency?

If he felt like this in the protection of the limo, how would he feel if that jerk-off mayor had his way about that Meet-the-Stars party he was cooking up? Of all the idiot schemes Barron had ever heard of, this was the worst.

"We've gotta do it to keep peace in the town, Heatter," the mayor had explained. "It's the only way. You wouldn't believe the crap I'm getting from the constituents."

Barron had looked at him like he was crazy. Constituents? Who did this guy think he was? Teddy Kennedy, for crissakes? He had tried to tell him it was a terrible idea to mix the townies with the stars. Oil and water. Hatfields and McCoys. Capulets and Montagues.

"Capulets?" Galitz had asked, looking puzzled. "Who're they?"

Barron tried again. "Mayor, you can't tumble the public with the stars. There's a whole image thing we've got to preserve."

Galitz had nodded. He knew from image. Even so, as mayor it was his responsibility to smooth ruffled feathers, and at this point, feathers were flying. Roger Ridgeway. Carlo Battista. Margaret Jensen. The mayor told Barron, "The people in town don't trust you. Well, maybe not *you*," he qualified hastily. "*All* of you. Together. They're afraid . . . They're afraid of what they don't know. Once they get to know you, they'll love you. Trust me."

Barron wanted to trust him. He had a lot riding on this picture. Like *everything*.

86

He sighed as Enrico slowed the limo.

"Are we ready, Mr. Heatter?" the chauffeur asked.

What is this "we" shit? Barron wondered. They weren't going to jump on *his* bones. He cleared his throat and closed his eyes. "Cream," he began to chant. "Cream . . . Cream . . . Cream," he sang in a steady monotone. It was his very own mantra, bestowed upon him by the maharishi back in 1973, and it had served him well. He felt calmer already and gave the high sign.

At the signal, Enrico stepped on the brakes and Barron bolted from the limo. A roar rose from the crowd. A sound so thunderous, so deafening, it was almost palpable. *"Bar-ron! Bar-ron! Bar-ron!"*

"Cream . . . Cream . . . Cream," he intoned desperately.

The door opened. Phyllis Sawyer grabbed him and pulled him inside to safety. "They're wild today, huh?" she said, peering over his shoulder.

"They're wild every day," Barron replied, unaware he was smiling.

He had barely stepped inside when Andy ffrench was on him.

"Barron, darling, thank God you're here! That Shapiro cunt is driving everyone up the wall. Six tantrums—*six!*" Andy complained, holding up five fingers. "And it's not even nine o'clock!" Together, they walked into the gym, where rehearsals were under way. "And *them,*" Andy moaned, pointing to the two old people in director's chairs marked *Zayde* and *Bubbeh.*

"Today they've got salami for lunch, and the

whole place stinks! Who *are* they, anyway, Barron?" Andy screamed.

Barron didn't answer. Come to think of it, he didn't know *who* they were. Maybe they were Barrbra Shapiro's grandparents, since the old guy couldn't keep his eyes off her. If so, he felt sorry for them.

He resisted a sudden impulse to run. Suddenly it all seemed too much, even for him. They were already behind schedule, all because of that cockeyed Mickey David. It had been a real coup when Mickey had agreed to do the score. But that was before Karly Huntly. Now Mickey wasn't into anything except the famous Huntly cunt. Any other time, Barron wouldn't blame him. But this was *Barron*'s time, *Barron*'s money—and *Barron*'s last-ditch effort to get his act together after one-too-many box-office flops. So all they had now was "Poor Little Us"—one fucking song. But one tune does not a musical make . . .

"So, Barron, you've gotta do something!" Andy was staring at him with his beady little eyes, a pleading expression on his flabby face.

This ffrench fag was a character, all right. Leave it to Nate Greene to come up with a guy who could play the Fourth Stooge. But Barron couldn't complain. Andy was working below scale, *way* below scale. Besides, he had to hand it to the guy. Somehow, some way, by some crazy fluke, he had found four fantastic Little Women! The kids were absolutely great: talented, unspoiled (except maybe for Galitz's daughter, who was a clone off the old block), and just perfect for the parts.

"Barron! Please! Come on . . ." ffrench's elbow made itself felt in his ribs.

Barron took a deep breath, squared his shoulders, and grinned, unleashing the full effect of the famous Heatter smile. "All right. I'll take care of it." He looked around. The Little Women were sitting on the stage, awaiting direction. The band waited, too, looking bored. The old lady with the rhinestone glasses was knitting; the man with her was peeling an orange. Where the hell was his female lead, Ms. Barrbra Shapiro?

"Where is she?" Barron asked.

"Who?"

Barron stared at Andy. "Barrbra Shapiro, for chrissakes! Isn't she the one acting up?"

"Oh . . . right." ffrench looked around. "She was here a minute ago, boss, honest."

He found her eventually.

She was in the girls' lavatory, sitting on the john, smoking a joint. "What the *fuck?*" she exclaimed when Barron burst into the stall. The roach disappeared beneath the heel of her shoe. "In case you can't read, Barron," she said, "this happens to be the little girls' room!"

She looked scared. He knew exactly what to do. He reached out his arms. "Oh, baby, come to Dada."

As always, it worked. She came into his arms like a moth to a flame. She melted against him.

"Tell Da what's wrong," he crooned.

Thank God they were alone. He leaned against the row of sinks with their dripping faucets. Dammit, the water would get all over his new apricot

89

raw silk slacks. Carefully, he maneuvered her body so that she was the one against the sinks. She was murmuring something against his chest, something about how hard it was to work with no-talent kids who walked over all her lines.

Barron patted her and rocked her and told her what a magnificent and talented actress she was, and that she didn't have to worry about a thing. He would take care of her.

He had to bend a little to catch his full reflection in the mirror above the sinks. He had to admit it, though. They made a nice couple, in spite of her purple hair.

The morning sunlight filtered hazily through the frosted glass window, softening all the angles. It was as good as backlighting. He'd have to mention that to Spyros, and maybe he'd get the cinematographer to use frosted glass for some of the interior shots when they finally got around to filming. If they ever did.

"You really think I'm talented, Barron?" she was asking.

"Of course I do, baby," he replied automatically. He winked at himself in the mirror. He smiled. Was it his imagination, or was one of his dimples deepening? God, he hoped so. In Hollywood, there was an old maxim: The deeper the dimple, the fatter the contract.

She lifted her face to his. Again he remarked to himself how much she resembled Streisand, especially around the eyes and the nose. Too bad the resemblance didn't extend as far as the vocal cords.

"Barron, get me out of this place," she implored

suddenly. "Let's go home to California where we belong. Why can't we shoot there, Barron? On a back lot? Like you did with *Tomorrow Is Another Day?*" She looked up at him hopefully.

Barron squirmed. Even thinking about *Tomorrow Is Another Day* made him uncomfortable. It cost forty mil to make and it grossed ten. He couldn't afford another *Tomorrow Is Another Day*. He said, "Barrbra, baby, I told you a hundred times. We want *authenticity*. The audience knows real from phony. This isn't just any Andy Hardy movie."

Barrbra's eyes widened. "Andy *who?*" she asked innocently.

If he killed her now, they'd have to go looking for another Marmie. It had been enough of a hassle getting this one. It was no secret that Shapiro was seventh choice, after Midler, Streisand, Cher, Diana Ross, Tina, and Aretha. Nobody wanted to play anybody's mother, at any price. And certainly not at the price Barron was willing to pay.

Then Nate Greene had called him one day and told him to turn on the television set. Shapiro's video, *Hot Little Tootsie*, was on MTV. To Barron's amazement, it wasn't bad. A little on the raunchy side, maybe, but better than some.

But even Shapiro had balked at playing Marmie. It had taken a couple of dinners at Ma Maison, a few drinks at the Polo Lounge, and a solid week of fucking at Barron's Malibu digs to change her mind.

Barron was sweating. He looked down. Barrbra was on her knees. His fly was open. She was sucking him. Hungrily. Like a baby with a lollipop.

91

How had that happened? he wanted to ask. But why talk? She was good. Better than good. *Great.* "Holy shit," he moaned.

The door burst open. Olivia Galitz stopped dead in her tracks.

"Mr. ffrench wants to know when you're coming back," Olivia said slyly. "What should I tell him?"

"Tell him I'm coming," Barron said breathlessly.

10

Peggy

IT was crazy, but she felt like a teenager again. And why not? This would be the first time she'd be going out with another man since she was sixteen. That was a long time ago. Sixteen years faithful to one man. Stupidly faithful. Never straying, although God knows she had good reason. How many times had Duke cheated on her? Well, it was her turn now. And since they were separated, she couldn't even call it cheating. So why did she feel so guilty?

Stop it, Peggy! She took a deep breath and looked at herself in the mirror. The coral cotton knit from Bliss Knits was exquisite. How generous of Bliss to sell it to her at cost.

The thought of Bliss made her smile. It was hard to believe that only three weeks had passed since the afternoon she and Bliss and Selma had become friends. How dramatically her life had changed since then. First, Morgie had won the role of Meg in the movie. And by an amazing coincidence, Bliss's daughter, Sunny, was Amy, and Selma's daughter—What was her name? Olivia?—had been chosen to play Jo. Peggy had immediately reread Louisa May Alcott's classic. She knew why the girls had been chosen. They were perfect! She didn't know the other child, Ruthie Miller—the one who was Beth—that well, but her father had seemed nice enough.

Peggy sighed. Should she try the pearl earrings instead of the gold hoops? Duke always liked the gold hoops better. That settled it. She would wear the pearls. Her hands were trembling. Easy, girl, she told herself. It's only a *date*. She shook her head. Nope, not a date. Morgie had told her they didn't say *date* anymore. Then what did they say? She'd have to learn a whole new vocabulary. To go with her whole new life.

The small pearl earring slipped from her fingers. "Damn!" she muttered, bending to pick it up. A sudden wave of nausea washed over her. She gripped the edge of the dresser. God! Don't let it be the flu.

Nervously, she glanced at the clock. Five thirty. She still had plenty of time. He was picking her up at six. *Plato*. For the thousandth time, she tried to recall the sound of his voice. On the phone, he had sounded so resonant and sexy, with that Greek accent of his. "My leetle goddess, I look so forward to meeting you," he had said.

Had she really gone and done it? Placed a personals ad in *The Marketplace?* The idea had lingered in her mind since that afternoon at The Royal Palm when the three of them had read the ads aloud. They'd all been tipsy, of course, and the ads had seemed funny then. But that night, after she and Morgie and Wayne, Jr., had celebrated Morgie's triumph with ice cream and pizza, and after Morgie had finally fallen into bed exhausted and happy, and Wayne, Jr., had gone into the garage to practice with Bondage, his heavy-metal group, Peggy had had an insight.

She was *alone*. Duke was out of her life for good. Her children were growing up, and it wouldn't be long before they would be gone, too. There was school, of course, but it wasn't enough. If she were to survive—and survive she must—she would have to pull herself together and meet new people. New men. And after Duke, it wasn't going to be easy.

She'd made a serious effort to study for her favorite philosophy class—"Socrates, Aristotle, and Dr. Leo Buscaglia: The Feelings Behind the Words"—but her mind kept wandering. Before she knew it, she'd begun to compose snippets of prose. She refined them until she'd said what needed to be said: "Irish-American Venus (with arms) seeks compassionate, intelligent Adonis . . ."

Quickly, before she could change her mind, she'd mailed it.

And then, after the fiasco in Dr. Schindler's office—Peggy still shuddered at the thought of it— she'd come home to find a thick envelope waiting for her. To her astonishment, there were twelve replies.

One was from a convict in the county jail. The letter was effusive with love and promises of passion. However, owing to the miscarriage of justice that had landed its author behind bars, it would be twelve years before he could deliver. Peggy didn't have twelve years.

Marcus Silver, D.D.S., on the other hand, who'd written on notepaper decorated with molars and bicuspids, promised her free dental work for life if she would join him for four days next week at the dental convention in Atlantic City, no questions asked. No, thank you, Peggy thought, crumpling the molars and bicuspids and tossing them into the wastebasket.

She'd gone through all the letters and decided to reply to the one that began: "Dear Venus, I, too, am lonely. I am lonely for the majestic land of my fathers, for the beauties I have left behind me in Corfu. I am sincerely looking for the Venus of my dreams. *Thelo na se gamisou . . .*"

The letter was written in an elegant hand, albeit on a grease-spattered invoice from the Agora Diner. It was a good omen. She knew that *agora* was Greek for "marketplace."

The letter was signed Plato Pappamichaelis.

She waited three days to dial the number. And then, fortified with a double scotch, she did it.

"Aalo! Agora! Waatchu want?" a voice hollered into the phone.

Almost losing her nerve, she whispered, "Plato?"

The phone banged in her ear. "Pla-to!" somebody shouted. "Eees for you!"

And then she'd heard his voice. "Aalo?"

Peggy swallowed. "This is Venus," she said.

They drove way across town to Short Falls, to a rundown section near the railroad tracks that he told her was known among his friends as "Greek Town." There, in an undistinguished-looking storefront on Zorba Road, they found the Never-on-Sunday Taverna. It was like entering another world.

On the walls were vivid murals of the Parthenon, the Acropolis, and Mount Olympus. Small tables were grouped around a dance floor, at one end of which was a platform. Two elderly musicians played bouzouki music that made Peggy want to tap her feet.

She smiled at Plato across the small square table, and he grinned back at her. "You like?" he asked. "Eees just like Greece, no?"

She shrugged. "I've never been to Greece," she replied ruefully.

He kept grinning at her. "I take you there, someday," he promised.

There was no doubt about it—he was *gorgeous*. As good-looking as Duke but in a completely different way. Where Dukie was lithe and wiry, Plato was solid and muscular. And tall. And broad. For a brief instant, Peggy wondered what it would feel like to lie beneath him.

He ordered for her. "First, we have ouzo with *mezedakya*," he instructed the chubby waitress who stared at Plato with undisguised longing. "And then, bring us *avgholemono soupa*, then *youvetsi* and a bottle of retsina . . ."

Peggy listened as the lovely syllables rolled off his tongue. "You speak the language so beautifully," she told him after the waitress had gone.

He reached over and took her hand. He raised it to his lips and kissed it. Peggy felt a sharp, unexpected thrill. He beamed at her. "I can't believe it," he said, shaking his head. "My Venus, at last."

They talked about everything and nothing. About Athens and the harbor; about her classes at the community college; about the Agora Diner and how Plato had scrimped to buy it, and how pleased he was that it was finally doing so well; about how proud she was of Morgie's getting the part in the movie; and about what a coincidence it was that Mr. ffrench had commissioned Plato to cater lunch for the cast and crew for the duration of the filming.

"Eees good, movie came to town," Plato said. "It brings people together."

Peggy agreed. In fact, she was in the mood to agree with everything he said; that ouzo packed a wallop. Her head swam pleasantly. The piquant, unfamiliar food, the joyous music, the gaiety of the crowd—all were affecting her.

The music stopped and suddenly began again. Plato stood, took her hand, and led her to the dance floor. The room tilted, but Peggy didn't care. She felt as though she were dreaming, following Plato through the intricacies of what he informed her was the *sirtaki*—the Greek sailors' dance. "The dance of my forefathers," he announced proudly.

The strange thing was that although she had never danced it before, she seemed to know ex-

98

actly what to do with her feet. There she was, the only woman in a long line of swarthy, smiling men, and she wasn't the least bit uncomfortable. In fact, she felt as though she had been doing this all her life. Who knows? Maybe in another life she had been a Greek peasant girl or a Greek sailor or . . .

She couldn't remember leaving the Never-on-Sunday Taverna. But here she was, sitting next to Plato in his old Chevy, watching the fluorescent Styrofoam dice sway as they turned onto Grover Cleveland Boulevard.

"Where are we going?" she asked sleepily.

Plato took his eyes off the road to grin at her. "Ah, my leetle Venus, you are feeling better?"

Actually, she was feeling just fine. A little woozy, maybe; a little out of focus, perhaps—but nothing major. She said, "I didn't pass out, did I?"

He slipped his muscular arm around her and pulled her to him. She inhaled his scent—a mixture of bay rum, shaving lotion, and some indefinable aroma she found frankly enticing.

"I thought you were going to. You looked funny . . . so white. Like a leetle dove . . ."

She closed her eyes and rested her head on his shoulder. She felt a shudder go through his body. The car shimmied, and her eyes fluttered open. The luminous dials on the dashboard winked at her. Jesus, Mary, and Joseph in white plastic stood guard above them. She felt safe and protected, totally at peace.

"Venus . . ." Plato whispered hoarsely. *"Ehkis kati visia!"*

It sounded so lovely. What a beautiful language.

99

Maybe she would take a course in Greek next semester.

She felt Plato's hand slide along her chest, cupping her breast effortlessly. She felt no compunction to ask him to remove it.

"Thelo na se rikso ena bootso!" he continued.

She could listen forever to the beautiful-sounding words. She wondered vaguely what they meant. She looked up at him and smiled.

Suddenly he spun wildly off the road and pulled to a stop beneath a grove of trees. What was happening? she wondered, sitting up.

And then his hands were on both her breasts, then they were under her skirt. *"Visia,"* he whispered, panting against her neck. *"Thelo na se rikso ena bootso!"* The urgency in his voice began to penetrate her comfortable haze.

"Plato, wait—please, what are you doing?" she asked. Weakly, she pushed against him.

It was like a flea pushing against an elephant. Her resistance seemed to fire his passion. He was like a madman now, his skin hot to the touch, his hands like burning coals as they found their way under her panties.

"Plato!" she gasped. "I think there's something you should know!"

He looked down at her, pausing momentarily in his efforts. There was the look of fear in his eyes. "My Venus," he said, "you don' have da herpes?"

"Plato, no, no, nothing like that," she assured him. "It's just that, Plato, *I don't speak Greek!*"

He heaved a sigh of relief, then he shrugged. "No problem. I teach you." He grabbed one of her hands and positioned it against his swollen groin.

100

"*Bootso,*" he instructed matter-of-factly, unzipping his fly. His engorged organ swung into her palm. "For you, Venus, see how he grows, my *bootso!*"

She was intrigued. He was even bigger than Duke! She hadn't known it was possible. But of course, she was hardly an expert on the sizes of penises. Or was the correct word *penii?* For a moment, she wondered how it would feel to have Plato's *bootso* inside her . . .

His fingers were in her. "*Moonie,*" he explained, probing her gently, tenderly. "My *bootso* seeks a meeting with your *moonie.*"

From the corner of her eye, she could discern the dashboard figures taking it all in with bemused expressions. Suddenly it was all too funny for words. *Moonie. Bootso.* Mary. Joseph. Fluorescent dice. The ouzo was watering her brain. She burst out laughing.

For Plato, her laughter had the effect of a cold shower. He drew abruptly away. She was laughing uncontrollably now, unable to stop. *What was the matter with her?*

He watched her for a while in sullen silence. "You laugh at da wrong time," he said disappointedly.

"I'm sorry," she offered weakly, trying to catch her breath. "I'm not laughing at you, Plato . . ."

He looked around. "No? I don' see nobody else in dis car," he pouted.

He was wrong. There was someone else here. Duke was here, hovering like a phantom, coming between them, realer than real. How could she explain to Plato?

She took his hand in hers and kissed it. There was a sweetness about the man that appealed to her. "I'm sorry, Plato," she said. "It's not your fault. Honest. It's me. I'm just not ready for you."

He nodded. "Eees your husband, right? You still theenk about him, no?"

"Yes," she admitted with a sigh. *"Dammit.* Yes."

11

Barron

IT had been the worst of days; it had been the best of days. Whatever kind of day it was, for better or for worse, it would be etched in Barron Heatter's mind for all eternity.

After auspiciously being blown in the girls' lavatory, everything had gone rapidly downhill. In the middle of the "Roll Dat Gauze" scene (for which they still needed the music), Sven Jorgensen, the six-feet-four janitor, brushes, buckets, and all, came raving into the gym.

Holding Barrbra Shapiro's ground-out roach aloft like a trophy, he proclaimed: "Ja, ja, looka vad I find! Who shmoka da pot? I gonna report you shmall vimmens!" he cried triumphantly.

Everyone stared, dumbfounded. Andy ffrench looked like he was going to faint. No one moved. It had been up to Barron to calm the crazy Swede.

"Now, now, Mr. Jorgensen, let's not jump to conclusions," he said, trying to grab the joint.

"Who's yumping? Sven knows pot ven he shmecks it!"

Barron stood his ground. He put an arm around Sven and whispered, "I've been meaning to speak to you, Sven. Have you ever given any thought to becoming an actor? With your looks, you could go far."

Sven's vacant blue eyes grew dreamy. The bushy blond mustache twitched. "Ja?" he mused. "Vonce, I meet Bergman in Malmö. He look me over gutt. But nuttin' ever come of it," he ended sadly.

"Gee, that's too bad. Bergman missed an opportunity."

"Ja? You 'tink I got talent, hah?"

"Definitely," Barron said. "There's a part in this movie for an intelligent, sensitive blond rascal like you. Let's talk later . . . What do you say?"

Sven left the gym happily mollified. Barron looked meaningfully at Andy ffrench. It wouldn't be too tough to create a part for the lunkhead. He could be an orderly in the battlefield scene. Why not? He'd leave the details to the fag. Who knows? Maybe Andy could even persuade the guy to use some underarm deodorant.

After Sven came the fiasco with the score that never arrived. Mickey David had promised that by ten o'clock sharp the music would be there.

But ten o'clock came and went. So did eleven. The musicians were falling asleep in their chairs.

An expensive nap. Barron's stomach churned every time he looked in their direction.

"Call that David sonofabitch!" Barron ordered ffrench. "Tell him if that music isn't here in half an hour, I'll haul his ass into court!"

Obediently, Andy ffrench ran from the gym, only to return two seconds later. "The office is locked, Barron. I can't get to the phone!"

Barron wanted to grab him and shake him until his stupid wig fell off. "Get *Sven!*" he snapped through clenched teeth. "He has the keys!"

Andy rolled his eyes ceilingward. Did Barron think he was stupid? "I tried that, B.H. But he's locked himself in the broom closet. He says he's gonna be a star, and he doesn't want to be disturbed."

Barron was beside himself. Millions were riding on an idiot janitor who was dreaming of stardom in a broom closet.

"There's a payphone in the hall," Barron said, digging in his pocket for change. All he came up with was a handful of lint. Shit. He'd left his wallet in the hotel again! He looked to Andy for help.

"Don't look at me, B.H. I never carry money when I work. It's against my religion."

In desperation, Barron had turned to the old guy in the green silk shirt, with the chains around his neck. "I'm sorry to bother you, Mr. Zayde," he'd said. With difficulty, the old guy tore his gaze from the stage where Shapiro was doing deep-knee bends. "We seem to be having problems with the phone. You wouldn't have any change on you, would you?"

The lady with the rhinestone glasses and the

105

orange hair stopped knitting. Squinting up at Barron, she said, "Look how gorgeous he is, Abe. Don't you think he looks familiar?"

"Of course he's familiar, dummy," Abe chided her. "You've seen him hundreds of times on the screen!"

Bea shook her head. "No, no, I mean from before that. Don't we know him from the Bronx, maybe?"

Abe laughed apologetically. "You'll have to excuse my wife," he began, digging into his pocket and coming up with a small leather change purse. "She thinks everyone comes from the Bronx. Here," he said, handing Barron a handful of quarters. "Make your phone call, and *zei gezundt.*"

"*A shaynum danke,*" Barron said reflexively, realizing too late what he had done.

Bea's mouth fell open. "You speak Yiddish?" she asked.

Hastily, Barron shook his head. "Afraid not," he replied in his best clipped tone. He backed quickly away. "Thanks for the change, Mr. Zayde!"

But Bea held him with her eyes. "Too bad," she said. She was smiling at him.

He had to admit it—the old broad had the best-looking set of caps he'd seen in many a day. They were almost as good as his own. He returned the smile.

She asked, "So, what do you think of my granddaughter Olivia?"

Barron gasped. "Olivia is your granddaughter? I thought—" He should have known. These were Galitz's people. Where had he gotten the idea they were relatives of Barrbra Shapiro's?

106

"A regular star, a natural, no?" Bea was saying. "Oh, my, yes. We're lucky to have her."

Mickey David was nowhere to be found. They'd had to stumble through the remainder of the day without music. That's when the miracle happened.

Ten minutes before they wrapped for the day, Morgie Corcoran, bless her little heart, tugged on his sleeve and said, "Uh—Mr. Heatter, my brother's been working on some music. It's really good, Mr. Heatter. Would you like to hear it?"

Barron's first inclination was to tell the kid to get lost. *Everyone* had a brother who wrote songs. But the day was wasted, anyway. The band had given up and was playing pinochle over in the corner. "Sure, kid," he replied amiably. "What have we got to lose?"

She walked over to the pianist. He listened while she hummed something. Then the pianist got up and walked over to the piano. The drummer followed. So did the string section. Before long, Morgie and the other girls were gathered around the piano, too, belting out this incredible number—"Bake 'em Some Bread"—that would fit perfectly into the Mission of Mercy scene.

Barron couldn't believe his ears. Judging from their expressions, neither could ffrench, Phyllis Sawyer, or Barrbra Shapiro, for that matter. All of them were listening, transfixed. When the music finally stopped, there was silence. Followed by wild applause.

Morgie smiled sheepishly at Barron. "Did you like it, Mr. Heatter?"

"Like it?" Barron exclaimed. "It's fantastic! Great!" Fuck Mickey David, he thought. This time he had himself some *real* talent. Raw and uncorrupted. "Where is this brother of yours? What's his name?"

"He's in the garage with his band," Morgie informed him shyly. "His name is Wayne Robert Corcoran, Jr."

12

More Barron and Some Selma

GETTING out of the gym wasn't going to be easy. He'd hoped that Galitz would have forgotten about the appointment to inspect his house. He should never have mentioned to the mayor that they were scouting for interiors. The minute the words were out, Galitz was on him like a swarm of locusts. "You'll thank me, B.H.," Galitz gushed. "The minute you lay eyes on my living room, you'll see how perfect it is. Better than perfect. Pluperfect!"

Galitz was like an elephant—he hadn't forgotten. When ffrench signaled the end of rehearsal, the mayor appeared like magic, grinning from ear to ear, his golden curls standing on end in anticipation. "So," he said, "are we ready?"

Heatter forced a smile. What he wouldn't give for some Valium! "Ready as I'll ever be," he answered with a sigh. He looked around for Enrico. "Where's my driver?"

"Oh, *him?* I sent him home. You'll be staying for dinner anyway, and then I can give you a lift into the city," Galitz explained.

The nerve of the *putz!* Barron didn't remember accepting any dinner invitation! And what was the matter with Enrico, not checking with him first? But what could he do? One thing he *couldn't* do was go outside and be mauled by the entire female population of West Falls. He took a look out the window. There they all were—still waiting in the rain, ready to pounce.

"Well, let's go," said the mayor, grabbing Barron by the arm. "What are we waiting for?"

The blood drained from Barron's face. "I can't . . . I can't go out there."

The mayor looked perplexed. "Whatsamatter, you don't like rain?"

"You don't understand. I have to go mufti."

The mayor's eyebrows lifted. " 'Mufti'?" he asked with a lascivious grin. "Sounds interesting, but can't you wait until later?"

"No, *no!*" Barron explained. *"Mufti!* You know, in disguise! Otherwise, they'll tear me to shreds!" He gestured to the mass of squealing women hovering beyond the door.

The mayor gave him a knowing wink, then he nodded. "Of course. Wait right here. I'll get you something."

So it was that Barron Heatter emerged from West Falls High School in a pair of Sven Jorgensen's foul-smelling overalls, a mop slung over one shoulder and the famous baby blues shielded by a moldy peaked cap splattered with white spots that he hoped were paint drippings and not the aftermath of an enormous bird's dinner.

Together they drove in Jared Galitz's white BMW with the bumper sticker: IF IT'S GOOD FOR WEST FALLS, IT'S GOOD FOR YOU, BECAUSE WEST FALLS IS GOOD FOR YOU. Past the joggers, past the library, down Coolidge Boulevard with the three liquor stores and the barbershop, and up into West Falls Heights. "Great town, isn't it! I'm gonna miss it when I get to D.C."

Barron looked at him. "D.C.? You're going to Washington?"

"Eventually," the mayor replied as the car started to climb a winding wooded road. He pointed to a grove of trees. "This is Nixon Park. The shadiest place in town. Nice, huh?"

Barron squinted. Galitz was taking him on a goddamn tour of the burg, for crissakes, when all he wanted was to get into bed with a joint and a hot babe. And maybe a pastrami sandwich. "Are the falls near here?" he forced himself to ask.

Galitz stared blankly. "Falls?"

"Yeah. The *West* Falls. Are they nearby?"

"There are no falls in West Falls," Galitz informed him matter-of-factly. "What gave you that idea?"

They rode in silence after that until they reached what looked like a back lot for an antebellum flick. Pseudo-Georgian facades with imposing columns. Statues of jockeys holding out lanterns. Boxwood separating one sprawling lawn from the next.

Barron leaned forward eagerly. Maybe the

111

mayor had a point when he suggested I have a look, he thought.

A good-looking, bare-chested, mocha-skinned stud was riding a power mower back and forth over what looked like an advertisement for grass seed. Galitz pulled the BMW up the winding driveway. Barron half expected Scarlett O'Hara to come traipsing out to meet them.

Instead, what came out was a black woman in Army fatigues and a red fright wig. She waved an envelope in Galitz's face. "Mayuh, Mayuh!" she called. "Ah think you shud see 'dis right away! Some crew-cut honkie from Washington was heah! He said ta be shuah y'all gits 'dis!"

Galitz grabbed the envelope. "Washington?" he gasped, tearing it open. He read hastily and stuffed the envelope in his back pocket. He looked ashen.

"Good news?" Barron asked. Maybe the guy really *was* on his way to Washington.

"Yeah, yeah." Galitz slipped an arm companionably about Heatter's shoulders. "Come inside and have a gander. I'm telling ya, B.H., it's perfect. Trust me."

They were barely across the threshold when Galitz threw back his head and roared, "SEL-MA! Where *are* you? SEL-ma! We have a visitor!"

Barron shuffled uneasily. That's all he needed, another fawning Galitz.

But then the woman called Selma swept into the living room.

He couldn't believe it! She was a breath of fresh air. Not beautiful, exactly—at least, not by Hollywood standards. But there was something about her that was so compelling he couldn't tear his eyes away. It was more than the fact that she didn't react like all the others—she didn't grab his collar or ask for his autograph or jump on his bones.

She stared at him, surprise registering on her face. "Oh, hello, Sven," she said. "How *are* you?"

That explains it, Barron thought in disappointment. He had forgotten he was in mufti. No wonder she was so cool. He couldn't deny a deep sense of letdown.

"I want you to know how much we appreciate the good job you're doing at the high school." She smiled at him. Then to Galitz, she said, "I'm sorry to be in such a rush, dear, but I'm late for an appointment. Princess will get you a bite to eat. Olivia is upstairs, studying her lines for tomorrow . . ."

Under his breath, Galitz hissed, "*Selma,* don't you know who this *is?*"

"Of course I do, Jerry. What's the matter with you? Listen, I'm really late . . ."

Galitz tried to grab her. "But, Sel, wait—"

But in a second, she was out the door. Apologetically, Galitz shrugged. "Women!" he muttered. "Sorry about that," he said to Barron.

"Don't be. She's lovely."

Galitz stared at him. Selma? Lovely? Jaclyn Smith is lovely. Linda Evans is lovely. Barbara Johnson is lovely. But Selma? Selma was just a wife, for crying out loud. A loony-tune wife, at that.

In the car, Selma turned on the ignition. Men! she thought. The least Jerry could have done was

113

tell her he was bringing Sven Jorgensen home for dinner. She fished in the glove compartment for her spare glasses. Of all times to lose her contact lens! Maybe it was God's way of punishing her for what she was about to do.

Deliberately and in cold blood, she was going to The Royal Palm to rendezvous with a man who wasn't her husband. His name was Fremont Bisch, and he had been the only one to answer the personals ad she'd put in *The Marketplace*. Over the phone, his voice had been warm and caring. She didn't know what he looked like. And she didn't care.

She wondered briefly what on earth had compelled Jerry to bring Sven Jorgensen, mop and all, home with him.

Probably he wanted a favor from Sven. Probably, it had something to do with his image.

13

Jared

THE bedroom reminded him of one of those cheap steak houses on Forty-second Street. All red brocade wallpaper and black lacquer furniture. It even smelled the same. The rancid odor of over-fried steak permeated everything. But no; this smell came from that *farshtinkener* oil Barbara insisted he smear all over her every time they fucked. It was like screwing a sardine. It was all he could do just to stay aboard.

It was different when his mother oiled a chicken. Jared's mouth watered, thinking about his mother's chicken. No one made chicken like Sadie Galitz. Certainly not Selma. He opened his mouth and licked and was bitterly disappointed. Barbara Johnson was one tasty dish, but she couldn't compare to his Sadie's chicken. He supposed it was the difference between kosher and *trayf.*

Absently, he put a finger on her clit and massaged. She wriggled responsively. "Mmm," she hummed. "That's wonderful, you great big powerful panther, you! You tiger-baby! You wonderful wild maniac, you! Oh, do it to me," she begged.

He slid his lips gently around her greasy nipple and sucked. If only he weren't so tired. Well, he had Selma to blame for that. He'd lain awake half the night waiting for her to come home. Then, when she finally *did* come in (at two in the morning!), he'd pretended to be asleep. He was damned if he'd give her the satisfaction of knowing that he'd waited up for her.

But where had she been? Hadn't he gone out of his way to make it up to her for the mishmash over her drunkenness? All right, he admitted: Maybe he *had* gone a little overboard in showing his displeasure—not going near her for almost two weeks. But why did she have to go and make that remark about his *schlong?* He was willing to let bygones be bygones. He had even brought her precious movie star home with him—the great Barron Heatter—right in her own living room! So what does she do? She ignores him and runs out to God knows where, no explanations, no nothing. If he didn't know better, he'd think she was fooling around. The thought startled him. Barbara's nipple slipped out of his mouth. Don't be *ridiculous,* he told himself, sucking again. Selma would *never* fool around.

"What's thirty-four and a half and thirty-four

and a half, Snugglebuns?" Barbara asked teasingly. She maneuvered her curvaceous hips so that now he was face to face with the niftiest nooky in town. *Oy.*

"Sixty-nine, Pussywillow," he answered automatically. Dutifully, he made circles with his tongue. Once upon a time, these little games of theirs would have given him chills and thrills. Now, they weren't much more exciting than a game of Scrabble.

He was vaguely aware of her busy tongue at work on his balls. His mind wandered like an errant gnat. It settled on, of all things, his father-in-law, Abe Moscovitz.

He still couldn't get over the fact that Abe had come up with the idea for the party. Who would have thought such a brainstorm could have come from such a peasant? Abe Moscovitz was a guy who could eat and fart at the same time and not even know it!

When Abe approached him at rehearsal one day and said, "Yonkele, I have a proposition for you," Jerry had shushed him. "In public, Abe, I'm Jared," he'd hissed. "Or Mayor. *Never* Yonkele!" He'd paused for effect. "So what's the proposition?"

He listened while Abe explained his solution to the town's furor over the movie. "Make a party!" Abe had said.

Galitz looked at him. "A party?"

"Listen," Abe continued, "all they want is to be a part of the action. So why not let them?"

Why not, indeed? They were in the gym. Barr-

117

bra Shapiro was doing her "Marmie's Melody" number up on the stage, and just looking at her was giving Jerry a hard-on. He hastily looked away. She was nothing compared with his Barbara, but she had a nice pair. A *very* nice pair. "Nice, huh?" he blurted, forgetting who he was talking to. Nervously, he amended, "Nice idea, Abe." He was astonished to find the old man's hands folded in front of his crotch, too. *Sonofagun.* Was it possible? Why not? Men were only human, after all. "Tell me more," Jerry urged his father-in-law.

"You can call it a Meet-the-Stars party, Jerry," Abe went on. "Give them food and booze and maybe a little entertainment. They'll love ya for it. Think of the publicity. Think of your future . . ."

For once, Jared was speechless. It was nothing less than a stroke of genius. He said, "Maybe. It'll take some doing. And some bread."

Abe said, "Yonkele, please, don't insult me. Your future is my daughter's future. What's good for you is good for her. I look upon this as an investment," he explained, thrusting a wad of bills into his son-in-law's open palm.

"My pleasure," Jared replied. "My pleasure."

"Do it again," Barbara moaned.

Do what? he wondered. He shouldn't let his mind wander like this. He slid his finger round and round.

"No, not *that!*" she protested. "You know. The *other!*"

He slipped an oiled finger into her asshole. "Come on, Jerry, get with it!" she demanded, definitely annoyed.

The pressure was on. How could such a beautiful woman be such a bitch in bed? He opened his eyes. Her long, silken black hair was spread fanlike across the pillow. Delicate cheekbones; long, curled lashes; and when she opened them, eyes the color of emeralds. If you asked him, she had it all over Joan Collins. Elizabeth Taylor, even. But what did she *want* from his life?

"Let's play horsey!" she commanded.

Oy. Not horsey again! He crawled beneath her and allowed her to straddle him.

"Giddyap!" she called eagerly. " 'Yankee Doodle went to London,' " she began.

Halfheartedly, he joined in. " 'Rid-ing-on-a-po-ny . . .' " She'd already had three orgasms. He prayed for a miracle. They'd been at it for an hour and he hadn't come. He was barely hard now, in fact. Maybe she wouldn't notice.

"What is it with you today, Puckeypoo?" she asked.

He knew what it was. It was Selma. He hoped to hell she wasn't going through the changes. Once they went through the changes, they—well, they changed. Even his own mother. One day she threw down her apron and never set foot in the kitchen again. Good-bye chicken.

But it was more than Selma. It was the movie. And it was that damn letter from the EPA in Washington, giving him fair warning to clean up Dove Hills Estates or else.

Barbara was glaring at him. "Are you going to tell me, Loverbunny? What's on your mind?"

What could he say? That land he'd developed was a toxic cesspool? That old people were falling

119

down like flies? That babies were choking in their cribs? It wasn't exactly an aphrodisiac to even think about such things, let alone talk about them. Of course, it wasn't his fault. Who knew who dumped the *dreck* in the first place? The EPA didn't care. And Barbara wouldn't understand.

But he had to tell her something. So he said, "Lovebuckets, I have a surprise for you."

Her eyes widened and she smiled. "Ooh," she squealed, "I love surprises."

"You're going to meet him," Jared began.

" 'Him'—*who?*"

"Him. *Him.* The one you've been pestering me about for weeks." He didn't know what women saw in that Heatter anyway. But they all wanted to meet him. Selma. His secretary, Estelle. Carlo Battista's wife. Margaret Jensen, even. Sure, the guy was handsome if you liked teeth and thick, dark wavy hair. And dimples. But there was something wrong with a guy who always went around smiling.

"Barron?" Barbara shrieked. "BARRON HEATTER? Oh, my God!" She flung her arms around his neck. "You really mean it? When? *When?*"

"In a few weeks," he told her. "At the biggest bash this town will ever see. The idea just came to me," he lied, snapping his fingers. "In a flash. Like that. It'll bring the whole town together. I'm going to call it: Meet the Stars! And just think of it, Sweetcups. You'll be there, standing right next to him, in the flesh!"

Barbara was beyond rapture. He'd never seen such ecstasy. "Ooh, Jerry, you're so good to me," she panted, riding him faster now.

He rolled onto his back and found himself face to face with her enormous tits. He felt his dick stir to life. Everything was okeydoke now. It was a good omen. This party would solve all his problems.

Yes. Yes. They were definitely on the right track. He closed his eyes. Faster. Faster. Exceeding the speed of light. Spontaneously, he began to whistle. The tunnel was just ahead. *Whew-whew-whew!* He would make it this time, for sure. No derailments.

14

Barbara Johnson

Femme fatale needs her furnace stoked.
Wants pyrotechnical expert for the cold winter ahead. Everything must be working. No
kids need apply. **Box 3232.**

SHE wondered when he was going to get around
to telling her about the party. If he'd waited much
longer, she'd have given him her ultimatum:
Leave Selma and marry me, or I'll tell the whole
world about us. Blackmail didn't thrill her, but her
biological clock was running out. The ticking was
getting louder every day. She was thirty-six years
old, and she wanted to be a mommy. It was as
simple as that. And what better place to bring up a
child than the White House? A whole rose garden
to romp in! A gorgeous pool to swim in. A bodyguard for life!

Of course, there would be some sacrifices on her part. No more dalliances with garage mechanics or gardeners. A First Lady must be above reproach. It was a shame, though. Cisco was *so* good! And the thought of Duke Corcoran made her wet all over again. Duke was definitely the best lay in town. No unnecessary foreplay, no middle-class hangups. Just a pure, sweet love of fucking. How long had it been since he'd been around? A month, at least. Well, the Mercedes was due for a tune-up, and so was she . . .

With Jerry, sex was never the important thing. With Jerry, the important thing was the Future. "You'll be the wife of the first Jewish president of the United States someday," he'd promised her. "Think of it."

She'd thought of little else for almost three years, ever since their first coupling in the stairwell of the Y, by the Twinkie machine.

Three years, and she was still waiting. How many times had he promised to leave Selma? How many times had he sworn he would divorce that mousey little millstone of his? He didn't love her. He stuck by her out of a sense of duty. "She'd be like a lost lamb without me," he kept saying. "It's gonna take time, Barbara. Have patience. Trust me."

Her trust was wearing thin. She was tired of waiting. Silas never made her wait. Absently, she fingered the gold locket she always wore. Inside it was a picture of Silas Goodfreund, her first husband, her one true love. It didn't matter that Silas was seventy-two when they met and she was an innocent eighteen-year-old who had never been outside Detroit.

Age was irrelevant to them. What mattered was that Silas loved her, and that she loved him. Silas had been her teacher, her protector, her best friend . . .

She'd been a typist at the Lukad-Eze Latex Manufacturing Company for three whole months before she met him. Day after day she typed bills of lading for six hundred gross of latex shields to places like Daytona Beach and Atlanta. Then one day it occurred to her to ask what exactly latex shields were.

Mary Beth Williams, the girl at the next type-writer, said, "They're *rubbers*, dope!"

Surprised, Barbara had asked, "Rubbers? Are you sure? That's a lot of galoshes!"

Mary Beth started to giggle. She leaned over and whispered something to another girl, and it wasn't long before the entire typing pool was convulsed in laughter. "Galoshes!" they cackled, nudging each other in the ribs.

They wouldn't let her in on the joke. Finally, Joe McIntyre, a tall, good-looking salesman with spar-kling eyes and an acne-scarred face, took her to lunch—room service at the Hotel Carlotta on Ed-sel Street—and gave her a free sample of the prod-uct: Joie de Vivre, #690, top of the line, with feathers, along with a demonstration she would never forget.

From then on, the entire Lukad-Eze sales staff requested her services. Then came the blessed day when Silas Goodfreund himself asked for her. She couldn't believe it—the founder, the president, the chairman of the board of Lukad-Eze Latex Manufacturing Company wanted her? He really did.

"Come in, my dear," he had said when she knocked. "I've heard a lot about you."

The office was dim—all gleaming mahogany, ankle-high carpet, heavy damask draperies masking the sunlight. On the massive ebony desk behind him, a solitary lamp glowed softly. In the half-light a naked Silas Goodfreund appeared phosphorescent and ethereal. "Don't be afraid," he said, gently reaching for her.

She wasn't afraid, but she was genuinely amazed. He had the whitest hair, the bluest eyes, and the longest dick she'd ever seen. Even limp, it hung midway to his thigh. So that he wouldn't feel embarrassed, Barbara quickly stepped out of her own clothes.

Silas appraised her appreciatively. "Lovely, lovely," he murmured, his tongue brushing his lips. And then she was in his arms.

He performed like he was seventeen, but with none of the groping awkwardness of adolescence. He was forceful but gentle, instructing her in the nuances of lovemaking as opposed to fucking.

"Never hurry," he said. "That's the first rule. In the world of love, there is no time, just the present. Everything else is unimportant," he whispered as he inserted himself slowly, *endlessly*, lovingly, inside her.

A sense of emptiness she hadn't been aware of until that moment was eradicated by Silas's incredible presence. He was filling every pore of her being with his essence, his unbelievable sensitivity, his huge cock. It was an endless orgasm for them both.

Afterward, he kissed her tenderly on the lips. "You're wonderful," he said softly.

"I was thinking the same about you," she replied, blushing.

He went to his desk and filled two glasses from a crystal decanter. "Here's to a genuine jewel among the rhinestones in my typing pool," he toasted.

Shyly, she took a sip. It was delicious—better than anything she had ever tasted. "What is this?" she asked. "It's very good."

He nodded. "It's nectar from my vineyards in France. I drink it only on important occasions."

She looked at him with renewed interest. "You have vineyards in France? I've never been to France. I've never been out of Detroit."

He put down his glass and took her into his arms once more. "Well, my dear, it will be my pleasure to show you the world." He kissed her.

The very next morning, he proposed. "I can't ever let you go," he told her. "I've waited all my life for someone like you."

Their wedding made international headlines. "Tycoon Robs Cradle!" was the most popular one in Great Britain, where Silas had three factories. Locally, the headlines were somewhat kinder: "Wealthy Industrialist Weds Teen!"

"Sticks and stones!" Silas said to her across the considerable length of the breakfast table. He tossed the paper aside and got up to embrace her. "We don't care, do we?" He nibbled at her ear.

"Oh, Silas, all I care about is you," she responded truthfully.

They had four glorious months together. He died the way he said he always wanted to—in the saddle, so to speak. He left her everything except the Detroit plant, which went to his four sons from a previous marriage.

So it was that at age eighteen and a half, Barbara-Lee Hawkins Goodfreund counted herself among the richest women in the world. At her château in Vevey, she was interviewed by Robin Leach of *Lifestyles of the Rich and Famous*. Barbara Walters spoke with her at length at her country home in Surrey. Suddenly, she was in the public domain, stopped for autographs in restaurants, trailed by paparazzi, voted Widow of the Year by *FOLK* Magazine, and lusted after by every fortune hunter and conniver who could read. It wasn't long before she met Barney Johnson at a baccarat table in Monte Carlo.

Barbara-Lee wrinkled her nose at the thought of Barney. How could she have been so stupid? She knew how come. She was a kid. She was lonely. She was horny.

She had too much money for her own good. Well, Barney took care of all that. He was handsome, fun-loving, and about as substantial as a paper lantern in a hurricane. Their life together had been pure chaos. Four years of fighting and loving and wild, wild sex.

And then, after Barney had gambled away most of Silas's fortune—the factories, the houses, the vineyards, and on and on—Barbara-Lee had finally had enough.

"Go!" she commanded him.

So Barney went, leaving her only a small trust fund he couldn't get his hands on. And a house he didn't want in West Falls, Connecticut. He had won it in a crap game in Atlantic City.

"Where the hell is West Falls?" she had wondered. She'd gone to the local gas station and looked at a map of New England. After about forty-five minutes she finally found it—a tiny dot just off the Merritt Parkway.

That was six years ago. It was time to move on. And where better than Sixteen Hundred Pennsylvania Avenue?

How much longer would she have to wait? She was going out of her mind with boredom. She'd already sampled most of the men in town worth sampling, and some who weren't. While Jerry was still her main dish, maybe it was time for a little snack.

Idly, she picked up a pen. Let's see, she thought. How to begin . . .

Femme fatale needs her furnace stoked . . .

15

Abe

HE put down the copy of the newspaper and looked at the stage. Who could concentrate on a newspaper while that vision was up there? Such a beauty! *Brusts* like creamy, milk-fed veal! Shanks you could die from. So she had purple hair—so what? On her it looked good.

"You want an orange, Abe? Abe? *Abe?*"

With difficulty, he tore his gaze from the stage. Bea was watching him carefully through those tinted lenses of hers. Those diamond-studded glasses cost him a pretty penny. Rhinestones weren't good enough for her. Oh, no. His wife had to have the real thing. Diamonds or no diamonds, she still couldn't see the nose in front of her face.

It made him uncomfortable, the way she kept staring. How much did she know? Abe shifted restlessly in his chair. Could she tell that he was in love? She had radar in those eyes. *Nah.* He was being foolish. How *could* she know? He'd been so careful, waiting until she was gone from the apartment before he even sat down to answer that personals ad. He'd run to mail the letter before she'd even gotten home. So how could she know?

Bea was still holding out the orange. "Well? Go on, take it!"

He took it. He bit into a segment and grimaced. "Icchhh! Bitter!"

"It's not bitter. Eat."

The music swelled. Barrbra floated across the stage like an angel from heaven and smiled at him. He hoped Bea hadn't seen that! Still, he was proud of himself. It was the first time he'd ever taken the bull by the horns and made a move. There was no doubt Barrbra had written that ad for him, and for him alone. What a clever girl. She knew he'd get the message: "Femme fatale needs her furnace stoked." Who else but Marmie, alias Barrbra, would need her furnace stoked? Her husband from the movie was off fighting battles in Vietnam and left her with no money to pay the oil bill. Good thing he paid attention to such details. Obviously, she was reaching out to him, asking him to heat her up.

In his letter, he'd asked that she be discreet and not call the Stamford condo before midnight, when Bea would be snoring away. Abe made a face. Forty-three years of snoring and cold cream on the pillow. It was time for a change. It was time for a little Barrbra Shapiro. He was entitled, no?

He felt Bea's sharp elbow in his ribs. *"Nu?* Eat it, already!"

"Leave me *alone,* will you? I don't want to eat it!" He hadn't meant to raise his voice.

Barron yelled, "Cut!" The music died abruptly. Everyone turned to stare at them. The blood drained from Bea's face.

The *faygeleh* in the pink turtleneck came running up to them. "Shame on you, people! Puhleese! We must have quiet on the set!" He wagged a finger under Abe's nose.

"My husband apologizes," Bea said, glaring at Abe. "You can rest assured it won't happen again!"

Barron walked over. He flashed his grin. "Are things under control here? Can we get on with it?"

The *faygeleh* nodded nervously. Abe noticed he was sweating. Why? Barron, his boss, might be a "big star," but he was nobody to sweat for. A nicelooking goy but not too much upstairs. Bea was crazy to think he looked like old Morris Horowitz's kid from Bathgate Avenue in the Bronx. *That* kid had crooked teeth. Bea must be going senile.

The music started up again. Bea leaned over and whispered, "Whatsa matter with you? Are you crazy? Why did you yell like that?"

"I'm sorry," Abe apologized. Once again he was mesmerized by the vision of Barrbra Shapiro on the stage. So near and yet so far. So why hadn't she called him yet? Every night, after Bea fell asleep, he sat by the phone, waiting. Twice, he'd even called the telephone company to make sure the phone was working. In the morning, he was so exhausted he could hardly move. Bea was convinced something was wrong with him. Well, there was something wrong with him. He hadn't felt

131

such a fire between his legs since—since he couldn't remember when.

Even now, right this minute, his member was stirring. Lately, it seemed to have a mind of its own, standing up, lying down, quivering and quaking every time Barrbra swung those luscious hips. *She would call,* he told himself, crossing his legs. *She had to call.* He began to eat the orange Bea had placed in his hand.

"Takin' the Washington Train" was some good song. A foot tapper if he ever heard one. That Corcoran kid might be young, but he knew how to write music. A real talent, just like Olivia, God bless her. Look at her, up on that stage, dancing while his lamb chop, Barrbra Shapiro, sang: " 'Chugga-chug-chug, chugga-chug-chug, off to see the old man, flyin' down the track! Chugga-chug-chug, chugga-chug-chug, dunno when I'll be back!' "

Abe tapped his foot in time to the music. He put another segment of orange into his mouth. All of a sudden he couldn't breathe. Something was stuck in his throat! It wouldn't go up, and it wouldn't go down. He opened his mouth and gasped. "Arghhh . . ." He tried to stand.

It was true what they said. Your whole life *does* pass in front of your eyes! There he was, a little boy in the *shtetl,* his mother feeding him a herring, his father out back plucking a chicken. Then the boat to America. Then under the *chuppa* with Bea. How pretty she looks! Then little Selma, with the curly red hair . . .

Someone was hollering, "He's dying! He's dying! Help him, help him! Somebody!"

Someone else was crying. *"Zayde!* Don't you dare die! Not now!"

And then. Arms around him, pressing. Something wonderfully soft pushing into his back. Only two things in the world could feel that good. Tits. *Brusts.* Big ones. Enormous ones. Not Bea's—of that much he was certain.

But wait! Now what was happening? Someone was hitting him! Hard, on the back! *Thwack!* Something flew like a bullet out of his mouth.

"Ahhhhh!" The sound came out in a rush.

"Mr. Zayde? Are you all right? Should we call an ambulance?" Barron looked pale.

"Of course, call the ambulance! He had a heart attack!" Bea screamed. "I knew he didn't look good! I knew—" She stopped abruptly. *"Oy vay!* What's happening to him, now?"

A hush fell over the gym. Everyone was staring. Not at Abe's face, which was ruddy and healthy looking. But at his crotch, which was bulging. Abe looked down. Instinctively, he folded his hands in front of himself and tried to smile.

"I've heard that happens sometimes when people choke," Phyllis Sawyer remarked.

"I've heard that, too," Barrbra Shapiro offered.

Abe spun around. There she was! This close to him!

She was staring at him, too. At *it.* She looked awestruck. *"In-fucking-credible,"* she said softly. Then she looked into his eyes. "Gee, I hope I didn't hit you *too* hard."

"You?" Abe said. "That was *you?"* Then it dawned on him. Those arms pressing into him were *her* arms! Those tits in his back were *her* tits!

"You saved my life!" he shouted. "Without you, I'd be dead!"

She flicked her eyes at his still-bulging crotch. "Well, you're sure not dead *yet*," she said with a sly smile. Then she winked. She leaned over and gave him a peck on the cheek. "Take it easy, Pops!"

Abe sank down in his chair. *Take it easy?* How could he take it easy now that he had actually felt her tits against his back?

Bea said, "Abe, come on. Let's go back to the condo and rest. Or better yet, let's go to the hospital."

He shook his head. What was she talking about, hospital? He wasn't sick. In fact, he'd never felt better in his life. What he needed now was a little less Bea and a lot more Barrbra Shapiro.

16

Max

IT had been a crazy couple of weeks. Nobody in the lab had gotten more than three hours sleep a night. Tops. Around the clock, they sat and watched the mice for signs of relief. Finally, after nearly a year of no results, they'd had a breakthrough. And what a breakthrough!

All because of Sheldon Menshikoff, that klutz, and his ever-present can of stale beer. What happened was, Sheldon accidentally dripped beer into a serum bottle. Instead of disposing of the "tainted" mixture, he had, on a whim, fed it to Number Forty-two.

"What the hay?" Sheldon had said. "Let the little mousey get high before he becomes a martyr for science."

The following day, while all the other infant mice were convulsing from chemically induced

135

colic, screaming and squeaking pathetically in their cages, Sheldon noticed old Number Forty-two sleeping like a baby. At first, they assumed he was dead. But when Sheldon reached into the cage, the creature yawned contentedly.

"What happened here?" Max demanded.

Sheldon, blushing and stammering, admitted what he'd done. "It was beer, Dr. Miller."

"Beer?"

Sheldon shrugged. "I didn't think it would matter. He was going to get the colic serum anyway. I figured, let 'im enjoy himself a little . . ."

"So you gave him *beer?*" Max asked in astonishment.

"Well, actually, some of *my* beer spilled into *his* serum. You shudda seen him lap it up!"

Who would have thought it? Day-old beer (Sheldon's beer was *always* day-old beer) the magical cure for infantile colic!

It had taken them only four days to extract the B-factor that worked the miracle, but when you're on the right track, things have a way of falling into place. Now *all* the mice were sleeping like babies despite ever-increasing doses of colic serum. So far, there were no side effects except a few hiccups. If anything, the mice were a little *too* sleepy. But when the dosage was decreased, the problem was alleviated.

Next they would try it on the monkeys. And if all continued to go well, maybe, just maybe, they would try it on a real, live, colicky baby.

Thinking about it, Max felt humbled. One tiny little accident, one tiny little enzyme! One simple, ubiquitous substance. Why had no one ever thought of it before? Well, such was the nature of research. Look at penicillin. Did Fleming, in his wildest dreams, ever imagine that moldy bread would save the lives of millions—no, trillions—of human beings?

Max's head was still spinning. Reluctant to leave the lab, he had finally given in to exhaustion. So here he was, coming home at nine thirty in the morning—rumpled, with a five-day stubble on his chin. Thank God for Mrs. Schotz, the housekeeper, who had graciously agreed to stay with little Ruthie.

Ruthie. A rush of guilt washed over Max. Ruthie was the most important person in his life. He should spend more time with her, he knew. But time kept running away from him. At least now, Ruthie was busy with that movie. He was grateful she had something to fill her days. But Ruthie was upset with him. Yesterday, when he'd called, she told him straight out: "I'm mad at you, Daddy. You *never* come to see me—and I get scarlet fever tomorrow!"

For a moment, Max's heart stopped. Then he realized that Ruthie was Beth in *Little Women,* and *Beth* was the one with the scarlet fever. "Sweetheart, I'll try my best to be there. I promise."

Instead of going to bed, where he belonged, Max showered and shaved and changed his clothes and went into the kitchen to put on a pot of coffee. He checked his watch. There was time for just one cup.

* * *

The minute he walked into the gym, he knew something was wrong. There was a crowd milling around an older man in a director's chair.

Ruthie came running over. "Daddy!" she called, throwing her arms around him. "You came! You came!"

He swept her up and buried his face in her hair. She smelled so good! But he was curious. He pointed to the crowd. "What happened?" he asked.

"Olivia's grandfather almost choked to death, Daddy. We all thought he was going to die."

Max hurried over. "Excuse me," he said, elbowing through the crowd. "I'm a physician. Is everything under control?"

The older woman with the spangled eyeglasses stared menacingly at him. "Where were *you* when we needed you?" she asked accusingly.

"Bea, please," the man said, extending a hand to Max. "I'm fine, now. I'm Abe Moscovitz. To whom do I have the pleasure?"

Max grinned. Now he knew who they were. Jared Galitz's in-laws. Galitz had mentioned they were coming. "Two more thorns in my rump," was how he'd put it.

"Max Miller, here," he replied, reaching for Abe Moscovitz's wrist. He counted. The pulse was rapid but strong. The man was looking at him and smiling. "What happened?" Max asked.

"Nothing," Abe said.

"*Not* nothing! He almost died!" Abe's wife yelled. She peered at him suspiciously. "What kind of a doctor are you, anyway?"

"I'm a pediatric researcher, actually," Max told her, satisfied that Abe was in no immediate danger. He smiled at the woman. "I know your son-in-law and your daughter, too. A lovely woman." It was the right thing to say. Mrs. Moscovitz leaned back and relaxed, then gave him a weak smile.

There was a sudden, loud clapping from the stage. "Pee-pul! Puh-leeze regain your composure! We have work to do! We've gotta get the show on the road. Sir! Sir!" The man known as Andy ffrench pointed at Max. "You'll have to find a seat or leave!"

Just as the music started up again, there was a frenzied shouting in the hall. In another second Hizzoner Jared Galitz came rushing into the gym. "How izzee? How izzee?" he panted. He threw himself on his father-in-law, nearly knocking the old man down. "Abe! Abe! You're alive! What happened?"

"Nothing, *nothing!* Get *off* me, Jerry." Abe flailed wildly. "You know how your mother-in-law exaggerates!"

Now that she had a new audience, Bea began to wail again. "He almost made me a widow, and he says it's nothing! Jerry, I'm so glad you came!" She sniffled and looked around. "Where's Selma?"

"I tried to call her at home, but she's out. She's probably shopping. You know how she loves to shop . . ."

Up on the stage, Andy ffrench was tapping his foot impatiently. "So whaddaya say, everybody? Honest to God, Barron, can we get some cooperation, or what?"

139

* * *

Eventually, the rehearsal resumed. From the shadows, Max watched little Ruthie grow faint with fever. "Oh, Marmie, the room is getting lighter . . . Everything is golden, you're so far away . . ." The music swelled to a crescendo as Marmie wiped the little girl's brow and began to move in an expressive display of grief. Little Ruthie's voice grew fainter and fainter.

Max gasped. She was good—*too* good. Tears came to his eyes. Where did she learn to act like that? He could hear Galitz sighing beside him. Even *he* was taken with her performance.

"Ain't she somethin'?" Galitz asked.

Max nodded. "I know. I can't believe it."

"What a pair," Galitz went on. "I'd give anything to *shtup* that one."

In horror, Max turned to look at him. "What did you say?"

"Look at that tush! She's really asking for it, ya know?"

Max felt the edges of rage curl around his gut. "I beg your pardon? That happens to be my child you're talking about!"

Now it was Galitz's turn to look amazed. "*Your* child? Barrbra Shapiro is *your* child?"

"Who the hell is Barrbra Shapiro?"

The two men stared at each other in silence.

"Aren't you talking about my little Ruthie up there on the stage?" Max asked.

"Hell, no! I'm talking about the *mother* up there, with the purple hair! That piece of ass who's wiping your kid's forehead with the *shmatte.*"

Max shook his head. "I'm sorry, Jerry. You'll

140

have to forgive me. I haven't slept in a week. My head is spinning."

Galitz put his arm around Max. The guy had a lot to learn, Galitz thought. He spent all his time in that *farshtinkener* lab of his, when he could be making big bucks right here in West Falls. Just look how he's dressed! Scuffed shoes, frayed collar, pants that must be a hundred years old, a button missing from his shirt. "Max, Max," he said, "I know just what you need."

Max yawned. "Yeah. I need some sleep."

"Well, you're *half* right." Jerry leaned closer. "What you really need, my friend, is some twat."

"Some *what?*"

"Not what. *Twat!*"

Max looked dumbfounded.

"Pussy, Max. Cunt."

Max cringed. *"Enough,* Jerry! I get the idea, but you're wrong."

Galitz shook his head and wagged his finger. "The mayor is never wrong," he said, reaching into his hip pocket and whipping out a folded copy of *The Marketplace.* He tapped the paper with his fat finger. "There's something here for you, Max."

Whatever Galitz was selling, Max didn't want any. There was something about Galitz that rubbed him the wrong way.

"I'm serious, Max," Galitz insisted. "Give a listen." He began to read from the paper:

Where've you been all my life? If you're male, over 35, and willing to take chances, we could make beautiful music together.

141

Galitz paused for effect. "Here's another," he said:

Vital, vivacious redhead seeks sensitive, mature counterpart capable of appreciating the better things in life . . .

Galitz waited for Max to react. "Well? You want me to read some more?"

But Max wasn't listening. From the corner of his eye, he'd seen Bliss Billington enter the gym. Even in jeans, she was beautiful. Across the room, their eyes met briefly. Max nodded. Did she smile back? It was dark and he couldn't be certain. Galitz kept insinuating himself between their lines of vision.

"So it's okay? I have your permission?" Galitz asked.

Max nodded absently. "Sure, sure." What a lovely woman she is. Should he ask her for her number? Would she give it to him? Should he write her a letter? Would she answer? What was the matter with him? He was acting like a schoolboy trying to get up the nerve to call a girl for a date.

"Good. Good. You won't be sorry. Trust me, Max," Galitz was saying. "You got a pen?" he asked.

Max fumbled in his pocket and found a pen. He thrust it at Galitz. He had no idea what the man was rambling on about, and what's more, he didn't care. There were only two things in life that he did care about: his daughter Ruthie and his work. He looked across the gym at Bliss Billington. No. Three things.

142

17

Princess and Cisco

"YOU sure collected a lotta stuff," Cisco said, handing Princess the cassette. She took it from him and crammed it into an overflowing portfolio. She shoved the portfolio back into the broom closet. Then she took a twenty-dollar bill from her apron pocket and thrust it into Cisco's hand. Little enough, she thought, for all the data he had collected for her. The thought crossed her mind about giving him credit in the intro to her dissertation. She wished she could mention it to him, but that was, of course, out of the question.

Without looking at the denomination, Cisco jammed the bill into his hip pocket. "You know, there's another way you can pay me for buggin' Johnson's bedroom," he teased.

She grinned. They had been bantering back and forth this way ever since she hired him. He was one of her best observers. He was also damn good-looking. She sighed and forced herself away from such unprofessional thoughts.

"So when am I gwana see 'dis here book?" Cisco asked, pouring himself another glass of Jared Galitz's Château Lafite-Rothschild 1972 into a mug with the words "World's Best Daddy" printed on it. He chugged it down and wrinkled his nose. "Dese honkies will drink any shit!" he complained in disgust.

Princess tried to conceal her amusement. "Ah heard it was 'sposed ta be good stuff," she said. "The old fart guards it with his life."

Cisco shrugged and moved toward her. "You want good stuff? I got good stuff," he enticed, slipping his arms around her and placing his hands on her breasts.

In spite of herself, Princess felt a tingle of excitement. Hold on to yourself, Ms. Armstrong, she thought. You've got to maintain your objectivity. But now Cisco's hands were caressing her. She could feel the warmth of his fingers through the thin cotton of her T-shirt. It had been so long since she'd been with a man. Ross Updike was thousands of miles away in Nairobi. And even though they were supposed to be engaged, and even though they wrote, it was increasingly difficult to remember how she was supposed to feel about him. She closed her eyes and sighed.

It didn't help that she was exhausted. She was nearing the end of this project, but at times, it seemed it would never be finished. Her adviser kept hounding her for results, and here she was, with mountains of notes on her doctoral dissertation still to be collated. Charts and graphs and conclusions awaited her undivided attention. She should be in her room right now, this very minute, sifting through all the data.

She could feel Cisco's lips on her neck. His breath was warm and sweet-smelling. Halfheartedly, she resisted.

"You want me. You know you do," Cisco crooned.

Well, she did. He might be a primitive, but he was a downright appealing primitive. Besides, she suspected he had more native intelligence than anyone she'd known at Harvard. Formal education wasn't everything. Hadn't her father always told her that? "Hizzoner's goin' ta be here any minute, fool," she admonished. "Yo' want me t'lose ma job?"

Cisco took her in his arms. He kissed her fully on the lips. Princess had never been kissed like that before. It was impossible not to respond.

"You don't need 'dis lousy job," he said. "They's lotsa jobs you could get. A girl like you . . . You could do anything. You could be a nurse's aide, for crissakes! A secretary, even. You could tell dese here honkies to stuff it—"

She closed her eyes. "Cisco, give me a break." She felt herself slipping. How had Margaret Mead ever avoided having sex with those Samoans? For all she knew, old Margaret probably did sack out with a few of them, but Margaret was Margaret and Princess was Princess . . .

Suddenly Cisco took something from his pocket. "Hey, I forgot to give you this before," he said, placing a small carved object in her hand.

She looked at him. "What's this for?" she asked.

He smiled sheepishly. "Happy birthday."

She laughed. "It's not mah birthday, dope."

Cisco shrugged. "Merry Christmas, then. Happy New Year, too. Happy Easter . . ."

She put her fingers to his lips. "Shut up," she commanded warmly as she looked down at the object in her hand. It was a small, intricately carved figure of what appeared to be a symbol of fecundity, *definitely* male. Was it pre-Columbian? Or a ceremonial object from an island culture?

"My sister sent it to me from home," Cisco explained. "I want you to have it."

She was moved. "Hey," she said, "you're sweet stuff." She stood on her toes and pecked him tenderly on the cheek.

Cisco grinned. Behind his back, his fingers were crossed. She couldn't know he had just presented her with the symbol of Agulei, the ancient Haitian god of lust. It worked every time, even on tough scores like Princess Armstrong. And she was nothing if not tough. He'd been trying to get her to bed for years, and none of his tricks had worked. Until now.

Princess was looking at him with new eyes. She took the empty wine bottle and stashed it with the other empties under the sink. She put the mug into the dishwasher.

Silently, Cisco intoned the Agulei chant: *Hegawakahooga. Hegawakahooga.* He tapped his left foot three times. Then he waited.

Princess reached out her hand. "Come," she said, leading him down the stairs to her basement room.

Hegawakahooga, Cisco intoned to himself. Once more for good luck.

Jared Galitz glanced around the empty kitchen to make sure he was alone. No sounds came from the basement. Princess was probably asleep. Likewise Olivia. God only knew where Selma was. He pulled the step stool from its niche near the broom closet and stood on the top rung. Reaching into the uppermost cabinet above the refrigerator, he felt around until he found it. His Twinkie stash. Safe and undisturbed. Quickly, he took three of the wrapped cakes and eased himself back down. Carefully, he put the step stool back in its place. He poured himself a glass of cold milk and shoved a Twinkie into his mouth. Its creamy sweetness enveloped his tongue. He opened another and popped that one in, too.

He closed his eyes. Heaven. Better than heaven. Better than almost anything he could think of at the moment. Somehow, with his mouth full of Twinkie goo, his problems seemed more manageable. It almost didn't matter that Selma and he had become strangers, that they hardly ever saw each other, and that when they did, they hardly ever spoke. He sighed.

And then he saw it. A small statue on the table. What the hell was it? Curious, he picked it up. It was the ugliest thing he'd ever seen. About three inches high, with a face that could stop a clock. But that wasn't all. The statue had a hard-on from here to Kalamazoo. An evil-looking thing it was. It gave him the creeps.

One of Princess's *chachkas,* no doubt. Some

crazy *shvartz* voodoo thing. They all believed in that crap, didn't they? She probably meant to put a hex on him. Quickly, he dropped it back on the table. Well, this was still his house, and he shouldn't have to look at such things. Tomorrow, he would tell Princess to keep it out of his sight. What if Olivia should see it? He drained the glass of milk and was disturbed to find that he was still trembling. Could the thing be having an effect on him already?

Maybe Selma was right. Maybe they should fire Princess after all. He switched off the light and got the hell out of there.

18

Peggy

PEGGY leaned up on one elbow and looked at him. Asleep, Dan Ogilvie reminded her of an innocent child. Reddish hair tousled. Freckles sprinkled Huck Finnish across his snub nose. Sweet, full lips . . . She remembered the pressure of those lips on hers last night, and the image of the sweet little boy faded. There was nothing childlike about Dan Ogilvie's lovemaking. On the contrary, he was an experienced, gentle lover, carefully attentive to her every need.

She still couldn't believe he was here beside her, that she had come so close to not answering his reply to her ad. But there had been *so* many letters. They just kept coming, day after day after day.

After Plato, there was that nice accountant from Hamden, Irving Stronghammer. Bald and so timid, she'd had to strain to hear every word he said across the dinner table. A decent human being, but not somebody she could go to bed with.

Then there was Seymour O'Reilly. Sy, as he liked to be called, was a police lieutenant whose wife had left him after eighteen years. He was a big man with a ruddy, pockmarked complexion and an affinity for dirty jokes about the Pope. Peggy was not amused, and she was glad when the evening was finally over.

The biggest surprise of all was Otto Schindler. She still couldn't get over it. A professional man. A doctor. A sex therapist! But then, she reasoned, Otto Schindler was a human being with human needs. As far as she knew, he wasn't married. Why *shouldn't* he crave female companionship? The more she thought about it, the more sense it made. She read his letter over and over:

> *Dearest Venus,*
> *I am a compassionate, intelligent Adonis, ready for dialogue and Dionysian pursuits. I am sincere and I, too, crave company. I am an accredited therapist with a thriving practice in West Falls, Connecticut.*

It had taken her a day and two scotches to find the courage to dial his number. She was unprepared for the recorded message:

> *Hello there. This is Dr. Schindler. I would love to talk to you, but I'm not available at the moment. However, if you leave your name and number, I promise to get back to*

you as soon as humanly possible. Remember:
Time and love and truth heal all wounds.

So she left her name (Venus) and her number,
and three minutes later the telephone rang.

"Do I know you?" Otto asked immediately.

"In a way, I guess you do," Peggy replied tim-
idly.

"Don't tell me!" Otto went on excitedly. "Let
me guess! You came to see me not long ago!"

"Yes," she admitted.

"*Yes!* The adorable ash blond with the corn-
flower blue eyes!"

"Uh—no, not quite," Peggy fumbled.

"Wait, wait! Give me a minute! The statuesque
redhead with the frigidity problem!"

"*NO!*" Peggy almost shouted.

"Got it!" Otto screamed suddenly. "Corcoran!
The magnificent brunet with the soulful eyes, married to the big baby!"

Peggy felt a twinge of disloyalty to Duke, but
she succeeded in stifling it. "Yes. Well . . . I've
filed for a legal separation . . ."

"Oh, my dear, I'm so happy to hear that. It was
only a matter of time before a sensible woman like
you came to see the light. Are you still at the same
address?"

"Yes."

"Good. I'll pick you up Friday, nine o'clock."

The phone went dead in her hand. Uncertainly,
she replaced the receiver. Was it ethical to date a
man who'd been her therapist, albeit only once?

Stop it, Peggy! she admonished herself. You're
not his patient. You put an ad in the personals. He

151

answered it. You called him. You're going out for a drink and some conversation. Simple as that.

When Friday finally came, she was a bundle of nerves. The fact that Otto beeped for her and didn't bother coming into the house didn't help.

"Holy shit, will you look at that car!" Wayne, Jr., exclaimed as he peered through the window. "That thing must be worth fifty grand at least!"

"Wayne, please watch your language!" Peggy scolded, looking over his shoulder. She'd never seen a car like it before. So white and shiny, it seemed phosphorescent in the dusk. "What is it?" she asked.

"1938 Packard convertible, mint condition, top of the line. *Incredible!*"

Peggy looked at Wayne, Jr., with pride. He was *so* like Duke. The best of Duke. A bittersweet yearning washed over her. She closed her eyes and forced herself to think of the evening that lay ahead.

Otto took her to The Royal Palm. He was even taller than she remembered and impressive in a white linen jacket, white slacks, and white leather thongs.

They sat at a small table in the rear. "Let's have something with rum in it," he suggested, scanning the cocktail menu.

Should she tell him that rum was not her favorite drink? She decided not to.

When Fred the bartender came to take their order, Otto said, "Two zombies, heavy on the rum."

"Whatever," Fred replied, shrugging.

Otto was sitting very close. He took her hand and began to massage her thumb. Slowly. Methodically. "You have a beautiful thumb," he said, lifting it to his lips and kissing it.

She began to feel very warm. No one had ever complimented her thumb before.

"Tell me about yourself," Otto said.

"What do you want to know?" she asked shyly.

"Everything," he answered dramatically. "I want to know *all* about you, everything you can think of."

He didn't let go of her thumb. The effect was incredible. She hadn't felt this wet about any man since Duke.

"Well," she began, "I have forty credits toward my bachelor's . . ."

He took her to Mount Olympus—the newest high-rise apartment complex in Short Falls. She'd driven past the buildings every day on her way to work and often wondered what they were like inside. Now she knew.

Otto lived on the twenty-third floor of the east building. In his living room, with its panoramic view of the Housatonic River, Peggy felt as though she were literally on top of the world.

"Oh, Otto, it's so beautiful!" she gasped. "And you've got a terrace, too!" She tried to open the sliding glass door, but it wouldn't budge.

"Forget the terrace," Otto said, gently leading her to the sofa. "It's full of nasty soot. I never go out there."

The living room was a study in white. White

walls, white carpet, white furniture. The pictures on the walls were of white asparagus stalks, white parsnips, white celery. On the tables were ivory elephant tusks and tall, tapered white candles in graceful white holders.

Otto pushed a button and suddenly the room was filled with the sound of the ocean.

Even white noise, Peggy thought, amazed.

She was in his arms before she knew what was happening. His touch was as light as air; his breath against her skin, silky and warm.

In seconds, they undressed each other. He touched her everywhere. Their naked bodies melted into a spectacular synthesis of desire.

He carried her into the bedroom effortlessly and set her down gently. She heard a faint gurgling beneath her. She felt a soft undulation.

"Waterbed," Otto explained frantically, between kisses. "You'll like it."

She opened her eyes to see a lone candle flickering, its glow reflected on the black satin sheets. She was in another world now. A black world. The walls were black. The blinds were black. But he was kissing her thighs now and all thought ceased. His lips against her clitoris burned the very core of her being. She lifted herself to meet his thrusting tongue. Someone screamed . . .

Otto cursed silently. It was going to be another one of those nights. Not even the beautiful Peggy Corcoran, the vision he'd been obsessed with for weeks on end, not even *she* could stimulate the stubborn Schindler cock to orgasm!

What a cruel trick the Fates were playing on

him! The first truly multiorgasmic woman in his bed in ages, and still he couldn't come!

And he knew why. Too many years of practicing his duality of response (above the desk, professional cool; below the desk, hot stuff!) had rendered him virtually comeless.

He closed his eyes and tried to concentrate. She was slithering beneath him like a greased eel, her magnificent tits jouncing and bouncing like electrified orbs.

Now she had him in her mouth. Her perfect lips clasped his organ like a gentle vise. He could feel the pressure of her tongue on his glans. *Let me come!* he beseeched silently.

Nothing.

He tried to visualize his desk and was rewarded with a brief flicker.

Again nothing.

It was no use.

He reached down and gently disengaged himself from her. She was *too* beautiful. That was why he couldn't come.

"Otto, is there anything I can do?" she asked plaintively.

"I'm afraid not," he said matter-of-factly. "But don't blame yourself. Sometimes it takes practice for a woman to know how to please a man."

Peggy smiled ruefully. Otto Schindler. What a creep! It had taken her two full days to realize that, doctor or not, Otto had a real problem, and it had nothing to do with her. She would chalk the whole crazy episode up to experience.

Dan Ogilvie, on the other hand, was as normal as

you could get. He stirred now and opened his eyes. In the early morning light, their blueness was startling. He smiled and reached for her.

"No regrets about last night?" he murmured into her ear.

"Not a one," she told him truthfully. Last night, though, there had been some hesitation on her part. Dan was the first man she'd invited into her bed since Duke. She wasn't sure how Morgie and Wayne, Jr., were going to take it. She could hear them now, in fact, getting ready for the movie, and felt a stab of uneasiness.

Dan had sensed her reluctance. Last night, after the concert, he'd said, "I really want to spend the night with you, Peggy. I want to wake up and see your beautiful face in the light of dawn."

"I don't know," she had hedged. "My children . . ."

He said, "They won't judge you, Peggy."

She couldn't be sure.

Dan had taken her into his arms and held her close. "Do you want me?" he asked.

"Yes," she had answered without hesitation.

And that had been that.

Now, he said, "Peggy, I think we could be good together. Let's see each other as much as possible."

She liked Dan, but she wasn't sure if she wanted a relationship right now. There were so many other things happening in her life. Morgie's movie. Wayne, Jr.'s music. The reporters following them everywhere. The instant fame . . .

She was beginning to feel the pressure. She was

beginning to feel sick to her stomach, in fact. Could it be the shrimp she'd had last night?

And what about all those phone calls from Duke? He was driving her crazy, calling three, sometimes four, times a day. Frantic, desperate calls that left her drained.

"I love you, Peggy!" he pleaded. "You're my only! I swear, Peg, it'll be just you and me! Give me one more chance!"

Her head throbbed.

"Peggy? Are you all right?" Dan's voice sounded as though it were coming to her from a great distance. "Is there anything I can do?"

"No-o-o—" she managed to gasp as she leapt from the bed.

She made it to the bathroom just in time.

19

Duke

THE sunlight hurt his eyes. His legs were stiff from sleeping in the car all night. He had to take a piss so bad that it was practically dripping down his leg. He opened the car door and took a quick look around. Good. Nobody in sight. It was still very early.

He'd nearly finished when he heard a voice. "Corcoran, my good man, when are you going to fix my carburetor?"

It was Roger Ridgeway, the biggest square of all time, gussied up in fancy jogging gear that probably cost more than a garage mechanic made in a month. *Just my luck to have that dork see me pissing in the neighbor's hydrangeas!* Duke thought.

"Don't worry, don't worry, Roger. You'll have it by today, for sure," Duke said, quickly zipping up.

"You don't look well, Corcoran," Roger commented as he ran by. "Maybe it's all that carbon monoxide you breathe all day. Try jogging!"

Jogging, my ass, Duke thought. It wasn't the carbon monoxide that was making him sick. It was this whole separation thing with Peggy. His wife. In his house. Right this minute. Making it with some guy, some redheaded creep, in his very own bed.

Christ! He hadn't planned to sleep in the car. He'd just wanted to talk to Peggy. He'd seen them go in together and decided to wait for the guy to come out. Except the guy hadn't come out!

Duke took a deep breath and got back inside the car. His stomach growled. He looked into the rear-view mirror and winced. A night's growth of beard covered his face. His eyes were red and wild looking. *God damn her!* Why did she have to let that wimp stay the night? He saw the front door open, saw the kids come out.

Halfway down the walk, Morgie stopped and touched Wayne, Jr.'s arm. "It's Daddy!" she called excitedly. She ran to him. "Daddy, Daddy, what are you doing out here?"

Duke stumbled from the car and flung his arms around his daughter. "Hey," he said, tousling her hair, "where're you two off to this early?" He looked at Wayne, Jr., who seemed edgy.

"Come on, Daddy, you know." Morgie smiled. "We're going to start shooting today! Down on Main Street. You wanna come see?"

Duke smiled. "Hey, honey, I'd like to—you know I would—but I can't. There are five cars waiting for me in the garage." He looked at Wayne, Jr., again. The boy was definitely avoiding

159

his gaze. Duke reached out. "Hey, fella, I hear they're using your music in the movie. Way to go, guy," he said, playfully punching Wayne, Jr.'s arm.

Wayne, Jr., smiled nervously and shrugged. "Yeah, well, didn't I tell ya, Dad? They liked my stuff."

Duke felt like grabbing him and hugging him. How he missed these kids of his! Why hadn't he ever noticed what a good-looking boy Wayne, Jr., was? He nodded toward the house. "So . . . who's in there with her?"

Morgie and Wayne, Jr., exchanged uneasy glances. "I dunno, Dad. She's only been out with him a coupla times."

"He got a name?" Duke pressed.

Wayne shuffled his feet. "Uh, well, I think his name is Dan. Maybe Don."

Morgie tugged at Wayne's arm. "Come on, Wayne, we don't want to be late."

The look of misery on her little face made Duke want to storm the house and yank that prick out of his bed. Once, he might have done just that. Not now, though. He was a changed man.

He sighed long and loud. "Get in, kids," he said. "I'll give you a lift to the set."

20

Myra

THINGS were much easier for Myra Schick when she was with *Insider's Gazette*. Nobody there ever let a fact get in the way of a good story. But now that she was working for *FOLK*, it was a whole different ball game. For one thing, Richard Wallingham, her editor, insisted on *taped* interviews. "No more inventing the news, Myra, my girl," he had warned when he hired her. "I'm giving you this job for old times' sake—and because underneath those tiny boobs of yours, there beats the heart of a damn good reporter. Ya got the killer instinct, Myra. I like that in a girl."

She hated when Richard called her a girl. And she resented his reference to her small breasts. They had slept together so long ago she could hardly remember. She was just out of J-School at Northwestern, trying to make it in the Apple, and as luck would have it, there was an opening for a typist at LOOK. Richard was in the mail room—but not for long. When he was promoted to reporter, he took her out for a drink. One drink led to another and yet another and they wound up in her small studio apartment. After that, they fucked off and on, whenever either one of them needed it.

She had to admit that somewhere, down deep in her heart, there was still a special feeling for Richard Wallingham. After all, he was the one who picked her cherry. Still, what did he know about working with these deadheads in West Falls? It was the shittiest assignment she'd ever had, and she'd had her share of shitty assignments. The kids were impossible. Brats like you couldn't believe. That glitzy mayor kept shoving his carbon-copy kid in front of her every chance he got. The other parents were not much better.

At least she'd managed to get twenty minutes with the world's newest brother and sister act—The Corcoran Kids. Big deal! She knew that the real story was the Billington girl, but there wasn't a chance in the world the mother was going to let her interview the kid. "I simply will not allow my child to be exploited by the media, *no way!*" was the way she put it.

Well, *la-di-da.*

Myra ground out her cigarette and drained her cup. "More coffee," she demanded. The only decent thing about this burg was its diner. What would she do without a decent cup of coffee? She'd faint dead away, that's what.

"So, my beauti-ful flower, how are you progressing?"

The big Greek leaned over the counter and grinned at her. His gold tooth matched the mass of chains around his thick neck. Myra met his gaze. Automatically, she visualized the size of his dick. She had her own system: twice as long as the nose and half as thick as the neck. According to her calculations, this was a Greek worth knowing. Too bad she didn't have the time right now.

"I'm progressing fine, thank you," she said coyly.

His eyes swept over her appreciatively. "So—you'll be at the party?"

Myra's ears pricked like antennae picking up radar. "Party?"

The Greek nodded. "Yeh. Da beeg bash for da movie. All da reporters got invites. Ya know. Da Meet-da-Stars party."

She nodded. "Oh, *that*. Sure."

He grinned and leaned even closer to her. "Guess who's gonna supply da food? Yours truly!" he said, proudly pointing to his chest.

She forced a smile. "I'm so happy for you," she managed through tight lips. Anger seared through her. It would be just like that Heatter sonofabitch to toss a party and exclude her. She looked at her watch. Where the hell was Al, the hotshot photographer? Had *he* been invited to the party?

She slammed a quarter on the counter and slid off the stool.

Outside, the huge crowd stood waiting. Today was the first day of outdoor shooting, and the good citizens of West Falls—most of them women— were ready. Barricades were up on both sides of

163

Coolidge Boulevard, and the police were on horse-back trying to control the mob. Cries of "Barron, Barron, Barron . . ." rose up periodically, then faded, then rose up again. Myra smirked. They had as much chance of getting to him as she did. *Zilch.* Granted, the man was gorgeous. But a real asshole! She'd been covering celebrities for twenty years, and not one of them had ever given her the trouble Barron Heatter had. Redford, Eastwood, Beatty, Newman—they were gentlemen, at least. Courteous enough to answer her calls, even if they refused to interview. Heatter was another story. Who was he kidding? This was his last gasp. He couldn't afford to exclude her. Or any other reporter, for that matter. Why, the guy'd had three flops in a row and had to finance this flick with his own bucks!

She couldn't believe he was still holding that grudge against her. It had happened so long ago. He was making *Belgian Affair,* and she was on a story for *Insider's Gazette.* Was it her fault she had to hide under the bed in his room in the Hilton International Brussels? She'd been sent to get an interview, so what else could she do? She was there the whole time he was making it with that French bimbo, Brigitte. So Brigitte was just a kid—no more than sixteen. So what? Who could know? She'd managed to snap a picture of Barron and the little nymph on her way out of the room. Barron had never forgiven her. Of course, he denied the whole thing when it hit print. Of course, he sued. But pictures don't lie, and the case was thrown out of court. It had been the real start of her career.

But that was then and this was now. She couldn't

believe he was still sore. Well, that was *his* problem. If there were a party, she was going to be there.

One way or another, Myra Schick always gets her story.

21

Selma

SHE'D been waiting for a solid week. Finally, this
morning, *The Marketplace* had forwarded the response to her second ad: a single plain white envelope with no return address.

Not again! Selma thought in a haze of disappointment. She'd hoped that this time, at least,
she'd get more than one answer! She had pur-
posely reworded this ad to avoid attracting another Fremont Bisch. Not that Fremont wasn't a
nice person. He was one of the nicest men she had
ever met. But he was too old.

166

"Ah's goin', Miz Gee." Princess rapped on the door and entered the room without being asked to. "Hizzoner wants me ta pick up his white flannels from da cleanuhs. Den he wants me to go down ta da Palm an' make shuah da 'rangements is goin' okay for da party . . ." Princess sighed dramatically. "Ah sweah he's runnin' me ragged dese days!"

Selma said nothing.

"You okay, Miz Gee?"

"I'm fine, Princess," Selma replied impatiently.

"Well," said Princess, "guess Ah'll be movin' on. Ya'll wants me to mail dat lettah fo' yo'?"

"No, thanks," Selma answered nervously.

"Yuh shuah?"

"I'm sure I'm sure," Selma said coolly.

"No need to get hostile, Miz Gee." Princess paused. "Well—Ah'm on mah way."

Alone at last, Selma breathed a sigh of relief. She was absolutely, positively reaching the end of her rope with that woman! She looked at the envelope in her hand. *Please, dear God, let this one be younger than Fremont!* Seventy-four years old was too much. But how could she have known?

She'd actually sat next to Fremont at the bar of The Royal Palm for twenty minutes before she realized who he was. He'd assumed she was waiting for someone else, too. It wasn't until Fred the bartender asked, "Will you have another stinger, Mr. Bisch?" that Selma put two and two together.

Her first instinct was to leave, but how could she do that? She said, "Excuse me, sir, but you wouldn't happen to be *Fremont* Bisch, would you?"

167

He cupped his ear. "Eh? You talking to me, girlie?"

Selma repeated it, louder. Fremont's kind, wrinkled face brightened. "Why, yes, I *do* happen to be . . . Now, don't tell me . . . You're *Selma?*"

She nodded half-heartedly. She tried not to let the disappointment show on her face. She extended her hand and said, "I'm so pleased to meet you, Mr. Bisch."

He took her to McDonald's for dinner. Over a Big Mac, fries, and a shake, he admitted, "I've never done anything like this before."

Selma nodded. "That makes two of us."

"All my friends at the home find these ads so stimulating," Fremont said, reddening slightly. He leaned forward. "Can I tell you a secret? I think I'm the first one to actually jump in and answer one of them," he boasted with a self-satisfied grin. "It seemed like an interesting thing to do."

Strangely enough, as the evening wore on, Selma discovered she was having a good time. Fremont was attentive, gentle, and he seemed to be genuinely fascinated by her. In fact, he treated her as though she were a princess.

"Any man would be proud to be seen with you, my dear," he told her over and over. "Why, you're almost as beautiful as my Mamie, may she rest in peace."

After dinner, they went dancing. Wednesday night was Lawrence Welk Night at the Happy Valley Home, where Fremont had lived ever since his wife Mamie had died. Selma didn't know what to expect. She was surprised to see how cheerfully the social hall was decorated. It was like *any* party

168

anywhere except that she was at least twenty years younger than all the other guests—a fact that didn't go unnoticed. All the men scrambled to dance with her. She was "queen of the prom." They taught her the black bottom and the Charleston and she taught them the frug and the bougaloo.

By eleven, she was exhausted. She kissed Fremont's cheek. "Fremont, I had a wonderful evening," she said truthfully. "And you're a dear . . ."

"Will I see you again?" he asked.

She blushed. "Of course you will."

And she had seen him again. Several times, in fact. They were partners in a Scrabble tournament (they came in second) the following Tuesday night, and just last week, on Movie Night (Thursday), they'd held hands and cried during a screening of *Wuthering Heights*. She knew that Fremont was a person she could count on if she ever needed a good friend.

It was Fremont who had recommended the cardiovascular man she and Bea had taken Abe to see after that "episode" at rehearsal.

Abe had resisted every step of the way. "There's nothing wrong with me," he kept protesting.

As things turned out, he was right. There *was* nothing wrong with him, at least according to the test results.

Bea remained unconvinced. "I'm telling you, Selma, he's not himself. He's not the same man I married."

"They're never the same man," Selma replied.

Bea gave her a peculiar, penetrating look. "Selma, what is it? There's trouble in paradise?"

Selma shrugged. "I don't care to talk about it, Mother."

"So don't talk. Listen." Bea lowered her voice. "This isn't easy for me to tell you. I think your daddy is fooling around."

There was a stunned silence. Selma's first instinct was to laugh, but she didn't. "Don't be ridiculous, Mother," she said. "Not Daddy."

"He's a man, no? When men get older, something happens to them. Something crazy . . ."

Selma could relate to that. Jerry was getting older, too. But the idea of Jerry with another woman had never occurred to her. The thought of it was preposterous.

She was trembling. Cautiously her fingers tore open the envelope. Inside was a single typewritten sheet of paper. It looked like a photocopy. In the upper-right-hand corner a blurry photo looked vaguely familiar . . .

Her heart raced. Something . . . A form letter . . . Incredible! Some creep had actually responded to her ad with a form letter! Phrases leapt from the page:

I am a socially involved public servant . . . A lonely voyager in a sea of doubt . . . I seek an understanding woman . . . Precious, intimate moments . . . Trust me . . .

Her tear-filled eyes darted to the signature. She read it. She read it again. It couldn't be. It was. *Jared G. Galitz, Esq.*

The bastard! The sonofabitch! The ungrateful Twinkie-eating pompous, arrogant fool!

She tore the letter into a million fragments and flushed it down the toilet.

Time ceased to exist. Her eyes felt like sandpaper. It hurt to breathe. How long had she lain across the unmade bed?

All right, Selma, she said to herself. *What now?*

22

Bliss

SHE was livid. The *People* article had been bad enough, but the spread in *FOLK* Magazine was more than she could take. While more space had been devoted to the Corcoran children, that brassy, pushy Myra Schick had somehow managed to dig up an old photo of her and Sunny at The Settlement! Even worse, she had divulged where Sunny went to school—Miramar-Bromley—and that she was the daughter of the owner of Bliss Knits in the West Falls Mall!

Where had that Schick bitch gotten that old picture? It was from another lifetime, and just looking at it brought forth a rush of memories better left forgotten . . .

Damn! Bliss tossed the magazine into the wastebasket. Had Myra Schick bribed Gladys to get the photo?

"Why, Ms. Billington, I would never do such a thing!" Gladys insisted indignantly when Bliss confronted her point-blank.

Bliss didn't entirely believe her. She was tempted to dismiss Gladys. But Sunny liked the woman, and the thought of finding another housekeeper was more than she could handle right now.

The bell over the door tinkled musically and shook Bliss out of her reverie.

A trio of overly made-up matrons entered the shop. "It's her! It's her! She's the mother! There, didn't I tell you?" Chattering, they converged menacingly on her.

"You're her, aren't you?" one of the women shouted accusingly. "Amy's mother?"

"Oh, my God, Agnes, it *is* her! She's fatter in person!"

The woman with the streaked blond hair and long red nails chirped, "So tell us, dearie, what's he *really* like?"

Bliss fought to maintain her composure. In spite of herself, she felt a genuine stab of fear. She wished now that she hadn't sent her assistant, Lynda, to the bank. In a tight, controlled voice, Bliss asked, "May I help you, ladies?"

They ignored the question. "We saw the article in the magazine, so we came all the way down here from Dove Hills Estates. We have to know: Is Barron Heatter really a sex fiend?"

Bliss swallowed. "I'm sorry, I haven't the vaguest idea what you're talking about. If you'd like to see some yarn, I'd be happy to show it to you. We've just gotten a new shipment of mohair from Scotland, and the colors are luscious . . ."

The women looked at each other. The short, plump one shrugged. *"Yarn? Who wants yarn? We want dirt!"* She laughed lasciviously.

Bliss squared her shoulders and opened the door. "I'm sorry, but I can't help you. You'll have to leave . . ."

The women looked angry now. "Well, I never!" the streaked blond said. "Uppity thing, isn't she? Who does she think she is?"

The short, plump one walked out the door, saying, "Amy is a crummy part, anyway. Her child obviously has no talent!"

They slammed the door behind them, hard enough so that Bliss was afraid the glass would shatter.

She locked the door quickly. It was almost closing time anyway. She felt drained, weak. She walked slowly back into her office, sat down at her desk, and fingered through the mail.

Among the bills and junk mail, there was an envelope with a Lake Forest postmark. Her hands trembled as she held it.

She took a deep breath and reached for her ivory-handled letter opener. Slowly and carefully, she slit the envelope. Her mother's familiar scent was instantly recognizable. Bliss felt light-headed as she read:

> *My dear Bliss,*
> *I can't tell you what an incredible surprise it was to see my granddaughter's photograph in* FOLK *Magazine last week. She is so beautiful, so like you at that age.*
> *I had no idea you were living in the East*

now. It has been so long since we've had any contact. I don't even know if this letter will reach you, but I'm hoping it does.

There are some things you should know: Father passed away two years ago June. His death was sudden and painless. I am remarried. Do you remember Farnsworth Carter, the gentleman who owned The Emporium in Evanston? He is a wonderful man, sensitive and kind in ways your father was never able to be. I am happy, as happy as anyone could be who has not seen her only child in thirteen years.

There is no much I would like to tell you, Bliss. The first is that I love you dearly. I always have and I always will. Can you find it in your heart to include me in your life again?

Not a day goes by that I do not think of you, of where I went wrong, of how I could have eased your pain in the past. I miss you and would give anything to see you and my darling granddaughter.

> *Your loving mother,*
>
> *Patricia Billington Carter*

Bliss put the letter down. Her cheeks were wet with tears. *So he's dead. Well, I'm glad.*

She sat at the desk for a long time, ruminating over her childhood in Lake Forest. She thought of the house, with its sun-splashed rooms, the growing shadow of her father gradually eclipsing her childish joy and replacing it with terror. She

175

thought of her flight to The Settlement and Sojourn and Eric . . .

The ringing of the telephone jarred her. *Oh, please, God! Don't let it be that maniac!*

"Mom?"

The sound of Sunny's voice filled her with relief. "Sunny? Baby?"

"We broke early today, Mom, and Gladys isn't home. Can you pick me up at the library?"

Of course she could. She turned off the lights and let herself out the back door. The late afternoon sun was warm and comforting.

It had been a week since Steve Gordon's last call. Maybe he'd gotten tired of bothering her. Maybe she'd never hear from him again. She felt a rush of optimism.

She thought she had learned a valuable lesson. So how could she have been foolhardy enough to answer yet another ad?

But the fact was that she had, only two nights ago. After the *FOLK* article came out, she'd been upset to the point of despair, and all the old, lonely feelings had come flooding back. She felt used and victimized. Without thinking, almost from force of habit, she'd scanned the personals ads in *The Marketplace,* all the while telling herself she was just *looking.*

And then she'd seen it—an ad that seemed to answer her unspoken longings:

Middle-aged doctor. Quiet, sensitive widower. A real thinker. I am tired of lonely nights and need a shining star to give my life

176

direction. I love children and dogs and elegant, poised women. **Box 1206.**

She'd dashed off an answer and mailed it quickly, before she could change her mind. Now, as she maneuvered her silver Porsche expertly around Eisenhower Circle, past the high school, to the library, she thought, What's done is done.

The crowds were gathered around the building. Women, as usual. Bliss shook her head. How ridiculous they were to stand in the hot sun day after day, just for a glimpse of a good-looking man. Personally, she couldn't understand what the attraction was. Barron Heatter was all flash and prefabricated macho. He didn't seem real, somehow.

But then again, what was *real?*

23

Phyllis Sawyer

Show-biz pro, female, tired of too much tinsel, seeks solid, respectable citizen. You
should be tall, clean, well dressed, feet
planted firmly on terra-firma. No phony
baloney, please. **Box 2067.**

THE Motel Pierre was a dump. There was just no
other way to describe it. Off the Post Road at the
end of the West Falls landfill, it had absorbed the
odor of a half century's rotting detritus. If Norman
Bates ever moved East, he would snap it up in a
minute.

Phyllis Sawyer looked around the room and
wrinkled her nose. When Nate Greene got her this
job as Andy ffrench's assistant, she'd been ecstatic.
The big time at last! Some big time! "Barron, you
piker!" she snapped in disgust. "Is this the best you

can do for your coolies?" Sure it was. Everyone knew Barron was so cheap he could squeeze buffalo milk from a nickel. It was no secret that he'd made a deal with the owner of this place—none other than that wild-haired letch, Hizzoner the Mayor.

Barron didn't give a damn. Right now, he was probably sitting in his marble tub in his suite at The Plaza, with the world's meanest purple pussy, Barrbra Shapiro, going down on him. Glub. Glub.

Andy ffrench was in the room next door. She could hear him now, practicing his diction, rolling his r's making *ow* sounds with his tongue: The fl*au*tist p*ou*ts on the *ou*ter b*ou*gh, w*ow*, w*ow*, w*ow*. Phyllis rolled her eyes. She would like to *wow* him. Throw a shoe through the paper-thin wall and shut him up. She decided to ignore him instead.

Two rooms down was Spyros, the cinematographer, and next to him, the camera crew and the makeup people. She considered knocking on their doors, inviting herself in for a drink. But it had been a rough day and she was exhausted.

The air conditioner began a loud rasping. Like a death rattle. *Oh, please! Don't conk out!* It was eleven at night, and ninety-two degrees! She needed her sleep.

They'd begun shooting with the Laurie character today. What a disaster. Too bad they hadn't been able to get Leif Garrett for the role. He would have been perfect. Then there'd been a frantic effort to get David Bowie, but Bowie was too expensive. Which explained why they finally wound up with Johann Paul Jones—superbrat.

Phyllis groaned. Johann Paul Jones was the latest

in a series of up-and-coming street-rockers to shadow Michael Jackson and Prince. Except JayPee, as he liked to be called, had not yet attained superstar status. This picture, he hoped, would boost him over the top.

Years ago they would have called JayPee a delinquent. Today he was the object of twelve-year-old girls' masturbatory fantasies. A puny, runty, sneering seventeen-year-old dropout with the most incredible pair of flashing blue eyes in a coffee brown face, JayPee knew how to belt out a song. He wrote his own music and lyrics and could handle eight or nine instruments. There was no doubt the kid had talent. He was sexy, too, in a weird, schizoid way. But his affectations could drive you up the wall. He favored pink sequinned jockstraps and a jangling collection of religious medals that decorated his neck: crucifixes, a Star of David, Buddhas of jade and ivory, unidentifiable relics from obscure sects—even a bronze medal that bore the likeness of Albert Schweitzer. All that *and* a mouth that could spew more obscenities than she knew existed.

Phyllis sighed and sat down heavily on the ancient bed. The springs protested noisily.

She forced Johann Paul Jones from her mind. She had more important things to think about. The answers to her personals ad, for instance. She couldn't put them off any longer—not that she wanted to—but something was holding her back. *Fear.* Suppose they were all awful? She was already disappointed that there were only two replies, but then, all she needed was one—the right one!

She studied the envelopes carefully. Which one

should she open first? "Eeny, meeny, miney, moe, catch a husband by the toe. If he hollers, give him blow, eeny, meeny . . ." Her finger landed on the thicker envelope. Inside were seven sheets of gray and white stationery, lined, written in a tiny, precise hand.

Someone had sent her a goddamn book!

She began to read.

> *Dear Professional,*
> *For many years—indeed, most of my life—I have resided in West Falls, Connecticut. It is a wonderful town, with good schools and a variety of churches; it is a fine place to raise children.*

Phyllis stopped reading. What the hell *was* this? Something from the West Falls Chamber of Commerce? She began again.

> *While, in theory, I don't approve of personals ads, I must say I found your advertisement irresistible. It reflected your displeasure with the superficialities of contemporary life and your preference for basic American values . . .*

She shook her head: she didn't *believe* this guy!

> *I am fortyish, an investment analyst with Lanham, Bixter and Bligh for the past twenty years. I am also president of the West Falls Board of Education, a trustee of the West Falls Library Association, and a senior*

181

member of the town council. I hold a bache-
lor's from Palmolive University, class of '65,
and an M.B.A. from Harvard University . . .

Her eyes were beginning to get teary from the strain of reading the minutiae of this guy's life. He may hold degrees from Palmolive and Harvard, Phyllis decided, but he sure wasn't going to get to hold her. *"Bor-ing,"* she said, ripping the letter in to shreds—but not before she glanced at the signature: Roger Ridgeway.

"Nice try, Roger. I hope you find your true love." She reached for the remaining envelope. "Next!"

This stationery was nondescript. Whoever wrote the letter liked musk; she was nearly wiped out by the scent as she tore open the envelope.

She crossed her fingers and prayed. All right, God, this is it. Next week is my birthday. My forty-fifth, as You well know. So come on, already. What's the big deal? All I'm asking for is *one man!*

The letter was printed. Easy to read. Thank you, God.

Dear Lamb Chop,
You must know how much I admire you.
Every day for weeks I've walked around ach-
ing for you. My wife (in name only) thinks
it's gas. Of course, she doesn't know my feel-
ings for you, but I'll make her a nice settle-
ment and she'll be happy.

Phyllis's heart started to pound. She sat upright in bed. Was she dreaming? She didn't think so.

From the next room, she could still hear Andy mumbling his *ow*'s. She pinched herself. How did this man know who she was? Who was *he*? She didn't need another married man, not now, not after all those years with Nate Greene. Still, he had specified "in name only." There was hope.

I long for the touch of your firm flesh, the feel of your tender loins, the mingling of our juices . . .

A fine film of sweat broke over her body. Who could he *be*? Her mind panned over the men she saw each day. Someone connected with the movie? Spyros? But he wasn't married. Andy? Never! Barron? Nah.
Who? Eagerly, she read on.

At night I dream about the feel of your fine, healthy brusts *against me . . .*

Brusts? Did that mean what she thought it meant? A fire was building between her legs. She shifted on the bed. Who cared if he couldn't spell? This man, whoever he was, was head over heels in love with her!

I want to stuff myself into all your sweet, adorable little places . . .

Phyllis couldn't go on. Her breath was coming in shallow gasps. She began to rock back and forth on the mattress, to the accompanying thwang of the springs.

Suddenly there was a pounding on the wall. "Hey! Cut it out in there!" It came not from Andy's room but from the other side.

"Fuck off!" she screamed. It was happening all by itself, just from the letter. She didn't even have to use her hand! What would he be like in person if his letter had this effect on her?

"Nice talk, Phyllis," Andy called from his room.

Well, too bad. She read the last two sentences of the letter.

So call me, little cutlet, the sooner the better. But make it after midnight, when the ball and chain takes a sleeping pill and is dead to the world.

The letter was signed with a maddening You-Know-Who.

She *didn't* know who! But it was already eleven thirty-three. In only twenty-seven minutes she would dial his number and find out.

24

Max

> Middle-aged doctor. Quiet, sensitive widower. A real thinker. I am tired of lonely nights and need a shining star to give my life direction. I love children and dogs and elegant, poised women. **Box 1206.**

IT was embarrassing. The woman was coming out of her dress, and he didn't know which way to look. Max was relieved when the waiter arrived at last with the lobsters.

"Bib, madame?" the waiter asked, his eyes bulging at the sight of Miriam Blavatsky's plunging neckline.

Miriam nodded. The waiter advanced eagerly, his hands lingering longer than necessary on her soft flesh.

"Sir?" he asked Max, coming toward him with a bib.

But Max shook his head and waved him away. "No, thank you."

Miriam, her mouth stuffed with food, looked up. "No bib?" she asked. "You'll get butter on your tie, Maxie. You'd better wear a bib!" When she smiled, there was lipstick on her teeth.

Max shook his head again and silently vowed to get even with Jared Galitz for this. How would he do it? Ship Miriam Blavatsky Air Express to his doorstep? No. He would hire a van and dump the endless stream of letters from that damn personals ad on Galitz's desk.

He still wasn't quite sure how it had happened. While Galitz had been jabbering at him that day in the gym, Max hadn't been paying attention. So maybe it wasn't all Galitz's fault. But still, how was he, Max, to know what he'd agreed to? It wasn't until the post office called to ask how he'd like all the sacks delivered that he realized the enormity of the deed. Two overflowing mailbags a day, four days in a row! And still coming! All from women wanting to meet the "middle-aged doctor" who loved "children and dogs and elegant, poised women." Max wondered where Galitz got the dogs part. He didn't have a dog and didn't particularly *like* dogs—except, maybe, in the lab . . .

"Eat your lobster, Maxie, before it gets cold," Miriam cooed, her lips shiny with melted butter.

Halfheartedly, he attacked a claw.

"So tell me again what kind of doctor you are," Miriam managed between swallows. Before he could answer, she offered, "My brother-in-law is a doctor, did I tell you? He's a proctologist. Do you know what that is?"

Max coughed and grabbed for his glass of water. "Ye—yes," he sputtered, "I know."

"That's an ass man," she went on. "Personally, I don't know how he can stand looking up all those tushies all day, even if he does make half a million a year."

Max blinked. Judging from her letter, Miriam had seemed like a woman he would want to know better. She had described herself as a widow, a schoolteacher, whose favorite authors were Shakespeare and Saul Bellow. She'd even quoted poetry. Something from Edna St. Vincent Millay about a candle being burned at both ends.

Apparently, she had a fixation with ends. Max glanced at his watch. How could it be only eight o'clock? Would he get through the evening? Why had he been foolish enough to phone this woman? He *knew* why. He was lonely and he couldn't get Bliss Billington out of his mind. He had to try, though, and this was one way.

Somehow they made it through the lobsters, but Miriam didn't let up. "What *kind* of research? Who watches your little girl? Do you iron your shorts?"

The finger bowls arrived. In utter fascination, he watched as Miriam, pinkies aloft, lifted the bowl to her mouth and drank. "Mmm, lemony," she said, smacking her lips. "Try it, Maxie. Drink up."

He didn't want to embarrass her, so he drank. People were staring. Let them.

For dessert, he ordered coffee, black. Miriam

wanted cherries jubilee. "Have some," she offered, extending her plate across the table.

Reluctantly, he complied. His arm jarred hers and the cherries spilled onto the table and into his lap. "Holy . . ." Max yelped and jumped up.

"Ooohh, did I do *that!*" she shrieked, dipping her napkin into a glass of water and rushing around to him. "Oh, I'm *so* sorry," she said over and over as she wiped the sticky substance from his pants. As her hand brushed his crotch, he responded, in spite of himself. "Ooh," she murmured appreciatively, winking up at him.

Max motioned frantically to the waiter for a check. He had to get out of here—*fast.* He wanted to go home and pretend that this evening had never happened.

In the parking lot, Miriam looked questioningly at him. "Your place or mine?" she asked.

With all the diplomacy he could muster, he told her, "I have an early day tomorrow, Miriam. I'll drop you off and then go right home."

"But tomorrow is Sunday," she pouted. "What doctor works on Sunday?"

"Researchers work every day," he said. "There are no Sundays for us . . ."

Somehow they made it to Miriam's house. She kept up a steady flow of chatter while Max drove, his hands clamped on the steering wheel, his eyes glued to the road. When Max pulled up in front of her house, he let out a silent sigh of relief. But alas, his ordeal wasn't over yet.

Miriam Blavatsky was a woman for whom a polite "no" meant "maybe." On her doorstep, Max declined her repeated invitations to "come inside for a little nightcap." When she realized he had no intention of coming in, her voice turned suddenly shrill.

"Who the hell do you think you are?" she shrieked.

Lights in neighboring houses turned on. A man walking his dog stopped to watch. The dog began to howl.

"All you men are the same! You lead a woman on and you drop her when you've gotten everything you want!"

Max backed slowly down her walk. He wished for a hole to swallow him up. He wished he'd never heard of Jared Galitz or *The Marketplace* or the U.S. Postal Service.

Her shoe got him neatly on the left shoulder. The lady had perfect aim.

Safely in his car, he berated himself for believing even for one second that he could meet the right woman through a personals ad. What a bunch of nonsense! What was meaningful to one person was meaningless to the next. Love, *real* love, was not anything you could order up like a businessman's lunch. How foolish to think that you could!

Fitting his key into his front door, Max sighed heavily. All the tension and exhaustion of the past weeks were converging on him. He felt totally devoid of energy, drained. A night with Miriam Blavatsky could enervate even Superman, he thought wearily.

Mrs. Schotz had left a lamp burning for him. He tiptoed across the living room to Ruthie's bedroom. She was sound asleep, bless her, her hair tousled, the bedclothes tangled as usual. She always had been a restless sleeper. His heart melted as he bent to kiss her cheek. Where had the years gone? In a few weeks, she'd be thirteen. He remembered, as if it were yesterday, when she'd been an infant, and he and Audrey had taken turns walking her back and forth from one end of the house to the other, trying to ease her colic. They thought it would never end.

Colic. That bane of infancy! But it was Ruthie's colic that had inspired his research. Because of *his* Ruthie, future generations of babies would be able to rest easy. Ditto, their parents.

There was one more thing he had to do before he went to bed. He walked into his study. There they were. Mail sacks, eight of them, standing upright like a miniature Stonehenge, letters spilling out of them onto the polished wood floor.

Resolutely, Max went to the fireplace and struck a match. The kindling caught immediately, and he fed the letters by the handfuls into the flames. He could feel the desperation of the women who had written them rising like a wraith of despair all around him. It was as if a thousand lonely voices were calling out: WANT ME! LOVE ME! MARRY ME!

Something—he would never know what—made him pause and look down at the letter in his hand. An ordinary blue envelope. Nothing unusual about it. Still, he felt oddly compelled to open it.

A thin sheet of paper, translucent in the firelight, fell into his lap. The handwriting was graceful and elegant. Almost against his will, he began to read:

I was so intrigued by your ad in The Marketplace *that I had to answer it immediately. Let me tell you a little about myself. I like children; in fact, I have a thirteen-year-old daughter. I also have a busy career.*

Although my life is full and satisfying, there are times when I miss the companionship of a kind and caring man. Are you that man?

Simple and straightforward, Max thought. He glanced at the signature. He looked again. *It couldn't be.* His hands were shaking. Was he hallucinating? It was late. He was tired.

He looked again.

It was fate. But he was a scientist and scientists didn't believe in fate. But how else could he explain this?

He closed his eyes and opened them again. Yes. It was *her* signature.

Bliss Billington.

25

Andy

IT was nine forty-five in the morning.

The narrow hips were swaying. The scrawny shoulders were gyrating. Andy stood mesmerized as he watched those shimmering jet-black coils of hair snapping and springing like snakes in time to the music.

Andy knew he was supposed to be checking the props, but he couldn't take his eyes off JayPee. The kid was something else. Tight jeans. *Very* tight. Andy tried not to stare, but it was impossible. Control yourself, he thought. The last thing you need is another San Diego! Think of something else—*quick!* He looked at Phyllis Sawyer. Immediately his erection began to deflate. God, what an ugly broad. And dopey, too. What the hell was she *doing,* anyway? She was supposed to be following the script; instead, she was staring at the crew as if she'd never seen them before.

"Wake up, will you, Andy! What is it with you people today? You're all half asleep! Time is money!" Barron's voice pierced the haze.

Andy hurried over to where Barron was standing in the bright sunlight. "Yessirree, Barron! What can I do you for?"

Barron grimaced. "Did you secure that tree like I instructed? It looks wobbly to me. I don't trust those prop guys!"

Barron Heatter, that paranoid prick, never trusted anyone, Andy thought. But *did* he secure the tree? He *thought* he did. *Sure.* "It's as secure as it'll ever be, Barron," he assured him quickly. "Want some coffee?"

Barron nodded. Andy edged away. God, it was hot. He could feel his shirt clinging to the small of his back. He wished this project were in the can. He wished he were back in California. He wished he could get JayPee into the sack . . . *Oops! Watch it, Andy!*

He walked across the set to the coffee van. Spyros was there, shooting the breeze with Plato Pappamichaelis, who was supplying the cast and crew with his shitawful greasy food.

"Hi, guys," Andy greeted them. "Two regulars, pronto."

The men were yammering to each other in Greek and didn't even look his way.

"Hey," Andy said, "two regulars. And a donut."

The two men looked at each other and guffawed.

Andy smiled uncertainly.

193

Plato scowled. "Whatso funny, you?"

"Two regulars," Andy repeated a third time. *"Please."*

He made his way back to the set, a Styrofoam cup in each hand.

She appeared out of nowhere. That chinless wonder who was always hanging around the set, giving Barron and everybody else a headache. She jostled his arm, and the coffee shot in a brown stream onto her white skirt.

"You idiot! You moron!" Myra Schick screamed. "Why don't you watch where you're going?"

"Oh, my word, I'm so sorry!" Andy effused, making a halfhearted stab at her skirt with a napkin. "It'll clean, sweetheart. Just put a capful of vinegar into the wash water, and if that doesn't help, maybe some lemon . . ."

Myra stared at him. She wanted to sock the old fag. But she had a better idea. He was Barron's toadie, wasn't he? He could help her. She pasted on a smile. "Don't worry about the skirt," she said. "Andrew ffrench, isn't it?"

Andy looked surprised. "Why, yes. You know my name!" He paused. "You're with *Time*, aren't you?"

"FOLK," Myra corrected him. "Andy, I've been meaning to do a story on you for weeks. When can we get together?"

He was speechless. She wanted to do a story on *him!* At last, someone who knew a good thing when she fell over it. He could use some good press. Maybe it would undo the San Diego damage. Reflexively, he put his hand to the wig-eroo. Nicely in place, although underneath it, his scalp

194

was soaking with sweat. "I'd love to talk to you, sweetie," Andy said. "Just name the place and I'm yours."

Myra grinned coyly. "Well . . . let's see. How about The Royal Palm? Around eight tonight?"

Andy nodded. He could hear Barron screaming at one of the cameramen. He smiled conspiratorially at Myra Schick. "Wouldja listen to him. He's got the rag on." He never heard a woman laugh so raucously in his life.

"That's a good one," she complimented him. "You're my kind of guy, Andy. Oh, by the way, when is that big party again?"

"Andy! Get your butt over here!" Barron bellowed.

To Myra, Andy said hurriedly, "The Meet-the-Stars party? Next month. Didn't you get your invitation?"

She shrugged. "It's in my other purse," she lied, her voice sweet and light. "At The Plaza, right?"

"Don't I wish!" Andy sighed. "No such luck. The Royal Palm . . ."

"Andy! Where the fuck are you, already?"

Myra knew where he was. He was right in the palm of her hand. If she couldn't get Barron, she'd get his Best Boy, or whatever they called him, to tell her everything she wanted to know. And more.

The morning had somehow slipped by. They had broken early for lunch. Shooting had been in full swing again for what had seemed like hours.

The "Ballin' Round the Hall" number was on its fifth take. The sun was beating down without mercy. Andy stood next to Barron, holding a large black umbrella over the Great One's head. Barron sure was in a lousy mood. *Everyone* was in a lousy mood.

They were grouped on the lawn of the public library—an imposing red-brick structure that was the closest thing to an antebellum mansion this one-horse town had to offer. (Besides the mayor's abode, that is. But Andy knew that Barron was saving that for interiors.)

No one would guess that the magnolia trees on the front lawn were plastic. Or that the flagstone path was foam rubber.

Andy watched, fascinated, as JayPee appeared at the front door and started to boogie across the lawn, shaking those nonexistent hips like a couple of maracas.

And then it happened. One minute JayPee was there, wriggling and grinding in the shade of the biggest magnolia tree on the set, and the next minute he wasn't. Where was he?

In the next second, they knew.

"Get this fuckin' tree offa me! I'll sue! I'll have your asses in a sling for this!"

Uh-oh, Andy thought. Maybe he *hadn't* secured the tree after all!

JayPee was small; the phony magnolia was big. It took a full five minutes to extricate the puny rock star from the broken plastic leaves and branches.

Barron was fit to be tied. "Andy," he seethed through clenched teeth, "you *said* you took *care* of the damned tree!"

Andy, trying to look innocent, whined, "But,

Barron, I swear, on my mother's grave, I took care of it! I did!"

"Will you shits stop yapping and help me up?" JayPee roared.

Andy was amazed that such a little person could have such a big voice.

The three permanent members of JayPee's entourage were on their knees beside him. Two of them were crying hysterically; the third looked angry enough to kill. Cindi, Candi, and Lula Mae. Not one of them over sixteen. They protected him with the intensity of bodyguards three times their bulk.

Andy moved in. Carefully, cautiously, he began to feel JayPee for broken bones. "What the fuck—" JayPee began. "Get your pansy hands offa me!" He swatted Andy away like a fly.

Was it Andy's imagination, or was there a hint of playfulness in JayPee's tone? "You sure you don't need a doctor?" Andy asked solicitously.

"Don't need no doctor," JayPee grumbled. "What I need is some snow."

"Snow?" Andy repeated. The middle of July and the kid wants snow?

JayPee looked up at him. He made a loud, sniffing sound. "Snow. Ya know—coke!"

Andy gestured futilely. He wished he could comply, but who could afford it these days? "Sorry," he said sadly.

"Forget it. Help me to my trailer, girls, willya?"

The girls obeyed. Andy had trouble telling them apart. They wore indentical outfits: skirts that cleared their cunts by a hair; white T-shirts that stretched tightly across their tits. One of them—

maybe it was Lula Mae?—stuck her tongue spontaneously into JayPee's ear. Andy felt himself go hard again.

"Hey, man, that's it for today," JayPee declared as he hobbled past Barron.

Barron looked at his watch. There were four full hours of good sunlight left, but what could he do? All he needed was a lawsuit from this wacky kid. A little pampering was in order. "Why not?" he said with a smile.

The crew breathed a sigh of relief. A long, tough, hot day in a series of long, tough, hot days was apparently over.

Andy looked longingly at JayPee's retreating back. It had been ages since he'd had sex with anyone but himself. Wouldn't it be wonderful if . . .

Then he had an inspiration. He ran after the rocker. "JayPee, I just wanted to say how much I love your latest album! I have a copy in my room. Would you be kind enough to autograph it for me?"

Wonder of wonders, JayPee turned and smiled. "You really like it? What's your favorite cut?"

Andy thought quickly. "The fast one, you know, the one where you go, 'Ooie-blewy-yah-yah . . .'"

"Oh. 'Do-do-do-me'? Yeah, I like that one, too. Whacha say your name is?"

"Andrew ffrench—with a small *f*."

The groupies snickered.

"Well, Andrew-ffrench-with-a-small-*f*, how's about joinin' me and my ladies for a drink later at The Royal whatsis?"

Andy felt faint. Was God answering his prayers at last? "Okay," he replied as nonchalantly as possible. "What time?"

"When I gets there," JayPee said, giving him a jaunty wave.

26

Peggy

PEGGY flipped through yet another old copy of *The New Yorker.* She'd been waiting to see Dr. Kravitz for nearly an hour, and she was light-headed. But at least she wasn't dizzy or sick to her stomach as she'd been so often lately.

Whatever was wrong, it was something bad, something serious enough to make her miss her period. Maybe early menopause? Maybe cancer? She shuddered.

Her grandmother had died at age forty-seven of what they used to call "women's troubles." Oh, God, she implored, please don't let it happen to me . . .

"You may go in now, Mrs. Corcoran," the nurse said at last.

"Thanks."

As much as she liked Dr. Emma Kravitz, she

could never get used to the indignity of the gynecological examination. "I hate this," she complained.

Dr. Kravitz's lightly accented voice replied, "I don't exactly love it myself, Peggy dear. Just relax. It'll only take a minute and then we'll talk."

Peggy closed her eyes. For the first time today, she thought of Duke. What was he doing now, right this minute? He no longer called every day, and when he came to pick up Morgie and Wayne, Jr., on Sundays, he didn't even bother to come inside.

She heard the snap of Dr. Kravitz's plastic gloves. "Sit up now, Peggy," the doctor said jovially. "I have some good news for you."

Peggy sighed in relief. "It's not cancer, then?"

Dr. Kravitz regarded her with a raised eyebrow. "*Cancer?* Wherever did you get that idea? A healthy woman like you? No, darling, it's not cancer. You get dressed now and I'll see you in my office."

Dr. Kravitz's office was all pink chintz and white wicker. Duke would have called it a real pussy joint. Peggy had to laugh. It *was* a real pussy joint!

Dr. Kravitz sat back in her chair and steepled her fingers. "You're preggers, my dear," she informed her. "Better than two months down the road. Congratulations."

Peggy's jaw dropped. There was a roaring in her ears. She shook her head. "I can't be," she protested weakly.

Dr. Kravitz's mouth turned up into a wry smile. "I should have those words engraved in gold," she said, laughing. "Tell me, dear, why can't you be?"

"B-b-because . . ." Peggy stammered, "my husband and I are separated . . ."

Dr. Kravitz leaned forward. "Oh, my dear, I didn't know. I'm sorry. How long?"

"Since the middle of May," Peggy told the doctor, her throat burning.

"And no fooling around since the middle of May?" Dr. Kravitz asked.

Peggy looked uncomfortable. She took a deep breath. "Two men," she said at last. "But one couldn't come and the other had a vasectomy."

Dr. Kravitz suppressed a giggle. "Well, *somebody* came," she said, watching Peggy's face carefully. She was grateful that *she* didn't have such problems any longer. Peggy Corcoran was a lovely girl. Personally, she thought she was better off without that loutish husband of hers. Still, the woman had a problem on her hands. She was Catholic, and abortion was probably out of the question for her.

Peggy looked crestfallen. "Back in May. Just once. With my husband."

Gently, the doctor said, "Once is all it takes."

"What am I going to do?" Peggy asked softly, almost to herself.

She couldn't believe it. Duke's baby! The irony of ironies. She thought of Dan and how much she was beginning to like him. What would *he* say about all this? More important, what would *Duke* say? Somehow, she was going to have to find the courage to tell him.

She left Dr. Kravitz's office in a daze, too preoccupied to notice Bliss Billington waiting on the chintz love seat in the reception area.

27

Barron and Selma

IT was a mistake to have gone back. He'd been fighting the impulse to visit the old neighborhood ever since he'd arrived on the East Coast. It was another lifetime, really. Yet his past remained vivid in his mind. Stickball on Bathgate Avenue. Going to movies at the Loew's Paradise on the Concourse. Sodas and caramel nougats at Krum's.

A good thing the bar was dim. He hated to cry in public, but whenever he thought of the past, he couldn't help himself. His eyes welled.

He shifted on the bar stool. God, these stiff overalls were a pain. But he had to admit: the Sven Jorgensen disguise was a brainstorm—even if it was Jared Galitz's brainstorm. With the peaked cap and the false mustache, not one person had pestered him for an autograph all evening.

"Here you are, sir . . . a double scotch, neat,"

the bartender said, backing away and watching him carefully.

Barron knew the guy was confused. Well, let him be confused. He didn't have much longer in this town, and it was a pleasure to be able to walk down the street without being mobbed. What freedom! Sure, once or twice, someone had murmured, "Hi, Sven." And he'd nodded and put a finger to the brim of the cap and walked on. He took a long draught of his drink. His throat burned.

His mind drifted back to yesterday. Cleverly, he'd rented an old Chevy and followed the Major Deegan to Fordham Road. There was relatively little traffic except for the zoo, where there was the usual Sunday mob. Some things never change.

Too bad he couldn't say that for *his* street. He'd circled the old block three times before he realized his building was no longer there. There was nothing but an empty lot surrounded by more empty lots. His whole past, vanished. He downed the rest of the scotch and signaled the bartender. "Another." Shit. He'd forgotten to use the Swedish accent!

The bartender was eyeing him openly now. "Excuse me, sir," he said, "but—are you related to Sven Jorgensen? You look just like him."

Barron nodded. "Ja," he said, pursing his lips. "He's mine brudder." He'd have to watch it. This guy was a sharp cookie.

The bartender shook his head. "You're kidding! I didn't even know Sven had a brother. Well, welcome to West Falls, Mr. Jorgensen."

Barron nodded. He had a crazy impulse to rip off the mustache and confide in the guy, to say to him:

"Hey, listen, guy, I'm not Sven's brother. I'm not even Barron Heatter. I'm Benjamin Ira Horowitz from Bathgate Avenue in the Bronx and I'm proud of it!"

But that would be professional suicide. No one even knew he was Jewish. When he arrived in Hollywood in 1953, things weren't like they are today. There were no Barbra Streisands or Bette Midlers or F. Murray Abrahams. There were Tabs and Rips and Rocks. Bernie became Tony. Issur became Kirk. Betty was Lauren, and Benjamin Ira became Barron.

Barron's gaze wandered to the far end of the bar. At this hour, it was practically empty, except for a woman who was sitting hunched over a glass. Out of habit, he appraised her. The legs weren't bad. Neither was the ass, what he could see of it. Something about her was familiar . . .

He forced his eyes away and took another swallow of his drink. He couldn't understand how the *goyim* ever got used to the taste of liquor. Drinking had been one of the hardest things for him to learn when he'd become Barron Heatter.

In his father's house, there'd never been more than one bottle of whiskey at a time. And that was reserved for Friday nights and holidays. His father would come home early on *Shabbes*, wash his hands, and put on his yarmulke, and then they would all gather round the table while his mother lighted the candles. Morris Horowitz would then tip the shot glass and down the stuff in one gulp. Then it would come—the sound that could be heard all across the borough as the sun set on Friday night.

AHHHHH!

The butchers, the bakers, the deli men, the tailors, the milkmen, the grocers, the candy store owners—all of them swallowing the ritual schnapps and going *AHHHHH!*

What would Morris Horowitz say if he could see him now, sitting in a bar on a *Monday* night, drinking scotch like it was water? He knew what his father would say. His father would say *"Feh!"* Another *"Feh!"* in a long series of them as far back as Barron could remember.

Morris Horowitz had suffered a permanent lack of empathy where his son was concerned. "An actor, Benny?" he would scream. "What kind of a job is that for a nice Jewish boy?" His face darkening with frustration and disappointment, he would go on to proclaim, "A doctor, yes! A pharmacist, maybe! Even a dentist . . . But an actor? *Feh!*"

"But, Pa," Benny would try to mollify, "Edward G. Robinson is Jewish. So is John Garfield. So is Paul Muni!"

His father gave him a *klop* on the side of the head. "Don't you compare yourself to Edward G. or Muni. You good for nothing *trombenik*, you bum, you lazy!"

Barron sighed. The drinks were getting to him. He pushed the glass away. He had enough headaches already. First, that brat JayPee was beginning to be a real prima donna. He thought about the tree incident and shuddered. And Barrbra Shapiro wasn't letting him live. Always grabbing for his dick. At least the Little Women were turning in good performances—with the possible exception of Olivia, who was on an ego trip, demanding that Spyros shoot her only from the left side.

Someone lurched into him, hard enough so that his glass tipped over.

"Oh, excuse me," the woman began. And stopped. She looked up at him in surprise. "Sven?" She squinted nearsightedly.

Where did he know her from? In a flash, it came to him. She was Mrs.—what's his name?—the mayor's wife. Olivia's mother. He'd met her briefly, once, when Galitz dragged him to see the house. He reached out to steady her. "Are you all right?" he asked.

"No," she said, shaking her head. "I'm not all right, Sven. I think I'm *shikker* . . . Point me in the direction of the ladies' room, will you?"

He did. And watched helplessly as she stumbled inside.

Selma hugged the bowl and heaved. At least this time, she was doing it in private and not all over the seat of an expensive car. No one knew she was even here, except for Sven.

She flushed the toilet twice and looked in the mirror. Her face was a mess. Her eyes looked like twin road maps, crisscrossed with red. Her skin had a deathly pallor. She fished a lipstick out of her purse and shakily redid her mouth. How was she going to drive home? Did she even want to go home? She thought again of why she'd come here. To forget. But how could she forget? What woman could forget that her husband had sent a form love letter in answer to a personals ad? She closed her

207

eyes and tried to keep the tears from coming. She had to get out of here.

Outside, the fresh air revived her a little. It was dusk and she could hear the birds chirping madly in the trees. She wondered what it would feel like to be as free as a bird, to flap her wings and fly away, wherever she wanted to go. Involuntarily, her arms lifted in simulated flight and she nearly lost her balance. She felt a strong arm at her elbow.

"Here," he said, "I'll take you home."

Where had she heard that voice before? She turned and saw him. Tall and mustached. She squinted in the darkness. "Sven?" she asked.

"No, I'm not Sven," he answered softly as he guided her to her car. She didn't protest. There was something about him that was reassuring and nonthreatening. He took her keys and helped her into the passenger seat. Then he got behind the wheel.

"Do I know you?" she asked after a while.

He nodded and, stopping at a light, turned to her.

"If you're not Sven, who *are* you?"

Slowly, with one hand, he began to tug at the mustache. Selma's heart lurched. He smiled. She knew that smile. She'd seen it hundreds of times in her dreams and fantasies. She felt her skin prickle as he maneuvered the car to the side of the road and turned off the engine.

Sweetly, he said, "I think you know who I am, Selma."

Oh, my God! she thought. It was *him*. The Gorgeous Goy. In the flesh. "I think I know who you are, too," she replied.

28

Abe

ABE tootled the Continental around the block a third time. Wouldn't you know? Tonight, of all nights, Selma's Volvo has to be in the parking lot! What was Selma doing in The Royal Palm at this hour on a Monday, anyway? Why wasn't she home, making *tsimmes* for her husband and Olivia? He remembered that just the other day Jerry remarked that Selma wasn't acting right. Well, he could sympathize. He remembered that when Bea was Selma's age, she started acting crazy, too. She had all kinds of *meshugayas*. Cha-cha lessons. Tarot cards. Vegetarian cooking.

"*Vegetarian?*" he'd raged. "Your husband's a meat man, and all of a sudden you go vegetarian? What happens if the customers find out?"

Bea didn't give an inch. "Meat is *poison!* It gets into your blood and clogs the arteries!"

Abe was stunned. "Since *when* is meat poison? It feeds you? It puts mink on your back! A million-dollar roof over your head!"

But he needn't have worried. Soon enough, Bea tired of sprouts and radishes and began with singing lessons. Which nearly drove him crazy altogether, but at least it wasn't veggies.

Women. Go figure.

Half an hour later, Selma's car was finally gone. Thank God. He eased the Continental into a parking space and looked at his watch. Seven forty-five. Fifteen minutes late. Lamb Chop had told the answering service she'd meet him at The Royal Palm at seven thirty. Abe wished he'd been home when the call came, but that night Bea had insisted on going to a new seafood restaurant in the city. Then they'd had a flat on the way back. It was after one when they'd finally arrived home.

He locked the car and inhaled deeply. He put his hand to his mouth and tested his breath. It seemed all right, but who could be sure? He took the breath spray from his pocket and fired a few shots into his mouth. A person can never be too careful . . .

Abe walked slowly to the entrance of The Palm. He couldn't remember the last time he'd been so nervous. Take it easy, Abie, he told himself. She's only a woman . . .

Yeah, but what a woman!

It took a while for his eyes to adjust to the dimness. Why the hell don't they ever light these places so a man can see where he's going?

He glanced at his reflection in the mirror behind the bar. Not bad for an *alter kocker,* he thought charitably. That afternoon, he'd managed to slip away from the ball and chain and gone to the only barbershop in town for a trim. "Make it sexy," he'd instructed the little guinea with the scissors.

The barber nodded. "Sexy you want, sexy you'll get."

Well, he wasn't exactly Cesar Romero, but close enough. At least it was neat. He'd even had himself a manicure. Which might have been a mistake. When Bea took a look, she shrieked, "What's that on your nails?"

"Nothing."

Bea shook her head. "Abe," she asked suspiciously, "are you wearing nail polish?"

He ignored her, and after a while, she gave up. Earlier this evening, when he'd dropped her off at her mah-jongg game, she'd mumbled something about his seeing a psychiatrist. "It doesn't mean you're crazy," she told him. "It would be for your own good, Abe . . ."

"Maybe," he'd answered. "I'll think about it."

Fat chance. He didn't need a psychiatrist. He needed love. He needed passion. He needed his Lamb Chop with the purple hair. He needed his Barrbra Shapiro!

But where was she? He glanced around the bar. Just a few people on the stools, all of them men. One was that fag from the movie, Andy—or whatever his name was.

Abe sat down and ordered a drink. He looked at the Budweiser clock on the wall. The big hand was edging toward the twelve. *Where was she?*

At last the door opened. A woman. Abe's heart thumped dangerously. He looked. He looked

211

again. *Oy vay.* It wasn't Lamb Chop. It was that Sawyer dame, also from the movie. What was this, a convention?

The Sawyer girl sat down and looked around. She appraised him briefly, then looked quickly away.

Everyone in this world must be waiting for someone, Abe thought philosophically. Waiting. Hoping. But how much hope could there be for Sawyer? He never saw such earlobes, except maybe on a cocker spaniel. A real doggie!

He finished his drink and ordered another. Eight fifteen. *Where was she?*

Then it hit him. Suppose she wasn't coming? Suppose, at the last minute, she'd gotten cold feet? Suppose she was sick?

No, today on the set she was healthy as a horse, God bless her. Wiggling and waggling that cute little rump of hers in front of his nose. Twice, she had smiled at him. He'd mouthed the word "Tonight!" and she'd nodded and given him a wink. Right in front of Bea, yet!

"Another drink, sir?" the bartender asked.

"Yes," Abe said.

After two more yesses, Abe realized there was no point in waiting. His head felt as if it weighed a ton. There was a burning in his stomach and a pain in his chest. His heart was breaking. Literally. He stood up and felt the floor move under him.

The bartender asked, "Are you all right, sir?"

Abe pasted a phony smile on his face and slapped a twenty on the bar. "I'm fine and dandy," he replied evenly.

He moved one foot woodenly in front of the

212

other until he was outside. How could he have been stupid enough to believe, even for an instant, that a beautiful young chicken like Barrbra Shapiro could feel anything for an old rooster like him?

29

Andy and Phyllis

ANDY stared into the shot glass. Amazing how the stuff kept disappearing. "Another!" he yelled to the barkeep.

He'd been waiting for JayPee for more than an hour. The pyramid of shot glasses on the bar before him was testament to this. He still couldn't believe it! Andrew ffrench, man of taste and distinction, stood up by a little runt rocker.

He realized now, of course, that JayPee never had any intention of meeting him here tonight. He'd been laughing at him—mocking him—all the time, along with those twittering groupies.

There was something to be learned from this. The question was, *What?* Here he was, his career hanging by a thread. This flick was his one last hope to get him back on track where he belonged. But he was beginning to have his doubts. Barron was botching the whole thing. First, Mickey David fails to deliver. Then along comes Barrbra Shapiro, that purple-haired cokehead, with her moods and her tantrums. And then, Johann Paul Jones, with *his* shtick.

Andy sighed and put his hand to the old peruke. If it were the real thing, it would probably be gray by now.

He signaled to the barkeep for another drink. The thought of returning to the Motel Pierre, that dilapidated sweatbox, was less than thrilling. Besides, he didn't feel like walking past Phyllis Sawyer, which he would have to do if he left now.

The barkeep said to him, "Take it easy, guy. That makes eleven."

Andy scowled. "Who are you? My mother? I can count!"

This wasn't his night. First, Mr. Zayde, that loudmouthed, orange-eating schmuck-of-a-mayor's father-in-law, had entered the bar, and for a while, it seemed like he was never going to leave.

And then Phyllis, looking like a walking florist shop in a hideous white dress splashed with giant red roses. A flower in her hair. Two enormous earrings shaped like tulips over those gross earlobes. Someone should water the pathetic creature . . .

He downed the last of his drink. Well, Andy old pal, the time has come to gather up your courage and vamoose. Then he heard it. An incredible wail from the front of the bar, like a moose in heat. He looked up.

It wasn't a moose. It was Phyllis. Her head was down on the bar and she was crying. Not just your

ordinary crying, either. She was *sobbing.* Openly.
Unashamedly. Uncontrollably . . .

She was mortified, but she couldn't stop. She
should have known better. One drink and she was
high. Four drinks, forget it!

It was finally dawning on her that she'd been
stood up. Again. You would think she'd be used to
it by now, that it wouldn't affect her this way. But
the guy's letter had seemed so sincere. She'd
called at midnight on the dot, just as he specified.
But he wasn't home. It occurred to her that the
answering service hadn't relayed her message. So
she'd called the answering service to make sure.
They had.

What had she ever done to deserve this? Was it
her fault she was no raving beauty? But uglier
women than she had managed to find husbands.
Have families. Attain some measure of happiness.
She wasn't stupid. She had a career. All right, so
she wasn't Lina Wertmuller. But for that matter,
who was?

She thought again of Nate Greene, although she
had promised herself not to think of him anymore.
She had loved him. He had been good to her, getting her that job with Pinky Lee. Paying for her
mother's dental work. Even getting her this job
with Barron. But she had eventually come to realize that Nate would never leave his wife, and if she
wanted a chance at real happiness, she'd have to
make her way without him.

Which was why she was here tonight. Except
that somehow she'd managed to lose her way

again. She didn't think she could take it any longer.

Blindly, she groped for her bag and tried to stand. Instead, her knees buckled under her.

Someone caught her just in time.

Someone said to the bartender, "Two coffees, black. And hurry."

Sniffling, she looked around. Andy ffrench! She started to say, "I don't need your—"

"Shut up and come with me." He pulled her to a small table in the corner and shoved her into a chair. When the bartender brought the coffees, Andy ordered her, "Drink up. You'll feel better."

She did as she was told. After the first few sips, she *did* feel better. A little. He was watching her. That absurd toupee of his was lopsided, but she didn't tell him. She didn't know why, but for some reason, she felt strangely comfortable with him tonight. Maybe she was drunker than she thought.

After a moment, he asked, "Well? You want to talk about it?"

She shrugged. He didn't look that happy himself.

"I will if you will," she said hesitantly.

30

Myra

THE nerve of that ffrench fag. How could he not have waited?

She'd arrived promptly at ten. Only two hours late. On purpose, of course. She knew from experience that the longer you made them wait, the happier they were to talk. The longer they'd been drinking, the looser the tongue . . .

She sensed the fag was ripe for the picking. In fact, she'd never seen anyone riper.

But where the hell was he?

She decided to ask the bartender. "Hey . . . *you.* I was supposed to meet someone here . . . Andrew ffrench. Do you know him? He's with the movie . . ."

The bartender's passive face brightened with recognition. "Oh, you mean the pansy with the rug?"

"That's him. Was he in here tonight?"

"Only for a couple of hours. Just left, as a matter of fact."

Sonofabitch! It wasn't often she read people wrong. Well, she'd fix him. She'd fix them all.

She, Myra Schick, had been pushed to the limit. First, by Barron, then by those spoiled-brat Little Women and their snooty mothers. And now the faggot gofer!

Seething, Myra turned on her sharp spiked heels and stalked out of the bar, the lust for revenge surging through her blood, flooding her with a sense of mission.

There'd be no stopping her now!

31

Jared

THE sweat poured from his brow. He dropped the envelope onto his desk like it was a hot potato. It *was* a hot potato! It was a subpoena ordering him to appear in court two weeks from today, and there was no way he could wriggle out of it. Not even Harry Houdini could escape from such a trap.

"Why *me?*" he said aloud, wishing for the hundredth time he'd never heard of Dove Hills Estates.

Why he had ever let Darren McDougal talk him into buying that rotten property was beyond him. Except, at the time, it seemed like a sure thing. "Jared, would I steer you wrong?" McDougal had gushed. "We'll go modular on quarter-acre lots. We'll triple our money in a year! It'll be the best investment you ever made!"

Yeah. Sure. In a year, McDougal was dead. A heart attack on the seventeenth hole at his country club in Boca Raton. Leaving Jerry holding the bag.

Not that the houses didn't sell. They sold like hotcakes. But who knew they were built on toxic waste? McDougal knew. Of that, Jared was sure. If McDougal weren't dead already, Jared would kill him.

He smoothed his hands through his golden curls. When word of this came out—and it would, because already he'd gotten calls from constituents asking if there was any truth to the rumors that people were dying in Dove Hills—he would be ruined. Good-bye mayor. Good-bye career. Good-bye White House.

His secretary, Estelle, came in and put a cup of coffee in front of him. He looked at her fondly. What would he do without Estelle? How long since they'd fooled around? He couldn't remember. Now they were just good friends. And she was loyal, which was more than he could say for Selma.

Estelle looked at him with concern. "Was the letter bad news?" she asked. When he didn't answer, she pressed. "You all right, Mayor?"

He had a wild impulse to tell her everything. Then he remembered that she had an aunt living in Dove Hills Estates. The same aunt who was now in the hospital with emphysema.

"Nothing I can't handle," he replied. "You can get started on those letters, Estelle. I'll buzz when I need you."

Obediently, she left. There was a lump in his throat the size of a cantaloupe. He hadn't cried in years, but he wanted to now. Not only was Dove

221

Hills Estates going down the tubes (and probably his career with it), but things weren't so swell in the love department, either.

Take Barbara Johnson, for instance. For months now, he'd been trying to wriggle out of her grasp. Enough was enough, after all. Why did he have to go and tell her he wanted to marry her? *Dummkopf!* If he knew then what he knew now—that her pussy was everybody's property—he'd have kept his big mouth shut. But Barbara was clinging to him like poison ivy, and she wouldn't let go.

As if that wasn't bad enough, there was Selma. More precisely, there *wasn't* Selma. She was never home anymore. She was out at the crack of dawn. Where did she go? God only knew. Those shiksa girlfriends of hers had corrupted her, he suspected. Isn't that when the trouble had started? Whatever, he and Selma hadn't *shtupped* in more than a month.

He got up and walked to the window. No way he could jump. His office was on the ground floor. What damage could he do? Stub a toe?

Outside, West Falls baked in the early August sun. Traffic snaked slowly up Main Street. Everything looked so normal . . .

He wished he knew how to put things right with Selma. Maybe he should apologize. Maybe he should tell Estelle to buy her a little present from him. He hated to admit it, even to himself, but he loved Selma. She might not be the best wife in the world, but she was *his* wife, the mother of *his* Olivia . . .

The phone rang. Estelle's voice came over the intercom. "It's for you, boss. *Her* again."

He picked up the phone. "What is it *this* time?"

"Snugglebuns, I have some wonderful news."

How many times had he warned Barbara Johnson *never* to call him at the office? All he needed now to make his life complete was trouble with the *tsatske*, his little plaything!

"Barbara, sweetheart," he said, "I'm in a meeting and can't talk . . ."

"You don't have to talk, Loverbunny," she oozed. "Just listen. This is important."

What did this bimbo have on her mind that was so important? he wondered. She was probably going to ask him what she should wear to the Meet-the-Stars party next week! "So what's so important?" he asked impatiently.

"I'll give you three guesses, Puckeypoo."

He wanted to strangle her. Three guesses? What did she think this was? A goddamn quiz show? "You bought a new pair of shoes?"

"No-o-o . . . Guess again," she chirped.

He rolled his eyes to the ceiling. "You won the lottery?"

"Better than that, Jerrykins. One more guess."

"I give up," he said at last.

"Jerry . . ." She giggled. "You're going to be a daddy!"

32

Max and Bliss

THE food was probably delicious. Max wouldn't know—he could hardly taste it. There she was, across the table from him—flesh and blood this time. How often had he fantasized this scene?

She was truly beautiful by candlelight. Her eyes were luminous, her hair was soft and loose against her lovely ivory shoulders. He raised his glass, toasting, "To a wonderful evening."

She raised her glass hesitantly and returned the smile. "I'm still not so sure this is a good idea. When I answered your ad, I didn't know it was yours. I usually don't date men from town."

What was wrong with dating men from town? Max wondered. He sensed that she was a very private and complicated person. Maybe that had something to do with it. He hoped he could put her mind at ease.

"How lucky for me that you *did* answer it," he said, looking into her eyes. Then, before he could stop himself, he added, "You're a very beautiful woman." He felt suddenly foolish. He didn't want her to think he was some bumbling schoolboy barely able to contain himself. But it was true. His arms ached with desire to hold her. He didn't believe in love at first sight. But what else could this be?

He watched her slender fingers lift the fork to her mouth. Pure poetry in motion.

She saw him staring and she blushed. "Excuse me," she said, "did you say something?"

"I'm glad our daughters are friends," he replied, thinking quickly. She looked relieved. Evidently it was all right to talk about the girls. Score one for Max. He went on. "Ruthie tells me that Sunny may be going to West Falls High next year."

She leaned forward. "I've been thinking about it, but I'm not so sure it's a good idea."

Max prompted, "Tell me more about Sunny."

The evening flew by. It was ten o'clock when they left the restaurant—too late for a movie, too early to go home. The oppressively hot day had evolved into a gentle, balmy evening. The sky was filled with stars.

"Would you like to take a walk?" he asked.

She would. And so, slowly, leisurely, they made their way from the restaurant on Dewey Boulevard, across Taft Drive, up to the duck pond in Citizens Park.

"You know something, Max?" Bliss began. "In all

225

the years I've lived in West Falls, I've never really walked around town."

He chuckled. "Nobody walks anymore. Someday all suburbanites' legs will atrophy from lack of use."

She laughed. It was a wonderful laugh, light and musical, like the trill of a rare and beautiful bird.

His hand found hers. They walked easily together, their rhythms in tune. He felt as if he'd known her all his life.

The park had never looked so beautiful. The stately street lamps cast shimmering reflections on the still water of the pond. Couples ambled past them, hand in hand. He felt as if he'd entered Paradise.

Without speaking, they seated themselves on a bench. Reflexively, his arm encircled her shoulders. She snuggled wordlessly against him. He closed his eyes. It had been such a long time since he had been with a woman like this . . . Her hair smelled like lilacs. If this were a dream, he wanted never to awaken.

And then his lips were on hers and the fire consumed him. His hand slid across her silky skin and rested on her breast.

At his touch, she shivered.

Should he suggest they go somewhere? Wasn't it too soon? It was.

But before he could say anything, he felt it. Under his fingers. Her left breast. A thickening that had no business being there.

"Bliss," he asked, "what's this?"

"It's nothing," she replied hoarsely. Suddenly she was still.

He could sense her fear. "How long have you known about it?" he pressed gently.

She sat apart from him. "I've already been to the doctor," she replied quietly.

"And?"

She took a moment to answer.

To her surprise, Bliss found herself telling him. Not all of it, of course. Not about Steve Gordon and how the lump got there in the first place. Just about the lump itself and her visit to Dr. Kravitz.

"But it's been *two weeks* and you *still* haven't called the surgeon?" he asked incredulously.

She shrugged. "It's late. I think we should go."

"Bliss!" he returned sharply. "I'm a doctor. Don't pull this on me. Now that I've finally found you, I don't want to lose you!"

She looked at him with frightened eyes. He had scared her.

In a small, little-girl voice, she said, "I don't want to die."

He pulled her toward him. "You're not going to die. Chances are the lump is benign. But the sooner you see the surgeon, the better off you and I are going to be."

33

Barron and Selma

OOH, it was delicious! That's so *good*—keep doing whatever you're doing! Don't stop! *Don't stop* . . .

Miracle of miracles, it *didn't* stop! Selma opened her eyes. It *wasn't* Jared Galitz, Esq., Hizzoner the Mayor, on top of her. It was *him! Barron Heatter! Hunk of hunks! The Gorgeous Goy!*

He was kissing her eyes. Kissing her cheeks. Kissing her lips. Her body was on fire. They were moving together now, smooth, synchronized, in perfect harmony, like the workings of a fine Swiss clock. Faster. Faster! Yes. Yes! Somebody screamed . . .

"Barron, Barron darling," she moaned, her arms tightening around him, her legs grasping his hips. He was inside her, he was part of her. She would *never* let him go.

"I love you," he said, kissing her again. "I love you, I love you, I love you."

After, they lay quietly in each other's arms. She could feel his heart beating furiously. She had done that to him! She, Selma Moscovitz Galitz, the butcher's daughter from the Bronx, the broad with the big nose and the frizzy red hair. Who would believe that a big-time movie star was in love with her? She closed her eyes and told herself not to question. Accept, she told herself. Accept and be grateful.

She replayed the scenario in her mind for the thousandth time. How he'd appeared out of nowhere that night in the parking lot of The Royal Palm. How he'd waited for her and taken her home. How, when she was feeling *so* low—so low she could barely move—*he* had been there, to lift her spirits and to give her new hope.

She reached up and drew her hand gently across his face. He was *so* gorgeous. But he did look tired, drained. He had so much on his mind, poor darling. Everyone thought that being a big movie star was all fun and games. But she had learned that nothing could be further from the truth. *Nobody* worked harder than her Barron. He worked from early morning until late at night, directing, revising, mollifying the prima donnas, editing the dailies, worrying about the budget. Maybe all this sex was putting an added burden on him. She felt a stab of guilt.

"Maybe we shouldn't meet every morning like this," she began. "Maybe it's too much for you."

He looked alarmed. "I couldn't get through the day if it weren't for you," Barron said.

She leaned up on one elbow and admired him. His torso was flawless, his muscles rippling invitingly beneath his skin. She bent down and slid her tongue softly across his nipple. He moaned in ecstasy.

"Oh, God, Selma. I want you *again!* Tell me that you want me, too!"

She'd never wanted anyone this much in her whole life. "You know I do, but—I wish things were simpler."

"Selma, everything is simple if you let it be," he replied matter-of-factly.

"No, it's not." She fingered her wedding band.

"Selma, do you want to spend the rest of your life being Mrs. Jared Galitz?"

She clamped her hand over his mouth. "Shh," she said. "I don't want to talk about him."

Barron sat up. "How can we *not* talk about him? He's always here between us like some . . . I don't know, some fungus!"

Selma had heard Jerry called lots of things but never a fungus! A fungus was something that grew on something else; something that served no useful purpose of its own. Selma smiled. A *fungus* was appropriate . . .

"Barron, honey, Jerry and I have been married for fourteen years. I can't just throw him away like an old sponge!"

He pinned her with his gorgeous blue eyes. "Why not? Everyone I know gets out of a marriage when it no longer works. Selma, love, people do it every day!"

She looked away. "Maybe where you come

from, they do," she said softly. "Look, Barron, I'm just a nice Jewish girl from the Bronx . . ."

He was staring at her. "You're from the Bronx? I didn't realize that!" he replied excitedly. "Whereabouts?"

She looked at him. "You know the Bronx?"

He smiled.

How could he know the Bronx? She'd always assumed he was from Iowa or someplace like that.

Uncertainly, she answered, "Bathgate Avenue?"

His eyes widened. "You're kidding! What was your address?"

What was going on here? Selma wondered. "Seventeen-twenty. Why?"

He shrieked. "Oh, my God! I'm from seventeen-twenty-four! We're *landsleit!*"

Her jaw dropped open. *Landsleit?* Bathgate Avenue? Was she hearing things? Was he putting her on? "What are you telling me?" she asked at last.

Taking a deep breath, Barron began to tell his story. The more he talked, the better he felt. It was as though a great weight had been lifted from his heart.

He hadn't meant to tell her. But now that he had, he was relieved. He wanted her to know everything about him. If they were going to spend the rest of their lives together, there had to be no secrets between them.

"Benny Horowitz?" she kept repeating, stunned. "Your father owned the grocery store on Washington Avenue by the El?"

Barron nodded. "And you were that funny-looking baby—always trying to climb out of your stroller!"

They stared at each other in astonishment. "Benny Horowitz," Selma repeated numbly. "Selma Moscovitz . . ."

"It's a small world," they said together.

34

Duke

THE miracle was, he didn't even miss it. Five months ago—even two, if you wanted the truth—if anyone had told him he could go without nooky for more than a couple of days, he'd have called them a liar.

But it was true. He simply wasn't interested, not even when opportunity knocked. And it knocked a lot. Yesterday, for instance, when that Johnson babe drove her cream Mercedes into the stall and asked for a lube job.

He had to admit it. Barbara J. was one of the juiciest cunts in West Falls. Especially in that white T-shirt, so thin you could see her nipples from three blocks away. "Dukie, sweetie," she'd cooed, sliding her tongue slowly over her full lips, "I've missed you. Where've you been?"

"Takin' care of business," he'd bantered lightly.

After all, he couldn't cut her off completely. She was a good customer.

She was also one ballsy dame. Right there, in broad daylight, she climbed out of her car and pushed her tits into his chest. Before he knew what was happening, she had him unzipped and in her hand.

The cable bell sounded. Outside, a Buick was waiting at the pump.

"Barbara," he said, "I gotta go . . ."

He had to push her away. It wasn't easy.

"What *is* it with you men?" she hissed, her eyes wild with fury.

What could he tell her? That he was still in love with his wife? It was corny . . . But why not? "I'm a married man, Barbara," he called over his shoulder.

"That never bothered you before!" she screamed after him. The next thing he knew, she was back in her car. "See if I care! I'll get my lube jobs somewhere else!"

You bet she would. He was through with the Barbara Johnsons of this world.

He opened his eyes. The sense of peace here was incredible. It had been too long since he'd been inside a church. St. Michael's was just as he remembered—sunlight filtering through the stained glass, bathing the smooth wooden pews in its comforting glow. It even smelled the same: incense and candle wax.

He sighed and crossed himself. Then he prayed: "Dear Lord, I know I have no right to ask favors of you. I haven't been much of a husband, and I'm no

234

great shakes in the father department either . . ."
He paused.

What could he say next? he puzzled. It occurred to him that God probably already knew what he wanted to say, what was in his heart. So why pray in the first place? *Because, jerko, that's the way it is!*

"So listen, Lord," he began again. "All I want is one more chance. I can't make it without her. Send her back to me, and, I swear, I'll do better this time around. I'll be the best damn husband you ever saw. No more pissing in other people's bushes, either. No more getting mad at the customers, even though they *are* jerk-offs . . ."

He stopped abruptly. Why had he called them *jerk-offs?* They were, after all, God's creatures. He shook his head and apologized. "I'm sorry, Lord. Forgive me." He said a hasty "Amen," crossed himself, and walked toward the confessional. Should he? Ah, why not? Might as well do it *right.*

Inside, the same stale smell of other penitents' sweat assailed his nostrils. The same claustrophobic feeling overtook him. God, he thought, maybe this *was* a mistake . . .

He heard movement on the other side of the partition. Shit! Too late to back out now . . .

35

Princess and Cisco

SHE reread the letter she had written to Ross. It was probably the most difficult letter she'd ever had to write. But she had no choice. She couldn't go on pretending to be waiting for Ross Updike when she was wildly in love with Francisco Williams.

How had she gotten herself into this? She knew how. She had let her emotions get the better of her. She had lost her objectivity.

Not that it was such a bad thing to lose. Cisco was the most magnificent man she'd ever known. Ever. In her whole life. There was no one like him at Harvard. Hell, there was no one like him anywhere!

She folded the letter and sealed the envelope. What would Ross think when he read it? A *gardener?* he would think. An uneducated Islander who'd never seen the inside of a library? A primitive no higher on the evolutionary ladder than the tribesmen he was studying in Nairobi?

Ross would probably think she was having a breakdown. Well, let him think it. She loved Cisco, and he loved her. At least, he loved Princess-the-maid, she thought uncomfortably. Would he love Princess-the-doctoral-candidate?

She forced her mind away from such thoughts. Upstairs, she could hear the racket of the camera crew moving their equipment inside. It was seven o'clock in the morning, and already she had the beginnings of a major headache. It was going to be a long day.

It was only seven in the evening, but that didn't matter. Anytime was a good time to make it with Princess.

Cisco watched her from his bed. She was putting on a show just for him. A damn good show it was, too. He was enjoying the biggest hard-on of his life.

She looked adorable in that dumb outfit. Little white cap on the close-cropped black hair. Frilly lace apron barely covering the thick bush. The luscious tits swinging free, jiggling like ripe melons.

"Would yo' care for a little somethin', honeychild?" she cooed, dancing around him, holding aloft an imaginary tray.

"You bet I would," Cisco said slyly.

"Ah got me some caviarrr, an' some paa-tayyy, an' some—"

He couldn't stand it any longer. He reached out and grabbed her and she came toppling over him, squealing with glee. God, she felt so damn good! Satin skin. Sweet as a rose. He'd never loved a woman like he loved her. He kissed her. "I hope you remember to wear somethin' *under* that apron for the party," he teased, nibbling at her ear.

"Maybe Ah will, and maybe Ah won't," she teased back, straddling him.

He entered her easily. He wished, as he always did, that they could remain like this forever. He once heard about a guy who got it in and then couldn't get it out and had to go to the emergency room in order to cut loose. Shee-it. If that ever happened to Princess and him, he wouldn't go to no emergency room. They'd go through life together like that forever. It might get a little complicated, though, Cisco allowed, especially when one of them had to use the bathroom. He had to laugh.

"Hey," she chided, squeezing him with her pussy muscle. "What's so funny?"

"Nothin'," he replied, closing his eyes. She was wetter than he ever remembered. God, she did him so good . . .

"Nothin', huh? Ya know what they call people who laugh for no reason?"

What did he care? He pulled her down against his chest. He was trembling. "I love you, Princess," he said, astounding himself. He'd never said that before to any woman.

But the truth was, he *did* love her. He loved her enough to want to marry her. He loved her enough to take her back to the Islands, where she'd never have to wear a degrading maid's outfit for any honkie party and where she could forget about writing that cheap novel of hers. Most of all, where she'd never have to work for a Jared Galitz again.

36

Otto and Roger

IT was hot, even for August. Even for seven in the morning.

Roger Ridgeway jogged down Eisenhower Boulevard, past West Falls High. For once, there were no cars in the parking lot, no throngs of frenetic women waiting to catch sight of that big-shot movie star.

Roger knew where the crowds were. They were in front of his neighbor Galitz's house, jamming the street, blocking the driveways, littering his lawn, and trampling his pachysandra. They had been there for three long days—and he couldn't take it much longer. In fact, he'd called Chief Daniels this morning, before he left, to complain. But the chief wouldn't be in until nine o'clock, they told him.

Ahead loomed the railroad tracks. The barrier

was down. Roger ran in place, waiting for the train to come. Behind him, he could hear footsteps. He turned and saw a tall bald fellow in tight white bikini trunks. Roger stared. The guy was naked from the waist up. Wasn't there a law against letting men run around like that in West Falls? He thought there was. In fact, he *knew* there was! Statute 34467A. He could make a citizen's arrest if he wanted to. The guy's privates were practically falling out . . .

Ten-to-one, the bikini was involved with that movie. Roger had been against it from day one, but naturally, nobody had listened. They all fell for that line of the mayor's: "If it's good for West Falls, it's good for you, because West Falls is good for you!" What malarkey! They didn't realize it, but he, Roger Ridgeway, knew what was happening in West Falls. Morals were crumbling. It was the Roman Empire all over again! And the mayor was responsible, of course. Well, that's what happens when a Galitz gets the office instead of a Ridgeway . . .

He wished the train would arrive, already. Suddenly, he watched, astonished, as the bikini skirted the barrier and ran right across the tracks! Statute 256 plainly stated that each citizen must wait for the barrier to lift before crossing. Two infractions in the space of a minute! Who was this white bikini, anyway? He looked vaguely familiar, but Roger couldn't place him. Where was that darn train?

He shrugged. He looked around. Nobody. He hesitated. And then he darted across the tracks. An overwhelming sense of guilt immediately as-

241

sailed him. In all his born days, he'd never as much as jaywalked. And now he'd crossed the tracks—literally! The moral decay was even getting to him!

He noticed the bikini heading for Nixon Park. *Darn!* He'd hoped to have the track to himself this morning. He resisted the urge to turn back. Why should he? Why should he let these weirdos cut into *his* self-improvement time?

As he ran past the tiny houses on Roosevelt Way, Roger instinctively wrinkled his nose. He hated this part of town. The proximity to the lower-middle classes always made him vaguely uneasy. Up ahead, the bikini was slowing down in front of Duke Corcoran's Cape Cod. Now *there* was an interesting case.

Just last week, Roger had driven his Buick into Duke's Royal West Service Station to be gassed up, and instead of having to wait the usual twenty minutes for the grease monkey to make an appearance, Corcoran had been prompt and polite. He'd even wiped the windshield! A good thing, too, because Roger had almost decided to switch to the Sunoco station at the other end of town.

The bikini was running in place now, staring at the house. Maybe he was trying to figure out what was happening to Corcoran, too. Roger passed him. Soon enough, though, he heard the footsteps again. Suddenly they were jogging side by side. The guy sure was peculiar-looking. A head shaped like a bullet and the knobbiest knees he'd ever seen.

"Nice day, huh?" the bikini asked.

Roger grunted. "Hot!" he gasped. The hill was always the most difficult for him. He tried to concentrate. What he didn't need now was some bozo making small talk about the weather.

"Do you do this route every day?" the bikini persisted. He didn't seem out of breath at all.

The guy was crazy to expect an answer on a day like this. Roger could feel the sweat pouring out of him, in the small of his back, under his arms—everywhere. He glanced at the guy. Not a drop of perspiration. "Yeah." Roger grunted again.

"Not me," the bikini said. "I usually run up the Coolidge Hills area. Gives a more aerobic experience, you know?"

The guy spoke with an accent. German? Roger wondered. It made sense. Krauts don't sweat.

They ran a while in silence, past the empty tennis courts, past the playground, finally into the shade of the picnic grove. Ducks were huddled under the shade trees, bespoiling the ground with their green excrement. The stuff was everywhere. In fact, a humongous chunk of it lay immediately ahead. Roger swerved sharply to avoid it. Something bony caught him on the shin, and he toppled headfirst onto the path. A tremendous weight was crushing his gut, cutting off his ability to scream. The bikini groaned. "I'm sorry," they said simultaneously.

So, there they were, sitting in the middle of the path, ducks cackling wildly all around them. "You okay?" the bikini asked.

"I think so," Roger replied cautiously. "You?"

"Nothing broken," said the bikini, grimacing at the glob of green duck shit clinging to his white trunks. "Yech! Anywhere I can wash this off?"

Roger swallowed. No, of course there wasn't. As

senior member of the town council, he'd led the fight against "profligate spending" and voted down the installation of water fountains in Nixon Park. Maybe he'd made a mistake.

"Sorry, the lavatories don't open until nine," he informed him. "Maybe we should call it a day."

Reluctantly, the bikini agreed. They helped each other up and hobbled slowly out the way they had come in.

"Are you a resident of West Falls?" Roger asked.

"Well, I have my practice here," the bikini answered. He extended a hand. "Dr. Otto Schindler, marriage counselor and sexual consultant."

Nervously, Roger introduced himself. "Ridgeway's the name. Roger Thaddeus. I'm in finance."

As they made it past West Falls High, Otto Schindler mentioned the movie. "What do you think of it?" he asked.

"A disgrace. That's what I think."

"But you're going to the big party on Sunday at The Palm? Right? Should be lots of good pussy there."

"I hate cats," Roger replied.

Schindler stared at him incredulously. "Cats? Who's talking about cats? *Pussy . . . Women . . .* You know . . ."

Roger blinked nervously. The only experience he'd had with the sort of thing Otto was talking about had been a disaster. His face still burned at the memory. *Barbara Johnson. Two years ago.* He would never forget.

They'd met by accident in the supermarket. Her cart had bumped into his, and he'd offered to carry out her groceries for her. She invited him

244

home for some banana cake, his favorite. To this day, he still didn't know how she'd gotten him into that heart-shaped bed of hers so quickly, but there they were, undressed, *naked*, behaving like animals. What was worse, he enjoyed it! He'd invited her home to meet his mother and she'd agreed. And then, the very next day, when he'd stopped by Duke's garage for a radiator cap, she drove her Mercedes right past him and into one of Duke's stalls. He'd watched, shocked, as Duke slipped his hand under her skirt and they'd kissed for what seemed like an hour. That very day, Roger made an appointment with a doctor in the city for a V.D. checkup. God was with him. He was clean.

No, pussy was not his cup of tea.

"I'm not into pussy," Roger informed Otto.

"Gee, that's too bad. . . . You like men?"

Roger looked genuinely horrified. "Of course not! It's just that the kind of woman I'm looking for doesn't seem to exist in West Falls."

"Ridiculous! Have you ever thought of trying the personals ads?" Otto asked.

Again, Roger was horrified. "You won't catch *me* writing to strangers. Besides, isn't advertising for love illegal? And if it isn't, it should be!"

Especially since it doesn't work, Roger thought. Why, he'd spent three whole days composing that letter to the show-biz professional who was tired of too much tinsel. And he'd waited an eternity to hear from her before he realized she was never going to call. Well, the heck with her. The heck with all of them. Who needed them, anyway?

At the next town council meeting, he was going to bring up the subject of personals ads. What were they doing in *The Marketplace*, anyway? There had to be a way people could be protected from getting their hopes up and having them smashed to smithereens.

37

Max and Bliss

SHE hated the bandage.

"You're beautiful," Max kept repeating. His hands on her skin were warm and gentle. He caressed her face, her neck. He pressed his lips against her shoulder.

She leaned back in his bed and looked up at him. The look in his eyes told her that he loved her. The touch of his fingers sent shivers through her body. She moaned.

Max quickly removed his hand. "Am I hurting you?"

Bliss shook her head impatiently. "No, no, I'm fine." She was more than fine. She was transported. Trembling. Losing control.

"Are you sure? You've only just come out of the hospital," Max said. His voice was filled with longing. "We can wait, you know."

No, they couldn't. *She* couldn't wait. She'd never wanted any man as much as she wanted Max Miller. All those others—Sojourn, Eric, the faceless, numberless men who had had sex with her—they all meant nothing. They were shallow memories, phantoms of a meaningless past.

How she wished the bandage were off. But suppose there was a scar? The doctors assured her there wouldn't be, but she didn't believe them.

The operation had gone well, they'd said. When she had awakened, the afternoon sunlight was streaming through the blinds of her hospital room, and Max was there, half asleep, in a chair beside the bed.

"You still here?" she'd mumbled, drugged and thick tongued. "When are they going to do it?"

He'd jumped out of his chair and grasped her hand. "They've already done it! You're negative!" he'd exclaimed, his eyes sparkling with unshed tears of joy. "Everything's great!"

She'd pulled her hand free and felt her breast. The bandage. In spite of herself, she felt afraid.

"I'm telling you the truth," Max had said, gently taking her hand into his again. "It's just a small bandage. In a couple of days, they'll remove it."

Could she believe him? All her life, she'd been lied to by men, manipulated by them, abused by them. She turned her head and saw the flowers. A dozen red roses. "You shouldn't have," she had said.

"And why not?" Max grinned. "You're my lady, aren't you?"

She nodded. "Your lady's thirsty."

"I know," he had answered, nodding. "I'll be right back."

He returned with a glass of ginger ale and held her head while she sipped. She'd never felt so cherished in all her life.

Now her breast was beginning to ache. She didn't care. There was a deeper ache inside her that she knew only Max could satisfy.

It had been her idea to come to Max's house right from the hospital, even before she'd gone to her own home. "I want to see where you live," she'd insisted. "I want to know everything about you."

Max seemed embarrassed. "The place is probably a mess," he'd apologized. "Mrs. Schotz is good with Ruthie, but she's no great shakes as a housekeeper."

"Don't apologize, Max. It'll be fine."

It wasn't fine. Dishes were piled in the sink. A pot encrusted with dried oatmeal was sitting on the stove. A layer of dust covered everything. There was an aura of benign neglect throughout the house that moved Bliss in a way she couldn't articulate. Max seemed oblivious to the disarray. He must be used to living like this, Bliss thought.

He offered to make her a cup of tea. He looked haggard and exhausted.

"Max, why don't you take a shower? Change into some fresh clothing. Let *me* make the tea," she offered.

He seemed hesitant. "But I'm supposed to be taking care of you . . ."

"I'm *fine*," she assured him. It wasn't true. A

249

pain was making its way up her side, along her ribcage, through her shoulder. She tried not to flinch. "See?" She smiled. "One hundred percent! Now . . . scoot off to the shower!"

When he had gone, she looked around the kitchen. She found herself wondering again about Max's wife. All she knew was that her name had been Audrey and that she'd died two years ago of cancer. Bliss found a kettle and filled it with water. She opened a cupboard and got the tea bags.

Then she saw it. High on a shelf above the counter. A small photograph in a silver frame. Max with his arm around a woman. Not a beautiful woman, but nice-looking, with a kind and open face. She was smiling up at a younger, happier-looking Max. Bliss felt a surprising stab of jealousy.

She put the tea things on a tray and carried it to the bedroom. Behind the bathroom door, she could hear the shower still running. The bedroom was a shambles: the bed unmade, the dresser top cluttered with remnants of Max's life—keys, crumpled tissues, pennies, half packs of breath mints, brushes clogged with hair.

She couldn't help herself. She had just started to clear the disarray when Max emerged from the bathroom, clad in a terry robe.

"Bliss, what in heaven's name are you doing?"

"Please don't be angry."

He laughed. "I'm not angry. Don't you think I know I live like a slob?"

He put his arms around her. She closed her eyes and rested her head against his chest. His nearness sent shivers through her.

He kissed her. "Oh, Bliss," he murmured, "why

have we waited so long for this? You're beautiful," he said again as he lovingly began to disrobe her.

For the first time in her life, she began to believe it. He made her feel worthy, good about herself.

Max was a sensitive lover, anticipating her every need, seeming to know intuitively what would please her. When at last he entered her, she was more than ready. They were making *love*. All those other times, she had been fucked, screwed, diddled, humped. The realization brought tears to her eyes.

"I love you, Max," she whispered, her hands pulling him tight against her.

"I love you, Bliss," he said as he exploded inside her.

Seconds later, she came. The world receded.

Only Max remained.

Later, it dawned on her what she had done. She had told Max that she loved him. She had never said those words to any man before. The implications of it frightened her. Nevertheless, she did love him. She looked over at him. He was smiling.

"What?" she asked.

"I can't believe it . . ." he began. "How close I came to throwing you into the fire."

"What?"

"Those letters. There were so many that I couldn't handle it. I didn't know about that ad until it was already in print."

She nodded. "Well, chalk another one up for the mayor."

They chuckled.

"I still can't get over it," Max said. "Who would

251

have thought a personals ad could have brought *us* together?"

She sighed. Who, indeed? Of course, he had no idea about her other experiences with the ads.

Come to think of it, there was a lot about herself that she hadn't told him.

38

Peggy

THE sun was just coming up. Its pale rays bathed the kitchen in a faint, roseate glow. Peggy poured herself another cup of fresh coffee.

Phyllis DeCaprio said she was crazy for going through with it. "Whatcha gonna do with a baby now? You don't even have a husband! Your life is just beginning!" Phyllis had even called the abortion clinic for her and made an appointment. But there was no way Peggy was going to keep it.

Absently, she put a hand over her belly. It wasn't noticeable yet, but in a few weeks, it would be. A February baby. A little valentine from Duke. And he didn't even know . . .

Peggy sighed. She would have to make a decision—and soon. Dan Ogilvie wanted to marry her right away.

"I love you, Peggy," he'd told her last night. "I'll

raise the baby as my own." He kissed her and held her.

He wanted to stay the night, but she sent him home. "I need time to think," she explained, trying not to see the hurt come into his eyes.

"It's *him,* isn't it?" Dan had accused icily. "Peggy, forget him! You don't owe him anything!"

But she did owe Duke something. She owed him the truth.

She stood and fought a wave of nausea. This pregnancy was so different from the others! With Wayne, Jr., she felt drowsy all the time. With Morgie, she hardly even felt pregnant. But this one! Headaches, fatigue, nausea—the works. It was almost as if the baby knew what was going on and was protesting.

She glanced at the telephone on the wall. If she called Duke now, this minute, would he be there? If he were there, would he be alone? A rush of jealousy flared briefly and then faded.

Phyllis DeCaprio insisted on giving her reports about him. "He eats breakfast in the diner every morning. He looks like he's lost his best friend. I'm telling you, Peg, it's pathetic! He's a changed man."

Could she dare believe Phyllis? Almost against her will, she remembered the Duke she had fallen in love with aeons ago: so full of the devil, so vibrant! To be near him was a high in itself. The way he moved, his sexy smile, the fire in his eyes! How she had loved him!

Who was she kidding? She *still* loved him.

She glanced at the telephone again. *Call him,* a voice inside her urged. Just as she lifted the receiver, Wayne, Jr., stumbled bleary-eyed into the kitchen.

"Mom? How come you're up so early?"

She shrugged. "Couldn't sleep. What about you?"

He yawned and opened the refrigerator door. "Too excited to sleep," he said, grabbing a carton of juice. He put the carton to his lips and guzzled.

She watched him with a mixture of amusement and annoyance. "Wayne, honey, how many times have I told you not to do that? Use a glass!"

He grinned. A Duke-like grin that clutched her heart. Suddenly he threw his arms around her and lifted her off the floor.

"Wayne! Stop that! What are you doing?" she demanded, giggling.

"Mom, you'll never believe it! I got an offer!" His eyes sparkled. "Last night, after the shoot, this guy comes over and hands me his card. I thought he was some weirdo salesman, but, Mom—guess what? He's a big-time record producer and he wants Bondage to do a demo!"

"Really?" She tried to smile.

"They want seven cuts—arrangements and everything! And if it takes off, they'll want seven more! Can you believe it?"

His excitement was contagious. In spite of herself, she began to feel happy for him. She had always known he had talent. "Oh, Wayne, honey, I'm so proud of you!" And then, almost as an afterthought, she heard herself ask, "But what about school?"

A look of exasperation crossed Wayne, Jr.'s face. "I *knew* it! I knew you'd bring me down! Who needs school when the world is knocking at my door?"

She turned away. "You haven't signed anything, have you?"

"Christ, Mom! He only asked us last night!" There was a pause. "We're supposed to go see him next week . . ."

Peggy closed her eyes. She wished Duke were here. "I think you should discuss this with your father—"

Wayne, Jr., slammed his fist against the countertop. "Hell, Ma, what does *he* know about the music business? He's always got his head under some car . . ."

She whirled. "Stop it, Wayne! Don't you dare talk about your father in that tone!"

Wayne, Jr.'s face darkened with rage. "What tone? When did you start defending my father? Cars is all he cares about! Cars and broads! Isn't that why you threw him out?"

She slapped him, hard. She saw first the fear, then the fury, come into his eyes.

"Feel better?" he asked quietly.

"Oh, Wayne, honey, I'm sorry . . ."

He shook his head. "It doesn't matter. I'm gonna *do* this. You're not gonna stop me. And neither is he." He rushed from the room, nearly knocking Morgie over.

How long had Morgie been standing there? How much had she heard? She looked miserable. Peggy reached out to her. Morgie rushed into her arms. "It's all right, baby," Peggy crooned. "Everything's going to be all right."

39

Revelations

"I want continuous hors d'oeuvres!"

Plato nodded.

"I want miniature quiches!"

Plato nodded again.

"I want . . ." He paused. What else *did* he want? He knew there was something else, but his head was swimming. This whole party was on him. No one was helping. All the details were his responsibility. He wondered if the Greek even understood him. He just stood there nodding at everything like he was one of those novelty birds dipping its head into a glass of water.

"Chicken wings!" he finally remembered.

The Greek nodded again.

Jared closed his eyes. His head was splitting open. The balloons! Oh, my God! He was supposed to pick them up at noon! How could he have forgotten? It was already one o'clock! When he opened his eyes, the Greek was gone. Jared was standing in the middle of The Royal Palm, talking to himself. Well, he was used to talking to himself these days.

He ran to the bar and asked Fred if he could use the phone. "Be my guest, Mayor," Fred said. "And have a drink on the house while you're at it."

"Thanks, Fred. I really need one." He dialed home.

Princess answered. "G'litz residence. Princess-the-Slave at yo' serviss."

Jared stared at the receiver. How was he going to live through this until he could fire her? With all the calm he could muster, he asked for Selma.

"She ain't home."

So what else was new? He took a deep breath and plunged right in. "Listen, Princess, I have a little favor to ask of you . . ."

Click.

He couldn't believe it. She hung up on him! Well, he'd show her. After the party, he really *would* fire her!

After the party, a lot of things would change. And not all of them for the good. The word *bankruptcy* flashed evilly in his brain. He sighed and grabbed the scotch Fred had put before him.

He was aware that Fred was watching him. Why didn't the guy stand somewhere else and let him suffer in peace? Evidently, something was on the guy's mind. But what? Maybe the *putz* ran another stop sign. "Something on your mind, Fred?" he asked.

Fred had a strange expression on his face. What

could be wrong? Jared glanced at his watch. It was getting late. In less than an hour, the entire town would be converging on this place, and there were still a million details he had to take care of.

Fred cleared his throat. "Well, Mayor . . . This ain't gonna be easy . . ."

What could it be? He hoped Selma wasn't getting *shikker* in public again.

Fred shifted nervously. "It's your wife, Mayor . . ."

Oy! Jared thought. She *has* been drinking again! That's all I need!

"She's been very cozy lately with a certain Swedish gentleman . . ." Fred began.

What was the schmuck talking about? What cozy? What Swedish gentleman? There was only one Swede he knew of in the whole town, and that was—

"A certain Mr. Jorgensen, Mayor. He and your wife have been loving it up something fierce. I felt it was my duty to tell you."

For a long moment, neither man spoke. Then, suddenly, the scotch came trickling up from Jared's gullet. With great difficulty, he managed to get it back down again.

"Tell me, Fred," Jared whispered hoarsely, "what exactly do you mean by 'loving it up'?"

Fred blushed and averted his eyes. "You know— kissing, feeling, the whole enchilada."

It *couldn't* be. Not Selma. Not Selma the Clean Queen, the woman who changed her undies twice a day, who kept air fresheners in every room!

Not Selma and that *farshtinkener* Sven Jorgensen you could smell from three blocks away!

Fred was mistaken. He *had* to be!

Then again, Jared hadn't seen much of Sven lately, either. Suppose it were true? Suppose Selma *was* shacking up with the Swede? The vision of them doing it flashed before his eyes.

How could she do this to him? Did she hate him so much? If she had to cheat, why couldn't she pick someone more presentable?

"I appreciate it, Fred," he managed to say. "Keep it under your hat, huh?"

"Will do, Mayor," Fred answered sympathetically.

Now more than the scotch was coming up. His sorrow. His faith. His *trust*.

He made it to the john just in time.

40

Steve, Sunny, Ruthie

HE had forgotten why he was here. But here he was. In his new Calvin Klein blazer, his new Guess jeans, his new Ralph Lauren shirt. And, of course, his Porsche sunglasses. He never went *anywhere* without the sunglasses.

He was sweating, but that was good. The voices said it was part of his punishment.

Now he remembered why he was here! To do penance. To apologize to Bliss Billington for upsetting her. *Tell her you're sorry!* the voices had demanded. Tell her you only wish her well. He had no choice.

He rang the bell.

A pretty young girl came to the door. She smiled at him. "Yes? Can I help you?" she asked.

This had to be Bliss's daughter. The same melancholy eyes, the same sweet smile. "Is your mother home?"

"I'm sorry, she's out," the girl answered. She was looking at him with interest. "Are you a friend of hers, or something?"

"You might say that . . ."

Another girl came to the door. This one was younger and skinnier. She was looking, too. "Who is he?" she asked Bliss's daughter.

"A friend of my mom's," the girl replied. To him, she said, "Have you known my mother long?"

He had to be careful. The angels were watching. He could see them sitting in the treetops, looking down at him. "We've known each other quite a while, yes," he answered. Suddenly the heat was unbearable. He reached into his jacket pocket for his handkerchief and wiped his forehead.

Bliss's daughter asked, "Would you like to come inside? I could have Gladys fix you a cool drink."

The other girl frowned. "You *can't* do that, Sunny," she whispered loud enough for him to hear. "He's a *stranger!*"

"No, he's not. He's a friend of my mom's," Sunny corrected her.

From the kitchen, Sunny heard Gladys call, "Sunny, is that Mrs. Corcoran?"

With a twinkle in her eye, Sunny called back, "It's okay, Gladys."

Sunny. That was her name. It was in the magazine. He'd forgotten. "So," he said, "I guess I'd better be going. Do you know when your mom will be back?"

"She's going directly to the party," Sunny told him. "It starts at two o'clock." And then, as an afterthought, she asked, "Are you going to the party?"

He nodded. "Yeah, sure." Party? *What* party? He hated parties! All those people watching, judging, whispering. He turned to go.

"Wait!" Sunny called. "You didn't tell me your name. It wouldn't be Eric, by any chance, would it?" She crossed her fingers behind her back. *God, she pleaded, let him be Eric. Let him be my father.*

Steve spun around. "How did you know?" he asked. He looked up and saw the angels nodding. Obviously, they were pleased. For some reason, though, his head was beginning to ache.

"Hey," he said on impulse, "I could sure go for an ice cream. How about you?"

A flicker of hesitation crossed Sunny's face. What if he weren't her father? But he was. He *had* to be! "We have time to go down to the Peppermint Parlor, don't we, Ruthie?"

Ruthie shook her head stubbornly. *"I'm* not going. *I'm* waiting right here for Mrs. Corcoran to pick us up!"

"Suit yourself," Sunny told her. *"I'm* dying for a soda. You can stay here if you want to, but I'm going with Eric."

Doubt clouded Ruthie's wan little face. "Oh, all right, Sunny," she agreed reluctantly, "but we just have time for one quick soda . . ."

Steve Gordon extended his arms to both girls. He looked up at the trees and was relieved to see that the angels were gone. He never even noticed that his sunglasses had fallen from his pocket.

41

Andy and Phyllis

THE idea of making love to a woman still felt strange to him. Strange but wonderful. Yes. He definitely liked it. He kissed Phyllis's eyelids and heard her moan with pleasure. He was glad they'd put the light on. Phyllis was self-conscious about doing it in broad daylight, so she'd pulled down the shades and drawn the dusty flowered curtains closed, and the tiny room had been thrown into darkness. "I want to see you," Andy murmured, switching on the lamp. "You're a vision to behold."

"Oh, Andy," she protested, "stop that!"

"I don't want to stop! I love you!"

"Oh, Andy, I love you, too. I love everything about you." Her hands caressed his bald spot. "You're the most exciting man I've ever known. You're sensitive. You're talented. You're brilliant. Why did it take us so long to find each other?"

He kissed her earlobes lovingly. How could he have ever thought they were unattractive? They were the best-looking lobes he'd ever seen. They gave her a specialness, a uniqueness, a wonderfulness. Oh, God, how he loved her.

Carefully, he slid his hand between her legs. He couldn't get over how soft it was. How soft *she* was . . .

He felt himself growing inside her, expanding with his love. Her legs tightened around his hips as she lifted her body in ecstasy.

The bedsprings were making their usual racket.

A husky voice bellowed from the next room. "You two at it again? Don't you ever get enough? What a pair of fucking animals!"

Andy ignored whoever it was. They moved faster now, both of them approaching the point of no return. He'd never known such intense satisfaction. But then, he'd never really been in love before.

"Andrew, Andrew, Andrew," she moaned. "My little teddy bear."

He never wanted it to end. They clutched frantically at each other. Their lips met softly, sweetly, at the point of climax.

"I want to marry you, Phyllis!" he screamed as he ejaculated.

"Marry him, already, Phyllis!" the voice from next door boomed. "Maybe *then* I can get a little rest!"

It wasn't the first time he'd proposed. Andrew had been asking her to marry him at least once a day, every day for the last three weeks. Every time he came, out would pop the proposal. But if she said yes, would he still want her? Or would he be like all those others, scared shitless of commitment? Well, she thought, she had to start trusting him sometime. Maybe today was the day. She had just decided to say, "Yes, Andrew, I'll marry you," when the phone rang. He picked it up.

"Andy ffrench speaking."

She watched as he paled. Frantically, he looked at his watch. "Yes, yessir," he said. "Right away, sir. My watch stopped, sir. We'll—I'll—be right there." He put down the phone and grabbed for his pants. Phyllis sat up.

"What?" she asked.

"The *party!*" he said. "We forgot about the goddamn Meet-the-Stars party!"

42

The Royal Palm

THE Royal Palm was bedecked with yellow ribbons. Giant heart-shaped Mylar balloons floated from the curled brass fronds of the massive plastic palm tree in the center of the dimly lit barroom. Across the mirror behind the bar, an enormous satin banner announced: MEET THE STARKS!

Jared Galitz frowned at the silver letters and shook his head. Damn those idiots at the Unique Party Favors Company! What was wrong with them that they couldn't get a simple little word like *STARS* right?

As if the sign wasn't bad enough, the five hundred balloons repeated the same mistake. "Who the hell are the *STARKS?*" Jared had raged when he had finally stopped retching and went to fetch the banner and the balloons. "It's *STARS,* dummy!" he'd shrieked at the gum-chewing shiksa behind the counter. *"S-T-A-R-S!"*

The girl looked at her nails and yawned. "I only work here, buddy," she informed him. "Don't lose your cool with me." And then she looked at him with her vacant blue eyes. "You want 'em or doncha?"

He took them, of course.

"Who the fuck are the STARKS?" Fred the bartender wanted to know as he helped Jared put up the banner.

Jared didn't bother to answer. It was already five minutes to two, and the parking lot was beginning to fill up. He'd already met with Chief Daniels to discuss security. Putting on a party for a whole town was no simple matter. The entire area for miles was carefully cordoned off to forestall traffic jams. Manpower had been borrowed from two of the neighboring towns, Short Falls and East Falls. West Falls police were stationed up and down Main Street.

For most of these schleppers, Jared knew, meeting celebrities like Barron Heatter and JayPee, even like Barrbra Shapiro, was a once-in-a-lifetime thrill. A dream come true. But there was always the danger that the dream would turn into a nightmare. That's what Chief Daniels was here to prevent.

Jared looked up and saw his father-in-law shoulder his way through the door, balancing two foil-covered trays. Abe looked up at the balloons. "Who the hell are the STARKS?"

Jared ignored the question and asked one of his own. "What's with the trays, Abe?"

"You know Bea. It was a party—she had to bake. It's only five dozen ruggaleh, a babka, and about thirty-five knishes."

Jared couldn't believe his ears. Selma should only be so concerned about this party. Before he could say anything, Plato Pappamichaelis emerged from the kitchen with a tray of hors d'oeuvres and glanced up at the banner. His swarthy face registered puzzlement.

"Da STARKS? Who' dem?" Plato wanted to know.

Barron Heatter took one look at the crowd and shivered. "I *can't!*" he quavered. "If I go in there, they'll rip me to shreds!"

Selma put her hand lovingly on his thigh. Then, noticing Enrico leering at them through the limo's rearview mirror, she self-consciously took her hand away. She'd have to watch it. She couldn't afford to throw discretion to the winds. *Not yet, anyway.* She still hadn't told Jerry she was planning to leave him. She looked at Barron. He wanted her to tell Jerry today, after the party. It wasn't going to be easy.

Barron looked petrified. Selma had an urge to take him in her arms and tell him again not to be afraid, that everything was going to be all right. She wouldn't let anything happen to her Benny. In her mind, he had ceased to be Barron Heatter the Movie Star; he was Benny Horowitz from the Bronx, a sweet, innocent naïf who was at the mercy of an overzealous public. She squeezed his hand. "I promise, darling, I'll be by your side the whole time."

He turned to her. Some of the fear left his face. He smiled that famous smile, the smile that sent chills through women all over the globe. "I love you, Selma," he said. He leaned over and kissed her. "What would I do without you?"

Enrico eased the limo into the lot. Selma saw her father's Continental with its FLANKEN plates parked in the no-parking zone in front of The Palm. She hoped Barron wouldn't notice. She wondered what her parents would say if they knew their only child was having an affair with a movie star. Would they rant and rave? Would they think she was having a breakdown? Would they have her committed?

She didn't even want to think about what Olivia would say. Olivia was every inch her father's daughter. When she found out, she would probably never talk to her mother again. Tears welled in Selma's eyes. She took a deep, shaky breath.

Barron's hand grasped hers tightly. "Okay, babe," he said. "I guess it's now or never!"

Peggy was beside herself with worry. Where could Sunny and Ruthie have gone? She'd called for them at the Billington house exactly at two o'clock, but they weren't there. The housekeeper —Gladys, Peggy thought her name was—had become hysterical. "She'll fire me for this!" Gladys had wept. Peggy had managed to calm her by suggesting that the girls had probably walked to The Palm by themselves.

But they were nowhere in sight. How was she going to explain to Bliss? Should she call the police? She wished Duke were here to tell her what to do.

Peggy squinted in the bright sunlight. There must be thousands of people here already. As soon as Morgie stepped from the car, she was surrounded by a mob of autograph seekers. In spite of her nervousness over the missing girls, Peggy felt a surge of pride to see how well Morgie handled the whole thing. Where had she learned such poise?

At the other end of the parking lot, Wayne, Jr., and the rest of Bondage were setting up their equipment. Peggy marveled. Duke had always downplayed his son's interest in music; but now, here Wayne, Jr., was on his way to becoming a rock star. Maybe school *could* wait. She decided not to think about it.

Absently, she placed a hand over her stomach. She wondered what this one would be like. A president? An artist? The options were unlimited . . .

She searched the crowd and saw Dan Ogilvie. Her heart plummeted. She was sorry she'd asked him to meet her here. But she had to level with him, and the sooner, the better. How could she marry him when she still felt the way she did about Duke?

Bondage launched into "Lost My Glove Over You" from the movie. People began to dance. Through a mass of flailing arms and legs, Peggy saw Dan start in her direction. She pasted a smile on her face and prepared herself for the confrontation.

Inside The Royal Palm there was hardly room to breathe. Bliss and Max had arrived twenty minutes earlier, but they still hadn't seen Sunny or Ruthie. Max, his voice tinged with worry, asked for the hundredth time, "Where can they *be?*"

They'd looked everywhere. The parking lot. The ladies' room. Even the kitchen. Then Bliss had called home. Gladys sounded peculiar. "You mean they're *not* at The Palm? I surely thought—"

Bliss cut her off impatiently. "What time did Mrs. Corcoran pick them up?"

There was a long pause. "Well, uh, actually, Mrs. Corcoran came at two, but the girls had already left. They decided to walk over by themselves."

Bliss tried to beat down a surge of panic. She slammed down the receiver. Max's face mirrored her alarm. She never should have gone to the lab with him this morning of all mornings! But he had been so heady with excitement over the success of his project that he'd wanted to show her everything in detail.

What he'd shown her was cage after cage of peacefully snoring monkeys. Max explained the implications: "Picture babies instead of monkeys! Bliss, you're looking at a colic-free world!"

Bliss was impressed. Sunny had never suffered from colic, but other babies at The Settlement had. The poor creatures had screamed relentlessly night after night while their sleep-deprived parents—and everyone else, for that matter—had been driven crazy with frustration.

She'd thrown her arms around Max's neck and told him how proud she was of him.

But now it all meant nothing. Now she was trembling with fear. *Where was her daughter? What had happened to her?*

Somewhere deep inside, Bliss thought she knew. She hoped she was wrong.

"Hey, babee!" Cisco called above the din. "You gotta help me wid dees tie!" It was at least a hundred and two in the kitchen. Sweat was streaming down his face. The crazy Greek in the chef's hat was screaming at his helper, Phyllis DeCaprio.

Princess set down a tray loaded with stuffed grape leaves. She wiped her hands on the skimpy white apron. "Here, honey, let me do it fo' you!"

Expertly, she proceeded to fashion the black satin strip into a perfect bow. Cisco eyed her suspiciously. "Hey, where'd you learn to do that?"

Princess smiled dryly. "They's a lot 'bout me yo' don' know, Cisco, darlin'!"

The very thought of what Cisco didn't know about her made her shudder. When was she going to get up the nerve to tell him who she really was? It would have to be soon, she knew. Her project was nearly over. In fact, she had written to her adviser yesterday, telling him so. She sighed as she gave the bow tie a final pat. She didn't resist when Cisco drew her close and slipped his hand under her short black skirt. *Today*, she promised herself. *Later.*

There was an ear-splitting crash behind them. *"Skata!"* Plato bellowed as an enormous platter of chicken wings slipped from Phyllis's hands to the floor.

Princess and Cisco watched, dumbfounded, as the two of them scurried about, retrieving wings from under counters and behind doors, then placing them neatly back on the platter.

273

"Remind me to stay 'way from dem chicken wings," Cisco whispered to Princess.

Such a tush! Such *brusts!* Abe could hardly stand to look. Thighs that melted like butter into the hips. Purple satin shorts so tight you could see her you-know-what plain as day. *Oy.*

The woman she was talking to was also not chopped liver. He'd seen her before around town. Long, shiny black hair, parted in the middle. A skin-tight dress made of metal bangles and spangles. When she moved, her *brusts* jiggled like a plate of *putcha*—jellied calves' feet. Abe's mouth watered. Looking at both of them together, he felt his member getting hard.

He folded his hand over his crotch and looked around. Wouldn't you know? There was Bea, staring at him through those glasses of hers. She didn't miss a thing, that Bea. "Lovely party, huh, Bea?" he said, forcing a smile.

"It should be, for what you're paying," she snapped crossly. There was a pause. "What's wrong? Why are you holding yourself like that?"

He wanted to wring her neck, the way his mother in the *shtetl* had done to the chickens. He wanted to tell her, "I've had enough, Bea! What I want—what I need—is a Barrbra Shapiro!"

Because even though the gorgeous Barrbra had stood him up, even though he knew she didn't love him, he was still smitten. She was still the woman of his dreams. He still saw her beautiful face everywhere he went. Every time he stopped for a traffic light. When he read the newspaper. When he watched television. It was like he had a disease. No

274

matter how hard he tried—and maybe he really didn't try so very hard—he couldn't get her out of his system. *Barrbra Shapiro!* Even her name sent shivers up and down his spine!

Chief Almanzo Daniels felt one of his migraines coming on. The back room of The Royal Palm was cramped and airless. The blinking fluorescent light didn't help, either. This Billington woman wasn't a bad looker, if you liked them skinny and blond, but she was driving him crazy.

"Tell me again, Mrs. Billington. When exactly did you last see your daughter?"

She fixed him with a stony gaze. "It's *Ms.* Billington," she said. "And I've already told you . . . I left the house early this morning. My daughter was asleep. Why aren't you questioning my housekeeper?"

Al Daniels did his best to contain himself. "I've sent my best man to do just that. Try to calm yourself . . ."

Max Miller put a reassuring hand on her shoulder. "Bliss, take it easy, darling. Al is doing his best."

Al threw Miller a grateful smile. He wondered what was going on between these two. An unlikely pair if ever he saw one. But what did *he* know?

Well, one thing he did know was that these kids picked themselves the wrong day to get lost. The Brinks job could be pulled off in West Falls today and nobody would care. Everyone was at this stupid party, trying to get next to the celebs. Whose dumb idea was this, anyway?

He looked up at Max and the Billington broad.

"Ms. Billington, we'll do everything in our power to find your girls. Try not to worry." He hesitated. "I'll need a description. Better yet, a picture."

Max dug into his wallet and retrieved a cracked and faded photograph of a toddler. He handed it to Al, who stared.

"This the best you can do, Max?"

"You already know what Ruthie looks like, Al," Max replied rather impatiently.

"Yeah, *I* do, but my men don't."

Bliss fumbled in her purse and came up with a recent clipping from *FOLK* Magazine. "Here they are," she said.

For a wild moment, Bliss considered telling Chief Daniels about Steve Gordon and all those threatening phone calls. She looked furtively at Max. He knew nothing about Steve. In fact, he knew nothing about her past except what she had chosen to tell him. Nervously, she looked away.

Fred the bartender was ready to explode. There was hardly room for him to move behind the bar, what with all these amateur barkeeps the mayor had hired to help him. The whole place was jammed to the rafters. More people than he had seen in The Palm since St. Paddy's Day. A whole lot more. And they kept on coming in. Like now, for instance. A busload of old-timers from the Happy Valley Home. My God, he thought, some of them could barely walk.

He recognized one of them. Fremont Bisch. A friend of the mayor's wife. Fred shook his head. That mayor's wife sure gets around! Poor mayor . . .

276

"How're ya doin' there, son," Fremont Bisch greeted Fred.

"Long time no see, sir." Fred smiled. "What'll it be? Another stinger?"

Fremont shook his head. "No . . . not today. Today, I think I'll have a zombie."

Fred hadn't heard anyone ask for a zombie this early in the day for a long time. Yessirree! This was going to be *some* party.

Fremont looked around. He hadn't been to The Palm since the night he met Selma. It was going to be wonderful to see her again. For a few weeks, she'd come to Lawrence Welk Night at the home and danced with him and all his friends, but lately she hadn't shown and he missed her. In fact, he couldn't stop thinking about her. What a woman! The most beautiful woman he'd met since his wonderful Mamie, bless her soul, had left him.

So where *was* she? Outside, he could hear loud music. It didn't compare with Lawrence Welk, but he felt like dancing anyway. There was a nice-looking woman over there in the corner who reminded him a little of Selma. The same red hair. The same distinctive nose. And she was standing all by her lonely, looking lost.

He walked over and bowed. "Excuse me, lovely lady, but will you give me the honor of this dance?" he asked.

Bea spun around. What lovely lady was he talking to? Her? Who was he, anyway? Actually, he wasn't bad-looking. And when was the last time Abe had asked her to dance? At Selma's wedding, probably, Bea realized. She smiled at the gent. "I'd love to," she replied.

Fremont made another bow, and Bea linked her arm through his. Together they made for the dance floor.

JayPee took a final snort and left the men's room. A group of shrieking young girls immediately surrounded him. It was a mistake not to have hired bodyguards, he knew. "Easy, girls," he said. "There's enough of me to go around."

They squealed with pleasure. "Oooooooh, JayPee, do-do-do me!" one of them shrieked. Another grabbed at his chains and started tugging. "He's Jewish!" she cried out. "No, wait a minute. He's Catholic. He's wearing a cross!"

JayPee was choking, gasping for breath, when a uniformed policeman parted the sea of arms ripping at him. In an easy motion, the cop lifted JayPee high above the horde and carried him across the room to the bar. "This okay?" the cop asked solicitously.

Trembling, JayPee nodded. "I owe you one," he said gratefully. Someone set a tray of drinks in front of him. He took the tallest one and downed it. Suddenly he felt a leg rub up against his.

"Will you do-do-do me?" a soft voice crooned in his ear.

Cautiously, he turned to see a sexy fox decked out in bangles. She had long black hair and the perkiest tits he'd seen in a long time. She smiled at him. Beneath the bar, her hand came to rest on his cock.

Should he do-do-do her? Why not? He looked around. Cindi, Candi, and Lula Mae were nowhere in sight. He hated to admit it, but he could use some variety. The fox was unzipping him. He had to think fast.

"Not here," he whispered, grabbing her hand. But where? He turned and saw a telephone booth near the john. Why not? It was as good a place as any.

Andy ffrench had never seen such chaos. Not even in Burbank. Not even in San Diego. This was true madness, and the rubes were wild and drunk, besides. The heat was melting their brains, to say nothing of the asphalt out in the parking lot. Andy was sweating profusely. How this "do" could help the film was beyond him. But, oh, no, Barron had to go along with that jerk of a mayor who thought he had all the answers. He looked around. Where was his Phyllis? *There she was*, at the other end of the parking lot, talking to some spade waiter with a crooked bow tie. Andy looked at his watch. Not even five o'clock, dammit. How long was this brawl going to last? He had better things to do.

Once this Little Women flick was in the can, he and Phyllis were heading back to Elay, where they belonged. Good-bye West Farts, hello future. Already Spyros had mentioned something about getting him a job on Newman's next project—a sequel to *Hud*, or something like that. Of course, before they signed on, he and Phyllis would get married. First things first.

Roger Ridgeway unbuttoned his pin-striped vest and extricated a linen handkerchief from his jacket pocket. He patted his forehead. "It's rather warm today, don't you think?"

Otto Schindler nodded. Warm? It was so hot that his sandals were glued to the asphalt. It was so hot that if he set the chicken wing he was nibbling on the ground, it would fry. "It's too hot to be standing here," he said, sucking the meat off the wing with a whoosh.

"Maybe we should venture inside?" Roger suggested hesitantly.

Otto shrugged. "Why don't *you* venture. I'll be along in a minute." He wished this Ridgeway would disappear, already. The guy obviously was too insecure to work a party on his own. He regretted ever striking up a conversation with him that unfortunate morning they jogged together.

Otto edged away. Relentlessly, Roger followed.

"So?" Roger asked in a strident voice. "Where's all that pussy you promised?"

People turned to stare.

Otto cringed. "Roger, *control* yourself!" he hissed. "Open your eyes. It's all around you!"

Roger looked. He shook his head. "Where? I don't see it," he said, puzzled.

Otto pointed to a stocky blue-haired woman standing nearby. "What about her?"

Roger crooked an eyebrow. "Her? That's Margaret Jensen, the town librarian. She's at least sixty-five years old!"

"Roger, Roger," Otto chided him, "you've got to start someplace. Now, go over and introduce yourself . . ."

Reluctantly, Roger obeyed.

Thank God, Otto sighed. He continued to scan the crowd for Peggy. Earlier he'd seen her talking to some Howdy-Doody type with freckles. Who was he? Not her husband, that's for sure. A brother, maybe. A cousin, maybe, he thought.

A red-haired black girl came up just then and offered him a meatball. "Why, thank you, my dear," Otto said appreciatively. She gave him a wink and sashayed away. "Now *that's* what I call pussy," Otto mumbled under his breath.

"*That?* Don't be ridiculous. That's the mayor's maid."

Oh, no, not Roger again, Otto thought miserably. He turned to him reluctantly. "No luck with the librarian?"

Roger looked embarrassed. "I couldn't get up the nerve."

Otto wondered if that was the only thing the guy couldn't get up.

Barron's arm hurt. His fingers were numb. He'd signed his autograph at least a thousand times this afternoon. "Barron Heatter" was scrawled across cocktail napkins, coasters, balloons, envelopes, even toilet paper. It always amazed him that people treasured these scribbles. What did they do with them? Probably put them under their pillows and got themselves off, he thought in disgust. He wondered what they'd do if he signed his real name. Maybe they wouldn't even notice.

He felt Selma's hand slip into his. Thank God she was here. True to her word, she hadn't left his side all afternoon. He turned to her. He wanted to grab her and kiss her here and now, in front of the whole damn town. "You're going to tell him tonight, right?" he asked, then immediately regretted it. A look of anguish clouded her sweet, pure

281

face. The last thing he wanted to do was cause her pain. Still, she was his woman now, and he wanted everybody to know it.

Suddenly he heard a rasping whine. *"Motherrrr!* Where did you get that awful dress? It looks like something from a thrift shop!"

Olivia! When he and Selma were married, he'd have to teach Olivia a thing or two about respect. Acting like a brat on the set was one thing. To her mother, it was something else.

"I think your mother looks beautiful," Barron said.

Olivia looked at him in disbelief. Then, a knowing smile appeared on her broad, florid face. "Oh, Barron, you don't have to be nice to her just because she's my mother!"

Barron wanted to slap her.

"It's all right, Barron," Selma whispered. "She doesn't mean anything by it."

Selma looked tense and worried. Barron decided to let it pass for now.

"So, Barron," Olivia pressed, "what about those close-ups you promised me? You were going to talk to Spyros about them."

"Olivia, darling," Selma urged, "now is not the time—"

Olivia ignored her. "I mean it, Barron. After all, I have my career to think about."

Well, it sure didn't take them long to become prima donnas, Barron thought. But this one was probably born a prima donna. He found it hard to believe she was Selma's daughter. "Did I promise?" he asked evasively. "We'll see . . ."

"Don't give me 'we'll see,' " Olivia growled.

" 'We'll see' is for amateurs like Sunny and Morgie. 'Yes' is for Olivia Galitz!"

The world was spinning. It wasn't just the dancing, although that was part of it. It wasn't just the drinks, though that was part of it, too. She'd had two zombies plus a piña colada, and she could no longer feel the tips of her fingers.

Bea Moscovitz was tipsy! What's more, she was having the time of her life. She'd come here today expecting boredom. Instead, she'd found a new lease on life in the person of one Fremont Bisch. He was some dancer, this Fremont! *He was some man!* He made her feel warm all over; he made her feel young again.

The music stopped, and he led her to a table. Gratefully, she sank down and fanned herself with her hand. "Whew!" she exclaimed, eyeing him appraisingly. There was a definite twinkle in his eye. When he smiled, there was a definite dimple in his cheek. She'd always liked men with dimples. The only place Abe had them was on his tush!

She wondered if Fremont was married. She decided to ask. "Fremont, do you mind if I ask a personal question?"

He leaned forward and grasped her hand. "I wish you would, my dear."

So sexy!

"Fremont, tell me . . . Are you by any chance married?"

Fremont sighed. "I was," he said, glancing at the ceiling. "She's gone now, my Mamie, may she rest in peace."

Bea felt a surge of sympathy, compassion, relief

—she wasn't sure what. "Oh, Fremont, I'm so sorry."

He was silent a moment, then he said, "Life goes on." And the music began again. Wordlessly, he drew her to the dance floor.

He held her very close. So close she could feel his hardness pressing against her. "Fremont—" she started to say, but then his lips covered hers. It caught her off guard. She'd never had a man's tongue in her mouth before.

So this is how the *goyim* kiss, Bea thought. *Amazing!* What had she been missing all these years?

Duke was late. After he'd finished fixing Battista's carburetor, he'd showered and shaved and tried his damnedest to get the grease out from beneath his fingernails. Yesterday, he'd gone out and bought a nail brush and a blow dryer for his hair, and then he'd shelled out twenty-five bucks for some fancy aftershave with a name he couldn't even pronounce.

All for the love of Peggy. *His* Peggy. He had a feeling that today was his last chance to win her back. *Please, God,* he prayed, *help me . . .*

When he finally got there, The Royal Palm was pure pandemonium. People crawling all over themselves, pushing and shoving and crowding the entrance. Duke elbowed his way inside toward the bar where Fred and some bartenders he'd never seen before looked like they were about to drop from exhaustion. He looked around tentatively. Where was Peggy?

He pushed his way through to the rear entrance

and stepped out into the parking lot. The music had a familiar sound to it. He looked up and saw girls, their faces rapt with adoration, gathered around the musicians, reaching up, trying to grab them. And there was Wayne, Jr.—his son!—right in the middle of it all. Those girls were screaming and wiggling their asses for *his son!* A surge of pride welled inside him. He caught Wayne, Jr.'s eye and gave him the thumbs-up sign. Wayne, Jr., grinned.

Duke stood listening. Dammit, they weren't bad. Why had it taken so long for him to realize that his son had talent?

And over there, in the middle of another huge crowd, was his daughter! Signing autographs, for crissakes, just like she was a real movie star! Well, she *was* a real movie star! She even had a union card to prove it!

God, you're a lucky sonofabitch, Duke Corcoran. Luckier than you deserve . . . But where was Peggy? He looked around. She wasn't in the parking lot. But there was that bald-headed asshole sex doctor, the one who'd set Peggy against him. He'd like to put his fist through that one's bony jaw. Instead, Duke controlled himself and went back inside.

What had happened to the air-conditioning? It was hotter than hell in here! A balloon floated in front of his face. Impatiently, he waved it away. Who the hell were the STARKS? he wondered. He picked up a scotch from a tray on the bar and downed it.

And then he saw her. Sitting at a table across from that freckle-faced creep he'd seen go into the house with her a couple of weeks ago. They were sitting head to head, oblivious to the world. *Like lovers.* He felt like he'd been socked in the stomach. Had he lost her, after all?

Bliss avoided Max's eyes as she spoke. They were in her car because that was the only place they could find. She shifted uncomfortably behind the steering wheel. Outside, all around them, people were milling about, dancing and laughing, and shouting to each other in the relentless heat.

The windows of the Porsche were up, and the air-conditioning hummed smoothly. She felt isolated from the rest of the world, even from herself. She tried to tell herself that the sunglasses the detective found on her doorstep could belong to anyone. *But she knew better.*

"What are you saying, Bliss?" Max said.

"I'm saying that I—I think I know what happened to the girls." She was trembling so badly she could hardly go on. She burst into tears.

"Bliss!" Max snapped, shaking her roughly. "What are you talking about?"

"I think they may have been kidnapped!" she screamed. "I think Steve Gordon has them!"

"Steve Gordon? Who's Steve Gordon?" Max yelled. "You're not making sense, Bliss!"

She forced herself to continue. "I met him a while ago. Through the personals ads. He's sick, Max. He's a real psycho . . ." She was hysterical again, sobbing uncontrollably.

He listened in stunned silence as she told him the rest of it. How, at first, Steve had seemed normal enough. How they'd had a drink at The Royal

Palm. How she'd taken him to her shop afterward. How he'd assaulted her.

She told him about the phone calls.

When she finally found the courage to look at him, he was ashen. "Why did you wait this long to say anything?" he demanded. "Why didn't you tell the police?"

Before she had a chance to reply, he opened the car door and left her.

The old fart in the Hawaiian shirt had attached himself to her like glue. And he made no secret of staring at her tits. Well, Barrbra thought, let him look. This party was one fucking bore. Barron was avoiding her like the plague. He was too busy sucking up to that dog-of-a-mayor's wife. She didn't realize Barron preferred them ugly and titless. Well, fuck Barron. As soon as this picture opened, she'd be able to write her own ticket. Streisand, Midler, Parton—move over! Here comes Shapiro!

The old guy shoved a drink under her nose. "I thought you might be thirsty." He smiled.

She took it gratefully. "How sweet of you," she crooned. What she could really use now was a snort, but she knew better than to ask this old *putz.* She downed the drink and licked her lips. Not bad.

One look at his crotch told her he had a hard-on. What's with this guy? she wondered, remembering the time in the gym when she'd performed the Heimlich maneuver on him. She'd never seen anything like it in her life. He must be the horniest grandpa in the history of the world.

Well, why not have some fun? she decided. He

obviously had the hots for her. He was practically drooling, for crissakes.

Without another word, she took his hand and led him to a booth at the farthest end of the room. He followed like a lovesick puppy.

Abe couldn't believe it was really happening. He was sitting next to his Lamb Chop at last. He brushed a purple curl from her forehead and shivered. Just touching her did such things to him! Lucky they had found a booth way in the back where no one could see. He could feel her thigh pressing against his. She had her shoes off now, and her toes were tickling his ankle.

"I knew it was you," he said.

She smiled vaguely, placing her hand tentatively between his legs. "Well, I should hope so," she whispered.

Hoo-ha! She was actually touching it! In all his forty-three years with Bea, never once had she touched it without him having to beg and plead.

"I understand now why you couldn't come," he said.

What was the old guy blabbering about? she wondered. She never had any trouble coming. Obviously, he was plastered. But not so far gone he couldn't get it up. "I'm glad you understand," she replied softly. *What a hard-on,* she thought, awestruck.

Expertly, deftly, she started to unzip his fly . . .

He had trouble breathing. He closed his eyes. She was actually holding it now! Squeezing it! His heart was beating like a motorboat.

She took his hand and put it *there*. She wasn't wearing any panties! *I'm dying!* he thought.

"Isn't this the juiciest pussy you ever touched?" she asked him.

He felt strange and tingly all over. He opened his mouth. "Pussy," he said.

Suddenly she wasn't sitting next to him anymore. She was under the table. She had him in her mouth. She let her tongue loll around and around the hot tip of his cock.

"You like that?" she asked.

"Pussy," Abe repeated.

It was some acting job. He, Jared Galitz, Esq., should get an Oscar for the best performance of a happy-go-lucky mayor. It was the campaign all over again: hand shaking, backslapping, cheek kissing. The works. Making sure everyone had a drink and a chicken wing. Hell, he wouldn't care if he never saw another chicken wing again for the rest of his life. He drained his glass and reached automatically for another. It didn't help. He felt like a drowning man, which, in fact, he was. His troubles rolled before his eyes like the credits at the end of a movie—a horror movie . . .

Dove Hills Estates was about to explode. Any day now, the EPA was going to make public the fact that the place was full of toxic waste, and that he was responsible. When the shit hit the fan, he was going to be up to his kazoo in alligators. Where —How?—was he going to find the fourteen million dollars to clean up all the crap?

And there was Barbara Johnson with a biscuit in

the oven. His biscuit! She sidled closer to him and smiled a coy smile.

"Hello, there, Puckeypoo," she whispered wetly in his ear. Mechanically, he put a hand on her ass. You could do that at a party, he knew. Besides, Selma was so busy playing the hostess to that Heatter that she wouldn't even notice.

"I like the dress," he said, staring into her cleavage.

"This old thing? Pretty soon it won't fit," she answered, taking his hand from her rear and placing it over her abdomen. The smile faded. "Well— have you told her yet?"

Oy. What was he going to do? He was torn. He'd always wanted a boy. Suppose the biscuit turned out to be a boy? The thought filled him simultaneously with pain and pleasure. "Soon," he assured her. "I'll tell her soon."

"You had better, Puckeypoo," she threatened. "Or you know what . . ."

He nodded. He was grateful when that skinny little *shvartzeh* punk rocker appeared out of nowhere with a drink for Barbara, and they turned their backs to him.

He looked around for Sven Jorgensen. He'd like to get his hands around that Swede's neck and squeeze. He hadn't had a chance to confront Selma yet, but for some strange reason, he had already decided to forgive her. Obviously, she felt guilty. Look how nice she was being to Heatter, and all for Jared's sake. So she'd let that dumb Swede seduce her. Well, everyone is allowed *one* mistake.

Where *was* that Jorgensen? Probably too afraid to show his face. And a good thing, too.

Ross Updike adjusted his silk ascot and stepped out of the rental car, woozy with jet lag. His psyche was still in Nairobi even though his body was here in this hamlet called West Falls. He didn't realize towns like this still existed. So quaint, so pastoral, so deserted. Like stepping into a Norman Rockwell painting. How smart of Princess to have chosen this place for her research.

Speaking of Princess, he'd already been to the address she'd put on her letters but found no one at home. No one seemed to be at home in West Falls. He'd driven down one deserted street after another until he'd come to a cordoned-off area and saw people everywhere. He stopped a policeman on a horse and asked what was going on.

"There's a party for the movie folks," he was told. "Down at The Palm. But you're going to have to park on Ford Place."

He recalled something in one of Princess's letters about a movie being filmed in town. So here he was. He made his way carefully through the throng. From the look of things, it seemed an orgy was in full swing. He hadn't seen so many inebriated souls since that puberty rite on the Algahura Peninsula.

Princess's letter was still in his pocket. On the plane, he'd read it over and then over again, and still he had trouble making sense of it. Well, he would talk to Princess and get to the bottom of whatever was up.

An uneducated gardener, indeed!

Inside The Royal Palm, confusion reigned supreme. It was worse than the fall of the Roman Empire, although he couldn't be certain. Worse even than Sodom and Gomorrah, although he couldn't be certain about that, either. Bodies were everywhere in various stages of foreplay. In every corner, in every booth, at every table, people were ogling, touching, thrusting. What was his Princess doing in a place like this? After all, how much could a scholar sacrifice for the sake of knowledge?

Ross stood for a moment, getting his bearings. Where *was* she? He had already rehearsed his strategy. First, he would get her out of here. Then he would buy her dinner. Then he would tell her that he loved her. And *then* he would present her with the ring, which was now in a velvet box in his jacket pocket. They would kiss and make up and discuss their plans for the future, and she would forget all about this aberration of hers.

But first he had to find her.

He wove his way deeper into the melee. He noted a pulchritudinous-though-distraught-looking woman talking earnestly to an all-American freckle-faced male at a table for two. Another man was bearing down on them with feral intent. Instinctively, Ross Updike turned in the opposite direction.

There on the dance floor, a vamp in a bangled dress was pressing her mammaries against a member of his own race—a skinny, bechained youth who closely resembled the Tsumba prince he'd written a monograph on two years ago. Dancing next to them was a bewigged fop in a turtleneck with a scarf. His partner was the most unusual

Caucasian woman he'd ever seen. Her earlobes especially. They resembled the distorted lobes of the women of the Imberateri tribe. How very odd! How worthy of further investigation!

He turned and nearly knocked over a slender red-haired woman who was dancing with a tall, superficially handsome Hollywood type with very white teeth. Perhaps these were the STARKS everyone was here to meet.

But where was his Princess?

Someone bumped into him. A buxom woman with a toothy smile and lipstick on her teeth accidentally elbowed him. "Oh, ex-cuuuse me," she gushed, appraising him. "Come along, Miriam." A constipated type in a pin-striped suit was tugging at the woman's arm. "We don't want to miss those chicken wings."

"I'm coming, I'm coming, already, Roger," Miriam said, flashing Ross an obsequious grin, which he took care not to return.

Suddenly someone thrust a tray of chicken wings under his nose. "Care for some horsey durves?"

He was about to refuse when something made him look at the offerer.

He blinked.

No! It couldn't be! It wasn't! Yes, it was!

"Princess?" he gasped. "Is that you under that fright wig?"

The tray dropped from her hands with a resounding clatter. They stared at each other in disbelief. "Ross?" she whispered.

His jaw dropped. What on earth was his Princess

293

doing dressed like a common domestic? Why was she wearing that degrading maid's outfit?

Before he could find his voice, a waiter with a crooked bow tie appeared out of nowhere and put a proprietary arm around Princess's hip. The waiter glowered at him. "Watchu doing, messing with my honeypot?"

Ross's jaw dropped. *His* honeypot?

"Cisco," Princess said in a small, shaky voice, "I'd like you to meet an old friend of mine—Ross Updike." She paused. And then she said, "Ross, this is Francisco Williams."

The two men glared at each other in stony silence. And then, in a single instant, generations of breeding were scattered to the winds as Ross Updike, A.B.—Harvard, M.A. and Ph.D.—Princeton, protégé of Margaret Mead and Gregory Bateson, author of four anthropology textbooks and seven monographs, clenched his fist and let go.

43

Bedlam

WHEN the good citizens of West Falls recalled the events of August 29, 1986—and recall them they would—all agreed that the trouble began with the dropping of a tray of chicken wings.

The agreement ended there. For every man, woman, and child had his or her own explanation as to why it happened and whose fault it was.

"Somebody putta da somet'in' inna da booze," Carlo Battista maintained.

"It was a virus in the air-conditioning vents," Roger Ridgeway insisted.

"It was that incredibly depraved music," Margaret Jensen said.

"It was the chicken wings."

It was all of the above.

And more.

5:00 P.M.

When Ross Updike's fist connected with Cisco Williams's jaw, Cisco, surprised, crumpled in a heap to the floor.

"What have you done?" Princess cried, lashing out at Ross, who slipped on a chicken wing and landed on the floor next to his prey. He felt a searing pain in his shin and yelped for help, but Princess turned a deaf ear. She was down on the floor with Cisco, his head cradled in her lap. "Oh, darling, darling Cisco, what has that beast done to you?" she wept over and over. To Ross Updike, lying wounded and stunned, she hissed, "Go away, you pompous ass! I never want to see you again!"

5:01 P.M.

The sudden noise at the other end of the room interrupted Peggy Corcoran midsentence. She'd already told Dan a thousand times that she wouldn't marry him, but he was behaving like a petulant child. Pouting and sulking, he gave her a dozen reasons why she should marry him.

She didn't even notice Duke approach. Too late, she saw Dan being lifted from his chair like a sack of laundry. The expression on Duke's face was fierce.

"Duke!" she shrieked. "What are you doing? Put him down this instant!"

But Duke was beyond hearing. "She's *my* wife!" Duke bellowed at Dan. "She's *still my wife, you fucking sonofabitch!*"

Peggy heard, rather than saw, the sickening thud as Duke's broad fist plowed into Dan's midsection. She saw Dan crash against Otto Schindler, who just happened to be innocently standing nearby.

5:02 P.M.

Duke, wild with rage, spun on his heel and grabbed Otto Schindler by his white shirt collar. *"And you, you bullet-headed bastard, you're the one who started it all!"*

Otto's high-pitched wail pierced the wall of noise with a stabbing suddenness. "No! No! No! Wayne," Otto bleated, "you're making a terrible mistake!"

"You're the one who made the mistake, buddy," Duke roared as he lifted Otto off the ground and sent him sailing above the heads of the stunned onlookers.

5:03 P.M.

Plato Pappamichaelis emerged from the kitchen in time to see something—someone?— whiz past him like a blur and land, between floating balloons, in the brass fronds of the giant plastic palm tree. Turning, he saw his Venus pounding her fists against the chest of the best mechanic this side of Athens. Why was his Venus crying like that? What was that mechanic doing to her?

Whatever it was, he, Plato, would put a stop to it. He was at her side in an instant, his trusty skillet at the ready.

"Dis jerk givin' you problems, Venus?" he asked. Not bothering to wait for an answer, he brought the skillet down, neat, on the mechanic's head and watched him sink slowly to the floor like the evening sun into the Aegean.

"Plato!" Peggy yelled. "What are you doing? *Stop!*" she cried, beating on *his* chest now. "Get your hands off my husband!"

5:04 P.M.

Andy ffrench couldn't believe his eyes. It was like something from a bad movie. It was a fucking cliché—that's what it was. Any minute, he expected John Wayne to come swaggering through the door, a six-shooter in each hand, telling everybody to freeze. Well, Andy ffrench wasn't going to wait for that. Andy ffrench knew a dangerous situation when he saw one. He grabbed Phyllis and headed for the door. "Let's get outta here, *fast,*" he said. "I don't like the looks of this!"

They almost made it to the exit when suddenly Carlo Battista, the barber, blocked their way. "You!" Carlo shouted, red faced. "You fairy! You sissy! You *tutti-frutti!*"

Andy looked around. "Who, *me?*" he asked weakly.

"You pansy!" Carlo ranted. "Dey oughtta putta you 'way for keeps!" The barber produced a rolled-up copy of *FOLK* Magazine. "*Que schiffoso!* You crazy! You *pazzo!* I gonna keep you 'way fromma my gran'bebe!" He swung at Andy's noggin with the magazine. Hard. Nobody saw the rock concealed inside.

Andy went down. The last thing he heard before his world went dark was Phyllis Sawyer crying,

"You dumb jerk! *You've killed the only man who ever loved me!*"

5:05 P.M.

Jared was stupefied. Who went down first? The gardener or the fancy *shvartzeh* with the ascot? It was hard to tell. But whoever it was, things happened fast after that.

He saw Corcoran go berserk—first knocking out a freckle-faced rube and then flinging Dr. Schindler into the tree. And who should catch the sex doctor? None other than the fastest pussy in town, his very own Barbara Johnson! It was a match made in heaven . . .

And now, fat little Carlo Battista had lost his mind and was attacking the *faygeleh* from the movie!

People were beginning to panic, scrambling like eggs for the exits. For the first time that afternoon, Jared Galitz, Esq., was tickled by the cold finger of fear. *Olivia!* Where was she! Then he remembered —she was safely outside in the parking lot with the other Little Women. Thank God.

Selma he didn't see at all. Maybe she was outside, too. He hoped so.

He was about to make his move out the door when an all-too-familiar odor assailed him. He spun on his heel. *"You!"* he exploded. "So you finally decided to show your face!"

Sven Jorgensen grinned from ear to ear. "Ja. I overslept . . ."

Jared yelled, *"I'll teach you to fuck my wife!"*

299

Sven blushed. "You vill?" He stood there blinking rapidly.

Jared swung. A fountain of blood spurted from the Swede's nose. "Maybe that'll teach you to fool around with married women!" Jared screamed.

He was about to swing again when Fred the bartender intervened. "No, no, Mayor! You got the wrong Jorgensen! You want his *brother!*"

Jared hesitated. He looked down at the bleeding Sven.

"I ain't got no brudder," Sven protested meekly. "Only shvesters . . ."

Fred, nonplussed, shrugged. "Well, he *said* he was his brother. And he sure *looked* like Sven. He even wore the same overalls . . ."

Jared considered. The same overalls? The only one *he* knew who was tall and broad enough to fill Sven's overalls was . . .

Oh, my God! His heart hammering in his chest, he turned to the spot where he'd last seen Barron Heatter standing with Selma. So she wasn't just playing hostess. She was playing *something else* . . .

A rage such as he never knew came over him as he made his way out to the parking lot.

5:07 P.M.

Barron stood at the center of a crowd of fawning women, signing autographs. Just as Jared suspected, there was Selma standing right beside him. She was watching Heatter with a rapturous, adoring look on her face. It was a look Jared hadn't seen in a long time.

300

They didn't see him coming. Vaguely, as though from a great distance, he heard his constituents greeting him: "How'ya doin', Mayor?" "Great party, Mayor!" "We gonna do this again next year, Mayor?"

He ignored them. Propelling himself onward, he made his way toward the loving couple.

Barron saw him and smiled. "Jerry!" he greeted him. "Good to see you!"

Jerry glared. He was going to kill the bastard. He didn't care if he had to spend the rest of his life in prison—he was going to do it.

"How *could* you, Heatter?" he rasped, grabbing the actor by the shirtfront. "After I let you use my town! My house! Did you have to use my wife, too?"

A hush fell over the crowd. He was satisfied to see the color drain from Barron's perpetually tanned face.

"Wait—wait a minute," Barron began nervously. "Can't we discuss this in private?"

"What's to discuss?" Jerry raged. *"You're fucking my Selma!"*

Selma had never seen Jerry like this. So totally out of control. So oblivious to his constituency. So indifferent to his image. If she didn't know better, she'd think he was actually jealous. That he still loved her.

"Jerry, honey—wait—" she began.

Barron turned to stare at her. *"Honey?"* he asked, sounding betrayed. "What's with the 'honey'?"

She felt confused. Light-headed.

In the split second she closed her eyes, it hap-

301

pened. She heard the awful crunching sound as Jerry's fist made contact with Barron's mouth. She heard the disbelieving gasp of the crowd. When she opened her eyes, she saw Barron on the asphalt, his million-dollar smile scattered like Chiclets all around him.

Barron was going to be sick, right here, right in front of his public. It wasn't just the pain, although that was bad enough. More to the point, it was seeing the handiwork of Dr. Irvin W. Supposnick, the best cosmetic dentist in Beverly Hills if not the world, being crushed beneath the feet of the mob. Fifty thousand dollars worth of reconstructed smile—his ticket to fame and fortune—ground to dust before his eyes. He ran his tongue tentatively over the jagged stumps poking through his gums.

"Galith!" he lisped. "I thwear I'll thue you for every lasth dollar!"

44

More Bedlam

THEY were almost trampled in the stampede of
bodies escaping from The Royal Palm. Steve
Gordon grabbed the girls' hands protectively and
said, "Stay close, kids!"

"What's happening?" Sunny asked worriedly.
"Was there a fire or something?"

"The party's probably over," little Ruthie Miller
grumbled. "I told you we should have left the Peppermint Parlor an hour ago!" She turned to Steve.
"It's all your fault, Stevie! You had to play all those
video games!"

Steve looked crestfallen. "I just wanted my
turn," he said petulantly. "It was only fair!"

The three of them were about to enter The
Royal Palm when Olivia Galitz ran over, shrieking,

"Where the hell *were* you? Barron's *livid!* Plus, your parents are having a shit fit. Would you believe, they called the cops?" Olivia glared at them. "Don't you know how important this whole thing is to the film?"

Ruthie put both hands on her hips and glared back at Olivia. "Buzz off, big shot! You don't scare me!"

But Sunny *was* scared. How could she ever have thought that Steve Gordon was her father? Steve could never be Eric. He was just fooling when he said he was. If you asked her, there was something a little bit wrong with him. He reminded her of a little kid—except he wasn't a kid. "Let's go find my mom," she suggested.

Steve Gordon hesitated. Try as he might, he couldn't remember exactly who Sunny's mother was. But he had a feeling he should know. He also had the feeling he should go home. "Maybe I shouldn't meet your mother right now," he said to Sunny. "After all, I wasn't invited to this party."

Suddenly Morgie Corcoran was at their side. "Sunny, where've you been?" she asked nervously. "My mother's frantic. Why didn't you wait for us to pick you up?"

Before Sunny could answer, Max Miller was pushing his way toward them. "Ruthie!" he screamed. "Thank God you're safe!" He scooped Ruthie up in his arms and began to weep.

And then, suddenly, they were the center of everyone's attention. Bliss Billington, disheveled and red-eyed, was sobbing uncontrollably and clasping Sunny to her bosom. "Oh, baby, are you all right? Did he hurt you?"

A phalanx of policemen surrounded them. Chief Daniels was at Steve Gordon's side. "You have the right to remain silent . . ."

But Steve was unable to remain silent. His lower lip was trembling. "I want my mommy," he said, softly at first, then louder. "I WANT MY MOMMY!" he screamed, bursting into tears.

"Here's something to cry about!" Max said as he hauled back and punched Steve in the eye.

It was a first for Max. In all his life, he had never had to resort to physical violence. He didn't like it one bit. His head was beginning to spin. His stomach was lurching up into his heart.

He hardly felt the ground come up to meet him.

5:11 P.M.

Barrbra Shapiro was getting tired. Her knees were numb. Her back was killing her. There wasn't much room down here under the table, but she sensed it was the safest place to be while all hell was breaking loose around her. At least nobody could see her here with her head between Abe Moscovitz's thighs.

For the past half hour, she'd been trying to make the old fart come. This had to be the longest hard-on in the history of mankind. By this time, even dynamite would have exploded.

She disengaged her lips from his cock. "Hello up there?" she called. "Are you close?"

"Pussy," he said.

She sighed. That's all he'd been saying for the last half hour. Talk about a one-track mind . . .

What did he expect her to do? Climb on top of him right here in a public place? Well . . .

"Pussy," he said again.

Oh, what the hell? The place was practically deserted anyway. And she'd never done it in a bar before. The thought began to excite her. The question was, How was she going to manage it? Maybe if he got under the table with her . . .

"Pussy," he said.

"All right, already," she replied impatiently. "But you're gonna have to cooperate, Abie."

She tugged at his pant leg. He didn't budge. Well, shit to this. He was all take and no give. In other words, a typical man. She crawled out from under the table to see that the bar was now nearly empty.

"Where is everybody?" she asked.

"Pussy," Abe said.

She looked at him. And then she took another look. His eyes were staring straight ahead. They were glassy and dazed. His whole body was rigid, exactly like his cock, except his cock was red and his face was as white as a ghost.

There was something definitely wrong here. She began to feel afraid. Tentatively, she touched his arm. "Abe, what's wrong?" she asked. "Should I do the Heimlich on you again?"

"Pussy," he said.

45

Myra

MYRA Schick stared. *Where the hell was every-one?* From the looks of things, it had been quite a party, but the party was definitely over. Silently, she cursed. On her way here, she had passed four shrieking ambulances racing in the opposite direction. Next had come a squadron of police cars, sirens going full blast. "There must have been an accident," she had remarked to Al Blaine, her photographer.

"Yeah. Maybe they actually found somebody alive in this dump," Al yawned, pulling into the parking lot of The Royal Palm.

It wasn't until she was inside the bar and saw the debris that she realized something had happened, all right. *And she'd missed it! Fuck!* She'd been looking forward to this moment all week. It was going to be her moment of triumph. But where

307

was Barron? Where were the bratty Little Women? Where was the ffrench fag?

Al was nudging her. "Get a load of that," he said, pointing to a back booth, where some bimbo was climbing all over an old guy.

"And that . . ." Al went on, pointing to the bar, where the frizzy-haired mayor was systematically emptying a dozen half-filled whiskey sour glasses into a pitcher.

Myra saw the mayor raise the pitcher to his lips and start to guzzle. "Al," she commanded, "get a picture of that." Not that a picture of the mayor getting plastered would compare with her story in this week's *FOLK*.

Cradled in her arms were two dozen copies of the issue, hot off the presses. It was all there, every seedy detail, beginning on page fifty-three and continuing for virtually the entire back of the magazine. Everything. All the dirty little facts and innuendos she'd managed to scoop up on her mission to destroy Barron Heatter and his filthy cohorts.

Earlier, she'd run into the rotund little barber and gave him a copy, just to get his reaction. She smiled now, remembering how the little guinea had first paled, then flushed, then paled again as he read about the homosexual exploits of one Andrew ffrench.

No, she sighed. A photo of the mayor getting plastered wouldn't have the impact of the fag's story. But it would sure make a nice sequel.

46

FOLK Magazine

Here's Hollywood!
LITTLE WOMEN FUNCTIONARY LIKES
LITTLE MEN
by Myra Schick

West Falls, CT—What happens when a convicted homosexual rapist is hired to assist the director of a rock musical cast with innocent young children?

Andrew ffrench, forty-two, who has worked on the fringe of show biz all his life, was hired by Hollywood has-been Barron Heatter to assist in the filming of his new rock musical *Little Women,* now in the final stages of production on location in West Falls, Connecticut. (See *Environment.*)

Heatter, washed-up matinee idol, is producing, directing, and—grab this, folks—*rewriting* the Louisa May Alcott classic into a raucous rock musical for the silver screen. (As if *anybody* could rewrite Louisa May Alcott!) This latest fiasco is an attempt to revive a comatose career that hit rock bottom three years ago with *Belgian Affair.* Rumors around Hollywood have it that Heatter has mortgaged himself to the hips with this one, folks, financing the entire production himself—with maybe some help from his "friends"?

But did Heatter go too far when he hired an assistant with a record? In San Diego, in 1984, ffrench was found guilty of raping a dwarf in a sailor suit . . .

Environment.
POISONOUS WASTE IN THE GARDEN OF EDEN?
by Myra Schick

West Falls, CT—On the surface, West Falls, Connecticut, is a Norman Rockwell painting come to life. Dig deeper, however, and you'll find something else.

Beneath the manicured lawns and sprawling suburban houses in this bucolic community there lurks a bubbling cauldron of—yes, folks—poisonous waste.

For years the unsuspecting residents of Dove Hills Estates, the town's newest development, have been complaining of various ills: nausea, headaches, upper-respiratory ailments—the works. It is only recently, however, that the EPA has discovered that the area is a toxic waste site. "Probably the worst in the country," says environmentalist Ernest Shale. "Possibly even worse than Love Canal."

The developer of Dove Hills Estates, one Jared Galitz, Esq., the mayor of West Falls (see *Life-*

styles) claims no responsibility for the hazardous conditions beneath his property. "I'm innocent! Trust me!" is Galitz's only comment.

Life-styles.
GETTING "PERSONALS" IN THE SUBURBS
by Myra Schick

West Falls, CT—Can you advertise for love? Ask any citizen of this provincial Connecticut bedroom (!) community and the answer will be a resounding "maybe."

Like many places in this id-oriented nation of ours, West Falls is experimenting with the latest fad to hit the fan since computer dating: *personals ads.* For some time now, the citizenry of this community has been attempting to fill its sociophysical needs through ads placed in the local newspaper, *The Marketplace.*

Do the ads work? Yes, no, and maybe.

"Answering a personals ad is an exercise in futility," says one bitter bachelor who requests anonymity. "Not that I've ever done it, mind you, but I have a very good friend who spent weeks composing a response to an ad and never even got an answer from the woman! It was downright humiliating."

Some citizens disagree. "I've heard of women meeting all kinds of nice men through the personals," says Barbara Johnson, an attractive brunet divorcée. "A good friend of mine does it all the time. After all, how else can you meet people these days?"

Miriam Blavatsky, a widowed schoolteacher, has, however, been "burned" through the personals. "If a girl doesn't jump into the sack right away, it's bye-bye baby! On the other hand," continues Ms. Blavatsky, "what else are you going to do?"

The town's mayor, Jared Galitz, Esq. (see *Environment*) approves of the ads. "I think they breathe new life into the community," he says. "They're good for West Falls, and I've always said, 'What's good for West Falls is good for you!' Trust me!"

But West Falls's police chief Almanzo Daniels urges caution. "As far as the police are concerned," he says, "we view the ads as a magnet for all kinds of weirdos. It's just like verbal hitchhiking. My advice is to stick to the old ways of meeting people—blind dates and bars."

47

Falls Memorial Hospital

BEA was all cried out. Selma offered her another tissue. Bea took it and crumpled it and threw it on the floor.

"Ma, what are you doing?" Selma asked in a hushed voice.

"What am I doing? I'm losing my mind! How will I ever survive this?"

Selma put her arm around her mother's shoulders. "Daddy will be fine, Ma. Even the doctor said he's going to live. With therapy, maybe he'll even walk again . . ."

Bea turned to Selma and glared. *"Walk?* I'll break both his knees, that no-good bum! How could he do this to me? In public, yet? In a bar! Better he should have died!"

"Shh! Ma! You don't know what you're saying!" Selma looked around. The waiting room was filled.

Everyone she knew was here. Peggy Corcoran. Bliss Billington. Phyllis Sawyer, from the movie. Even Princess, who was pacing back and forth nervously. Selma still couldn't get over how different she looked without the wig. She even *sounded* different!

Selma shook her head. How had all this happened? It seemed like a bad dream. Would she wake any minute and find that her father was home in Stamford where he should be—healthy, normal, *monogamous?* She pitied her mother. What a shock it must have been for her to find Daddy sitting like that in The Royal Palm with his fly unzipped and his thing sticking out a mile while that trampy Barrbra Shapiro was punching his chest in an effort to revive him!

"An insult to the brain," the doctor had said.

"An insult to *me,* you mean!" Bea had raged.

"A stroke," the doctor elucidated. "With an unfortunate aphasic correlation—"

"Unfortunate" was putting it mildly, Selma thought. Her father would have to be isolated, put in a room where no one could hear him utter the obscenity over and over again: *Pussy. Pussy. Pussy.*

A bell sounded, signaling the start of visiting hours. Everyone stood and rushed to the elevators.

Peggy Corcoran smiled wanly at Selma, and Selma smiled back.

Bliss Billington nodded. She said, "This is like a bad movie."

"Don't mention movies to me," Peggy said wearily. "I've had enough of movies to last a lifetime."

Phyllis Sawyer edged toward the group. "Well,

ladies, don't worry," she said, holding up a copy of *FOLK* Magazine. "After this, there won't *be* any movie. Myra Schick saw to that."

The women nodded.

"That bitch," Bliss said. "Someone should take her out and make her live in Dove Hills Estates."

Selma felt her cheeks redden. The mere mention of Dove Hills Estates made her cringe. How could she hold her head up around here after this? Of course, Jerry insisted that he was innocent. Well, maybe he was and maybe he wasn't. Whatever, his political future was ruined. Only yesterday, he'd received a letter of chastisement from the Connecticut Bar Association.

How could she think of leaving him now, when his life was such a mess? Did Pat leave Dick after Watergate? Of course not.

The lower half of Barron's face was swathed in bandages. "Umghrrmfth," he muttered as Selma entered his room.

"Some water, darling?" Selma asked as she planted a kiss on each of his eyelids.

Barron nodded. Carefully, she inserted the plastic straw in the gaping hole that was his mouth. "Umghrfufslagh?" he asked.

Selma sighed. "No, Barron, not yet. I haven't the heart to tell him. He's not himself. He sits in his chair all day, just staring out the window. He won't answer the phone. He won't talk . . ."

Barron thrashed angrily in his bed. "Mdglgrmahr!" he insisted. "Mghrelgurghh!"

He was sounding better to her. The surgeon had put thirty-two stitches in his gums—one for each mutilated tooth. She took his hand. "Don't be silly, Benny," she assured him. "Of course I love you. I'll always love you. But he's still my husband, and I owe him something . . ."

"Bbaooobeeee?"

"But you're stronger," she explained softly. "You're a survivor. I'll bet there are a million scripts waiting for you right this minute in Beverly Hills!"

The nurse came in smiling, carrying a tray of syringes. "And how are we doing today?" she chirped.

"Whhhhhh?" Barron looked at Selma with terror in his eyes.

He was petrified of needles, she knew. "Darling, be brave," Selma said.

The nurse looked at Selma. "I'm afraid you'll have to leave for a few minutes." She was a buxom woman in her late thirties, with yellow hair and a hungry look in her eyes.

Selma nodded. "I'll only be gone for a little while, darling. I'll look in on Daddy."

Barron nodded. "Murrrugle," he said.

"I love you, too," Selma replied as she breezed out the door.

Dr. Otto Schindler was immobilized, his wrists attached to a pulley over his head, his ankles hooked to the frame of the contraption that was stretching his body back into shape. Despite his discomfort, he was smiling. The best lay he'd ever had, besides Peggy Corcoran, was back in his life.

"I brought you something, honey," Barbara Johnson said. She was wearing a black low-neck dress that clung to her body like a second skin. Tiny pearl buttons marched enticingly from her cleavage clear down to her navel. Slowly, and with great deliberation, her graceful fingers proceeded to undo the buttons, one by one.

Otto groaned. "Don't do this to me," he begged. "Can't you see I'm in traction? Can't you see I can't move?"

"Mmm," Barbara said, licking her lips. "You'd be surprised what you can move when you want to, Otto baby."

What had he done to deserve this? He had been innocently enjoying himself at that ridiculous party when suddenly that Corcoran maniac slugged the redheaded stranger with Peggy. And then the next thing he knew, he, Otto Schindler, was flying through the air like a guided missile. When he came to, he was in Barbara Johnson's lap, her mammaries pressing up against his face. When he tried to sit up, a jagged pain ripped through his torso. He couldn't move!

Barbara had stayed with him all the way to the hospital. And here she was again today.

Her dress was falling around her waist, her amazing spherical breasts swinging free. He broke out into a sweat. "Please . . ." he begged feebly. "The nurses . . . the doctors . . ."

She smiled seductively. "I thought of that. I locked the door."

She was pulling off the sheet that covered the lower half of his body. The hospital gown came only to his navel. Despite the fact that he was totally helpless, his member had a mind of its own. It was standing at attention, saluting, ready for action. What would he do if he couldn't ejaculate? But wait . . .

Her mouth was moving closer to him. He caught a whiff of her tantalizing perfume as her breasts swung against his body. Her hands caressed his testicles, her fingers explored him with expertise.

He was trembling. He felt totally helpless.

And what's more, *he loved it.*

Duke's head was splitting, and none of the pain-killers could ease the pounding. If this was only a mild concussion, he hated to think what a severe one was like. He turned his head and squinted. The room swayed. Two Peggys stood at his bed-side and both of them looked worried.

"Duke?" Her voice was soft, loving. "Duke, dar-ling? Are you awake?"

Was he awake? He couldn't tell for sure. Maybe he was only dreaming that she was here, looking more beautiful than ever. He thought he'd never see her again after he acted like such an asshole at that party. But just the sight of her talking to an-other man had driven him wild.

She leaned over and kissed him tenderly. She smoothed the hair from his brow. Her cool hand felt like a feather against his skin.

"I'm sorry," he moaned. "I'm sorry I hit him— them. I shouldn't have done it."

"No, you shouldn't have, Duke." Her tone was only mildly scolding.

He found the courage to look into her eyes. "Are you mad at me?"

She grinned. "You big lug!" she laughed. "You cave man. You went totally berserk! First Dan, then Dr. Schindler." She shook her head. "He's here, you know. Schindler. Upstairs, in Orthopedics. Half the town is here. It really was *some* party!"

For the first time in days, Duke laughed. His head threatened to burst open. "Ow!"

"Are you in pain?" Peggy asked, suddenly serious.

Together they chorused, "Only when I laugh."

He grabbed her hand and pulled her to him. "So what's the story?" Duke asked. "Are you going to marry that jerk—or what?"

"Or what," Peggy replied impishly.

"That means . . ."

"That means you can't get rid of me so easily, Dukie."

She leaned forward. Their lips met. Fire flared between them, strong and hot, surprising both of them. He pulled her down onto the narrow hospital bed and drew her to him.

"Oh, Dukie, it's been so long," she moaned as his hands deftly found their way under her skirt.

He rolled off her panties. She kicked them to the floor. She was lost now. Lost in the ecstasy only Dukie could bring to her world. Lightly, she mounted him. In seconds, he was inside her, their bodies working together in sweet harmony.

"Peggy," he panted, his eyes never leaving her face, "I love you."

His hands cupped her breasts with a tenderness she couldn't remember. It was almost too much . . . too much . . . Her body shuddered in monumental orgasm.

An instant later, he came. "Oooohhh, God!" he

gasped. And then he said, "Look what you do to me, Peg . . ."

Afterward, when they were lying in each other's arms, she decided to tell him. "Duke," she whispered, "I'm carrying your baby. Duke, honey, we're pregnant."

The words entered his mind like the answer to a prayer. He smiled. Tears of joy welled in his eyes. Somehow he wasn't surprised. This was God's way of forgiving him. He was getting another chance with the only woman he'd ever loved.

"Peggy . . ." he said. "Oh, Peggy, you're my *only*."

Rules were rules. When you checked into the Cardiac Unit at Falls Memorial Hospital, you weren't permitted to leave for forty-eight hours.

Max was livid. "But I'm a *doctor*. I can read cardiograms as well as anybody. I know I'm okay!" he had insisted over and over.

The staff was unimpressed. "We can't be responsible, Dr. Miller, unless you follow our rules," one of them said. "Nobody, not even Dr. Denton Cooley himself, gets out of our Cardiac Unit in less than two days!"

Max watched their retreating backs in mute frustration. "Idiots," he muttered.

The door opened again. For an instant, Max thought the doctors had changed their minds and were going to liberate him. Instead, he saw Bliss Billington, looking vulnerable and waiflike. she was still beautiful, though, damn her.

"Max?" she said meekly.

"Come in," he replied uncertainly. He was still

320

all mixed up about her, but he'd thought of no one else since the episode with Steve Gordon. How could he have slugged that poor bastard? He was a physician. He should have known better!

Bliss walked tentatively toward the bed. There was an awkward silence between them. "I asked the doctors and they said you could have visitors . . . They said your tests so far are negative. You're looking well, Max—"

"I *am* well," he interrupted. "But these morons won't let me go home for another twenty-four hours!"

She sat down gracefully in the chair next to the bed. Her gray cotton knit dress looked as soft as a cloud. Her legs were crossed at the ankles. Such a lady. She was perfect. But even perfection can be flawed, Max thought.

"I've seen Ruthie," she said. "She's fine. Mrs. Schotz is taking very good care of her."

Max nodded. "That was nice of you. Thank you," he answered, his voice tinged with formality.

She studied her polished fingernails. He heard a gentle sigh. It cut through him.

"Max," she began, "I know what you must think of me . . ."

"How do you know what I think of you when *I* don't even know!" he snapped. "My God, Bliss, how could you have taken a chance like that? Gone out with a total stranger?"

She avoided his gaze. "I told you," she said quietly, "I had no way of knowing what he was like. He seemed perfectly normal at first."

"But you met him through the *personals ads!*"

She looked up at him. "Max, aren't you forgetting something? *We* met through the personals ads!"

"That's different," he mumbled. "I knew who you were, you knew who I was . . ."

"Did we really? We'd seen each other, but we didn't *know* each other. People always take chances. You could have been a hatchet murderer for all I knew!"

"Well, then, maybe you shouldn't have gone out with me," Max pouted.

"Do you really mean that, Max?"

For a long moment, he didn't reply. Then he said, "No. I don't mean it." He sighed. "I'm glad we met. I'm glad I fell in love with you."

Her face brightened. "And—do you still love me?"

He flung aside the covers and attempted to get out of bed, but she ran to him and held him down. "What are you doing? The doctors don't want you up yet! Please, Max."

He put his arms around her and pulled her against him. He buried his face in her hair. It smelled of roses. He *did* love her. He loved her more than he loved anyone, except maybe Ruthie.

"Bliss," he said hoarsely, "I shouldn't have hit him. I never hit anybody before in my whole life. I'm not a violent man."

"Don't you think I know that, Max? That's one of the reasons why I love you so much! My life has been filled with violent men, from my—my father all the way to Steve Gordon," she confessed, her voice breaking. "Oh, Max, you're the best thing that has ever happened to me, and I don't want to lose you."

Slowly, gently, he had begun to undress her. She was so vulnerable, so fragile. He wanted to protect her from all the ugliness the world had to offer.

Naked, their bodies melted one into the other, a smooth-flowing union marred only by the insistent ringing of the telephone.

"Let it ring," Max murmured.

"Maybe it's important . . ."

"Nothing is as important as we are, the two of us, together, right now," he whispered softly.

It was true. He knew it was. He would marry her and protect her and her past would cease to exist. There would be only the future ahead of them.

Somebody was prying open his eyelids. A harsh beam of light blinded him. *What the hell did they think they were doing?*

Now somebody was fiddling with his toes. It felt as if they were—*OUCH!*—they were sticking him!

From afar, he heard a voice say, "Good. He felt that one."

Of course I felt it! Andy screamed. Funny, though, he couldn't hear himself. He tried again. *What do you think I am, a pin cushion?* Still nothing. What was going on here? Why was it so dark? Why couldn't he open his own eyes? Why couldn't he move?

"Doctor, you've got to save him! I can't live without him!"

Andy *knew* that voice. At least he thought he knew it. Oh, God, what was wrong? Why couldn't he remember? Again, he tried to open his eyes. No soap. His lids wouldn't budge.

"Don't worry, Ms. Sawyer," he heard someone

323

say. "He'll come out of this any day now, probably with some minor memory loss. He was very lucky to be wearing that hairpiece. It absorbed a good deal of the trauma."

Andy's hand inched tremorously up until it reached his skull. His head seemed to be encased in a gauze helmet. Where was the old wig-eroo he'd paid fifteen hundred smackeroonies for?

"I still can't believe they had to cut it out of his scalp," the woman said sadly. "All that blood—the wig is ruined."

"RUINED?" Andy shrieked. He sat bolt upright. His eyelids sprang open. He stared at their shocked faces. "What do you mean 'ruined'? I'll sue!" he screamed. And then he fainted.

Cisco's face was turned to the wall. He refused to look at her. She'd been at his bedside, pleading with him to forgive her, ever since he'd arrived at the hospital.

"Leave me alone," he said. "You ain't nothin' but an Oreo—black outside, white inside."

Princess thought, an *Oreo?* She hadn't heard that one in years! But maybe he had a point. Then again, maybe he didn't. Had all those years at Harvard really changed her? She didn't think so. She was always the way she was. Her parents were both teachers. Her brother, Lincoln, was a physicist at Los Alamos; her sister, Aurelia, was a cellist with the Boston Symphony. She, Princess Delphine Armstrong, had been taught from the very beginning that there were no such things as "white" feelings and "black" feelings; people were people, and the color of one's skin didn't matter.

324

Oh, but she had learned that to some people—Cisco, for one—it *did* matter. Well, it would be *her* job to show him that he was wrong. She reached out and hesitantly touched his shoulder. He shrugged her off.

"Don' you start workin' on me, girl," he mumbled. "You betrayed me. You betrayed your whole race."

"I did no such thing!" Princess insisted. She hadn't meant to raise her voice, but he was the only man she knew who could make her lose control. "I just couldn't jeopardize my project and reveal my identity, Cisco, but my feelings for you are genuine."

Cisco turned to face her. His black eyes burned with fury. "Jes' listen to yourself! 'Project!' 'Jeopardize!' 'Genuine!' What *is* that shit you talkin', girl? That's honkie talk!"

Princess stiffened. "You know what your trouble is, Cisco? You're prejudiced! You're as bad as any redneck bigot honkie!"

"Come over here and say that, bitch!" Cisco sputtered. He tried to sit up, but the pain in his gut pushed him back. "Jeezus!" he moaned. "Uptight really packs a wallop!"

"Cisco, Ross Updike is a narrow-minded, shallow bourgeois, and I'm sorry he hurt you, baby . . ."

Cisco bristled. "Hurt me? Him? That wimp?" He made another attempt to sit up and groaned.

She came closer, then, and embraced him gently until his head was cradled against her bosom. "Baby, oh, baby, I *love* you. Don't do this to me."

"To *you?* What'd I do to you? All I did was fall in

love with a sweet, innocent li'l girl who turns out to be a big-time an-*thro*-pol-o-gist. Shee-it!"

His words stung her and she started to cry. Exasperated, Cisco sighed, then said, "Oh, no. Whachu cryin' for, girl?"

"Because I love you," Princess wept. "And I don't want to lose you."

"It's no use," he insisted stubbornly. "We live in two different worlds."

"It doesn't have to be that way," she said through her tears. "You'll come back to Boston with me."

There was a long pause. "I ain't never been to Boston," he answered finally. "What's it like?"

Princess sat down on the edge of the bed. She took his hand and put it to her heart. "It's beautiful," she told him. "It's got the Charles River and Faneuil Hall and Filene's and stately houses with big green lawns . . ."

Cisco's hand slipped inside her blouse. "Lawns?" he repeated dreamily. "Really big ones?"

"Enormous," Princess whispered.

She threw back the covers and climbed in beside him. He was wearing one of those idiot gowns that covered only the upper part of his body. Below the waist, his skin was silky smooth as her hand found its way between his thighs.

"The longest, biggest ones you ever saw," Princess crooned.

48

Peggy, Bliss, and Selma

THERE was a definite chill in the air. It was only the beginning of September, but already the afternoons were getting shorter.

It was almost four o'clock and shadows were lengthening on the hospital steps. Selma took a deep breath of the crisp, fresh air. She didn't know how people ever managed to get well in hospitals, breathing in that awful disinfectant all day long.

Peggy Corcoran was right behind her. "Hi, Selma," Peggy greeted her. "How's your father? How's Barron? How's the mayor?"

Selma sighed. "Not too good, getting better, and it remains to be seen." She paused, then remembered to ask, "How's Duke?"

Peggy's eyes lighted up. "He's wonderful. He's better than ever. He should be coming home any day." Peggy was beaming.

Selma smiled. "Coming home? Does that mean you and he are back together?"

Before Peggy could reply, Bliss Billington caught up with them. "Who's back together?" she asked. The two women turned to her. She was elegant, as usual—not a hair out of place.

"Duke and me," Peggy said gleefully. "We've decided to give it another go." Then she smiled a Mona Lisa smile. "I'd like you girls to be the first to know . . . we're pregnant!"

Both women stared. Selma and Bliss exchanged looks. "*Mazeltov!* . . . I guess," Selma said uncertainly. "It's what you both want?"

Peggy nodded. "More than anything."

Bliss felt a small flicker of envy. Wouldn't it be lovely to be carrying Max's child? she thought. "Congratulations," she said, hugging Peggy. "I think this calls for a celebration."

The three women giggled.

"Shall we?" Peggy asked.

Selma shrugged. What did *she* have to celebrate? Her husband was depressed. Barron, the dear heart, was despondent, and with good reason; *Little Women* would never be finished after the scandal ignited by Myra Schick.

Still, the thought of going home to Jerry's funk was more than she could handle right now. Besides, she liked Peggy and Bliss. They were her friends.

"This time," she suggested, "let's take *my* car."

EPILOGUE

One Year Later

SELMA Galitz hated to turn off the Bondage tape —she loved their latest hit, "Tie Me Up in Ribbons"—but it was time for Olivia's commercial. She boogied into the den of the two-bedroom Cape Cod in Bardener, Maryland, turned on the television, and eased her body into the chair. She looked at her watch. Only three minutes to go. It was only a thirty-second spot, but, Selma had to admit, Olivia made the most of it. Uncle Jerry's Poultry Palace was now almost a household name in Bardener. Soon, Jerry promised, it would be known throughout the state, as well. Eventually, there would be Poultry Palaces all over the country, like McDonald's, like the Colonel, like Burger King.

Her eyes glazed as she watched the last segment of *Bon Jour, Baltimore.* Reginald Phillips, the effer-

vescent host of the show, was gushing to his guest
—a familiar-looking black woman. Who was she?
Diana Ross? Nah. Shari Belafonte? Selma didn't
think so.

"So you lived in that suburb for how many
years?" Phillips asked.

"Almost three," the woman said. "Reggie, it was
quite an experience."

Selma leaned forward. She wished she had her
glasses. That voice! She knew that voice!

"I'll bet it was," Phillips agreed. "And a profit-
able one, too, judging from the incredible success
of your book, *Current Sexual Mores in Suburban
Society.*" Phillips held up a copy. "Tell me, Ms.
Armstrong, how has your life changed since the
book's publication?"

Selma gasped. Oh, my God! It was Princess! *Her*
Princess, of the *shmattes* and the Army boots! Except that now Princess looked like she was straight
from Saks Fifth Avenue. Wait'll Jerry heard about
this!

Phillips was addressing his viewing audience
now. "We'll be back with Ms. Princess Armstrong
in a minute, folks. But right now, a word from our
sponsor . . ."

Selma, in a state of shock, was only vaguely
aware of Olivia's spiel:

*Hi, there, all you chicken lovers! Have you
made it down to Uncle Jerry's Poultry Palace
yet? Have you tasted our breasts? Our wings?
Our thighs? What are you waiting for? Take
it from Olivia—our parts are awesome! Remember, Uncle Jerry knows what's good for*

you . . . [The camera slowly panned to a close-up of Olivia grinning from ear to ear.] Trust me.

Selma sat there, stunned. Had that really been Princess? Maybe she'd better get herself a copy of that book. Maybe she'd better call Jerry and tell him . . .

Maybe she should call Peggy and tell *her*. She decided against it. Peggy had enough to worry about, caring for the twins, Mona and Lisa. They looked so adorable in that photo she'd sent last month—Duke, safety pins in his mouth, actually changing diapers!

She turned up the volume on the set. Now Princess was talking about her new husband. "He's at Harvard, you know, studying botany. He's a very talented man, and I'm proud of him," she said.

Phillips looked at the camera. "For the record, Ms. Armstrong's husband is Francisco Williams, to whom her book is dedicated."

Selma almost fell off her chair. Cisco? At Harvard? In all her years in West Falls, she had never heard Cisco utter a single coherent sentence!

She wished she could tell Bliss, but she knew the Millers were at the Nobel ceremonies in Sweden this week. How incredible that Max, dear, sweet Max, had won the prize for medicine.

Jerry wasn't taking it very well. "How can it be?" he'd railed after Bliss had told them. "The poor schmuck can't even button his shirt properly! He spent his whole life in a *farshtinkener* laboratory with mice and monkeys—and for that, they give him a prize? Only in America!"

331

"But, Jerry dear, it's Sweden, not America," Selma informed him. "Besides, he made a big contribution to society. Don't you remember how Olivia used to scream with that colic?"

Jerry shrugged. "Colic, schmolic," he said mournfully.

Poor Jerry, Selma thought. He wasn't too happy about the fact that next month she was going to visit the Millers in their big new co-op apartment in New York City. But Selma wasn't about to miss the baby shower Bliss's mother was throwing for her. Selma closed her eyes and tried to visualize what Bliss looked like, eight and a half months pregnant. Probably as beautiful as ever.

The phone rang. "Hello, darling!" Bea's voice rang jubilantly. "How's everything? How's my granddaughter, the TV star?"

Selma coughed. "Fine, Ma. I just saw her commercial. She loves it."

"What's not to love? She's on television round the clock! And how's my son-in-law the businessman? Every morning, I thank my lucky stars he was able to take over the chicken end of the business!"

Selma closed her eyes. "How's Daddy, Ma?"

Bea's voice suddenly turned icy. "He's the same filthy-mouth. I don't want to talk about him. Fremont says the time has come for me to put all that behind me."

Selma shook her head. She couldn't get over the fact that Fremont and her mother were openly living together in the Stamford condo. She liked Fremont, but it just wasn't right for her mother to brazenly shack up like that while her father was languishing like a vegetable in a nursing home in Brooklyn!

"I can't talk now, Ma. I'll call you back."

"What, I can't mention Fremont without you getting mad? I know all about you and that movie star!"

Selma hung up. She refilled her coffee cup and thought about calling Barron in Santa Monica. She decided against it. He'd call her eventually; he always did. They were good friends now. She had a special place in her heart for Benjamin Ira Horowitz, but there could never be anything more between them. Barron knew it, too.

He and Barrbra Shapiro had been together now for how long? Six months. It was a record for him. And for Barrbra, too.

"She's good for me," Barron had written Selma. "She knows what I need. And she's a damn good bookkeeper!"

Barron's used car lot on La Cienega was doing much better than he'd expected. And he assured Selma he didn't miss the glitz of show biz as much as he thought he would. Selma believed him.

She knew how a person could pick up the jagged pieces and put things whole again after one part of life goes sour. She and Jerry were living examples.

At that very moment, Jared Galitz, former mayor of West Falls, Connecticut, disbarred attorney, bankrupted builder, sat in the back room of Uncle Jerry's Poultry Palace and lighted his first cigar of the day.

He closed his eyes and inhaled the rich aroma of his father-in-law's carefully humidored Cuban stash. He almost felt sorry for Abe, stuck away in that nursing home while Bea put horns on him.

He picked up a copy of yesterday's *Times*. Funny, how both items appeared on the same day, on the same page. The birth announcement of Nathan Greene ffrench, born to Andrew and Phyllis Sawyer ffrench in Edmonton, Alberta, Canada. And, wonder of wonders, the marriage announcement of Barbara-Lee Hawkins Goodfreund Johnson to Dr. Otto Bernhardt Schindler . . .

Jerry threw down the *Times* with an exclamation of disgust. He fought a wave of queasiness. Barbara Johnson, who was so hot to marry the first Jewish president of the U.S. of A. that she popped an imaginary biscuit into her oven, had deserted him like a rat on a sinking ship. Well, good riddance to bad rubbish!

Eagerly, he picked up a copy of the *Bardener Bulletin*. There, on page thirteen, was the ad for Uncle Jerry's Poultry Palace. And there, opposite, was the *other* ad:

Dynamic entrepreneur, new to area, seeks magnetic lady for social interaction. Must be slim, fun loving, adventurous. If you believe, as I do, that life is good and great and a whole lot of fun, we can make our own magic. Trust me. **Box 832**

Jerry read it once, twice, nodded in satisfaction, and smiled.